Praise for *The Tar Baby*

"*The Tar Baby* is a tour de force, and deserves recognition (it has been out of print for several years) with Nabokov's *Pale Fire,* Malcolm Bradbury's *Mensonge,* R. M. Koster's *The Dissertation,* and David Lodge's academic parodies as a sendup and commentary upon contemporary intellectual life."

—Patrick O'Donnell, *Review of Contemporary Fiction*

"Jerome Charyn has long ranked among the most talented, intelligent, and persevering of my contemporaries; and his fiction has established a solidly developing body of achievement. However, *The Tar Baby* represents a leap ahead, both conceptually and stylistically, and the sheer hilarity of the sustainedly marvelous invention ought to win for the book the audience it deserves."

—Richard Kostelanetz

"Clever, witty, and different. . . . Ribald, tongue-in-cheek, Nabokovian. Charyn's ingenuity and versatility are evident, and he will undoubtedly entertain sophisticates with his sly digs, buffoonery, and mazelike plot."

—*Publishers Weekly*

"An object lesson in how visionary idealists become mired in mundaneness, and an ingeniously scatological and funny celebration of unsubduably dirty life forces. . . . Charyn makes it all work, howlingly, in a brilliantly managed surrealistic collage, not much inferior to those of Barth and Nabokov—for me, the year's best novel so far."

—Bruce Allen, *Library Journal*

"An important book . . . an experiment in complex impressionistic and involutional form, striking and original in the extremes to which it juxtaposes comic stereotype and real suffering."

—Albert J. Guerard, *TriQuarterly*

Other Books by Jerome Charyn

FICTION

Little Angel Street
Montezuma's Man
Maria's Girls
Elsinore
The Good Policeman
Paradise Man
War Cries over Avenuce C
Pinocchio's Nose
Panna Maria
Darlin' Bill
The Catfish Man
The Seventh Babe
Secret Isaac
The Franklin Scare
The Education of Patrick Silver
Marilyn the Wild
Blue Eyes
Eisenhower, My Eisenhower
American Scrapbook
Going to Jerusalem
The Man Who Grew Younger
On the Darkening Green
Once upon a Droshky

NONFICTION

Movieland
Metropolis

THE TAR BABY

JEROME CHARYN

Dalkey Archive Press

First Dalkey Archive Edition, 1995

Originally published by Holt, Rinehart and Winston.
© 1973 by Jerome Charyn.

Library of Congress Cataloging-in-Publication Data
Charyn, Jerome.
    The tar baby / Jerome Charyn. — 1st Dalkey Archive ed.
    1. Literature—Periodicals—Humor. 2. Criticism—Humor.
I. Title.
PS3553.H33T37   1995   813'.54—dc20   94-25163
ISBN 1-56478-078-3

Partially funded by grants from the National Endowment for the Arts and
the Illinois Arts Council.

NATIONAL
ENDOWMENT
FOR THE
ARTS

Dalkey Archive Press
Illinois State University
Campus Box 4241
Normal, IL 61790-4241

THE TAR BABY

The Tar Baby

PUBLISHED ONE–FOUR TIMES A YEAR AT
GALAPAGOS JUNIOR COLLEGE
GALAPAGOS, CALIFORNIA

Editor: W.W. KORN

Editorial Assistant & Business Manager: NINA SPEAR

Former Contributing Editor: ANATOLE WAXMAN-WEISSMAN

Member Council of Little Magazines of the West

Subscription: $2.00–8.00 a year

Claims for missing numbers will be honored only if made within two years following date of publication.

At the moment no payment can be made for contributions to *The Tar Baby* other than ten complimentary copies of the same.

Distributed in San Francisco, Oakland, Los Angeles, Yuba City, Portland, Seattle, Vancouver, B.C., Missoula, Boise, Cheyenne, Reno, Salt Lake City, Denver Phoenix, Albuquerque, Oklahoma City, Dallas, Houston & Little Rock by W.W. Korn.

THE TAR BABY

A SOMETIMES QUARTERLY REVIEW

Memorial Number gathered by the Editor,
W.W. KORN

ANATOLE WAXMAN-WEISSMAN
1931-1972

Summer-Fall, 1972

VOLUME XXIX, NUMBER 1   Special Issue, $2.75

ANATOLE: IN MEMORIAM

from GALAPAGA, *the official handbook to Galapagos*

The president arrived with a party of fish-eyed valets, bodyguards, and baggagemen. They gave him two floors at the Brandy House. We saw him from the pantry, Ida and I. He had three chins. He was irritable and mumbled something about an attack of dropsy. His retainers had to heave him through the narrow doors. The house doctor advised him to lie down, but he wanted to go to the Spring. His bodyguards cleared the area of bathers and loungers, and his personal attendants brought him over to a bathhouse, but he couldn't fit in. So his baggagemen surrounded him, and one valet stood in the middle and undressed him. I winked to Ida. We had never seen a naked man before. We stayed behind our bush. The water was shallow, and the president seemed disappointed. He had orange moles on his back. He felt better after emptying his bladder. Odd that this alone should have pleased him: the sight of his piss smoking in the water. He called for a cigar.

—MIMI SKEDGELL,
  "Grover Cleveland Stops at Galapagos"*

* from *Woman-Child in Barbaryland* by Mimi Skedgell. Copyright © 1971 by *The Tar Baby* and the Trustees of Galapagos Junior College. Reprinted with the kind permission of Patchquilt Press.

A Waxman-Weissman Chronology

1931   Anatole born on November 20 in Vienna to Benno [a lexicographer attached to the Nationalbibliothek and a teacher of philosophy at various adult education centers] and Sophie Ender Waxman-Weissman.

1933   Anatole's sister Helene is born on February 9 during an influenza epidemic; dies of heart failure on April 11 stemming from acute bronchitis.

1934   The Waxman-Weissmans leave "red Vienna" after the abortive Austrian Nazi *Putsch* of July 25; reach America sometime in October; arrive two months later at Galapagos in northern California, where Benno begins work as a carpenter for the lumber company owned by his half brother Ulrich.

1936   Anatole enters Galapagos elementary school.

1938   Benno refuses position offered to him as lecturer in German at Galapagos Junior College.

1942   Benno chokes to death on July 24; autopsy performed; his lungs are found to be impacted with sawdust.

1943   Anatole enters Galapagos junior and senior high school; remains an indifferent student.

1947   Sophie Waxman-Weissman disappears on April 23; found dead on July 13 in a Yuba City motel; Anatole comes under the care of his half uncle Ulrich.

1949   Anatole runs away from Galapagos at the beginning of the year without graduating from high school; returns to Galapagos at the end of November, after his eighteenth birthday; settles in a Galapagos rooming house; performs odd jobs.

1950   Anatole has final break with his half uncle, after Ulrich has him imprisoned for vagrancy in an attempt to restore him to propriety.

1951   Anatole shows first signs of the manic-depressive psychosis that is to plague him for the remainder of his life; detained at Minerva State Hospital for two weeks in July; released on July 29 and put under the cognizance of Drexel Fingers, Sheriff of Galapagos and former acquaintance of the Waxman-Weissmans.

1953   Anatole begins work on his biography of the Austrian-English philosopher and logician, Ludwig Wittgenstein.

1954   Drexel Fingers finds job for Anatole as security guard at Galapagos Junior College; uses College library extensively in his research on Wittgenstein; amasses two thousand foolscap pages of notes.

1955   Selections from Anatole's notes are published by W.W. Korn in the Autumn '55 number of *The Tar Baby;* Anatole becomes a contributing editor of this review.

1957   First hundred pages of Anatole's untitled biography of Wittgenstein appear in *The Tar Baby*'s fourteenth anniversary number; Anatole severely attacked by numerous logicians, philosophers, linguists, grammarians, and literary critics of the Western states; awarded an honorary diploma by Galapagos high school on December 23.

1959   Drexel Fingers is killed on March 12 while apprehending a burglar-rapist from Oregon.

1961   Anatole abandons his Wittgenstein biography, condenses his material into a ten-page story-essay, "Wittgenstein Among the Redwoods," which is greeted with an outburst of venom by most Western critics after it appears in the Summer '61 number of *The Tar Baby*.

1963   Anatole, while remaining a campus policeman, teaches an elementary philosophy course at the College.

1965   Anatole begins to revise "Wittgenstein Among the Redwoods," a project which will occupy him until the end of his life.

1967   Anatole marries Cynthia ["Cindy"] Chace, seventeen-year-old daughter of Mother Margaret Chace, owner of the Redwood Motel, where Anatole has been living for the past eighteen years.

1969   Anatole's only son, Bruno, is born at the Redwood Motel on October 22.

1970   Cindy abandons Anatole and her baby, runs off to southern California with Anatole's savings and Millard Stokie, a twenty-three-year-old plumber, on May 11.

1972   February 9: Anatole is run over by a touring bus while walking in Galapagos. Dies on the spot.

Cruelly, sadly, what was meant to be a *festschrift* in honor of Anatole's fortieth birthday has now become a commemorative issue, still respectful of Anatole's work and life, but without his participation, and in the knowledge that he will never read its pages: so, in place of birthday, a deathday, and an issue to Anatole in memoriam. Those indifferent to *The Tar Baby* and unfamiliar with our past numbers, will find it a curious, perhaps unfeeling, issue, because I have included in it articles of an unfavorable bent. Readers, consider my own quandary: would it have been proper—to you, to Anatole, to myself—to paper over the life of this complex and contrary man with bombast, lists of platitudes, sentimental remembrances that would have glorified Anatole, yes, but shown you the contours of a narrowed, one-eyed man? The carp of Anatole's enemies cannot be stuffed inside a shoe to be forgotten, ignored. His severest critics, unfortunately, were often more insightful about him than his devoted friends. That Anatole's behavior was erratic, that he could be excruciatingly unpolitic, that coupled with his generosity and love was a capacity to turn away from his friends, to hurt them, deny them, and make enemies of them, is a fact commonly known in Galapagos. And I would be falsifying my own relationship with Anatole if I did not admit that I too had a falling out with him during the final years of his life. Here, then, are the detractors and the faithful, bitcheries and love notes, critiques by confidants and men who never met him, the gossip and crisp evocations of his teacher, his wife, a rodeo clown, and mother-in-law, comments on his work and illness, in an attempt to celebrate *and* grasp my one-time friend and contributing editor, Anatole Waxman-Weissman.

Readers will please note that because of the length of this number I have been forced to cancel my own column, "With Korn," and curtail our letters department, "Cries to The Tar Baby." Your indulgences will be appreciated.

—The Editor

CRIES TO THE TAR BABY

Dear TB,

Appreciate your generous note asking me to contribute to the special number you are planning on Mr. Anatole Waxman-Weissman's life and work to date. I would like to honor Anatole along with you, but have had a very gassy stomach this year, due to the poor quality of prison food, I guess, and my own excesses in regards to soft candy, which I love, and I can't seem to get comfortable when I start

---

CRIES TO THE TAR BABY

to write. This letter has already cost me a belly-ache. If I recover in time, I will certainly reconsider your offer—since the warm little peccadillos of Anatole's work and all his funny characters have kept my brain from rotting in this sink.

Please hand out my apologies to Anatole. I only met him once, under unfavorable circumstances. Maybe if that fat mother-in-law of his didn't come along, I would have liked him better. I can't abide people who give old clothes to convicts.

Sincerely yrs.
McNabb
State Prison Farm
Coeur d'Alene, Idaho
November 1, 1971

THE TAR BABY ANSWERS:

Dear McNabb,

We are disheartened to learn

of your recent stomach ailment. Our best wishes for an instant recovery.

*

Dear Tar Baby,

All of us here are shocked to see your name on the list of sponsors for the new Royal Sponge Freak-Out at the Flea Market. Surely you have some sense of the Royal Sponge's destructive attitude towards our daughters, our parks, and our town. They are a vile and shifty group of young men. We trust you will retract your sponsorship.

With sincere regards,
GALAPAGOS BUSINESSWOMEN'S BUREAU

THE TAR BABY ANSWERS:

Dear BUSINESSWOMEN'S BUREAU,

Grateful acknowledgment for your disturbing letter. We have authorized our name for no such purposes.

*

July 7, 1971

Dear Tar Baby,

I am outraged by your most unkind and ungentlemanly treatment of your own colleague at the good Galapagos, the venerable grammarian and naturalist, Seth Birdwistell, who was born and raised in my home State and has a large and devoted following among us and elsewhere. Nina Spear's excoriation of this tough old fighter for the causes of tradition and natural history in America is unforgivable. I quote from your Autumn '70 number: "Seth Birdwistell is ignorant, bigoted, and senile. I would remain indifferent to these qualities were it not also true that he is a mean-spirited fraud with a gift for slanted strategy, innocent-sounding footnotes and asides, who has not only reversed recent trends in linguistics, but corrupted our language as well. He has sniped at, and villainized, *les hommes de métier*—the literature scientists, the ethnographers, the neurolinguists, the psychosomaticians, the neo-algorists, the dialectologists, the computer teachers, the parapsychologists, and the decentrists who have bored into our linguistic heartlands to nose out the physiognomy of human speech and map the geographic and psychic boundaries of a given word, who have pissed on ethics and freed themselves of our cultural hangups by choosing algebra over metaphysics, who have not been afraid to invent new verbal systems where the old ones have gone stale. In short, this Birdwistell of ours has pledged himself against the significance of language games, constructs, and myths, and has done irreparable damage to the study of American

(continued on page 195)

Contents

W[OODROW] W[ILSON] KORN

Speculations on Benno, Anatole, Sophie, and Drexel Fingers

W.W. Korn was born outside Macon, Georgia, in 1919. He holds the A.B. degree from Giovanni Teachers College in Chicago, having earned his degree at the age of seventeen, under Giovanni's experimental "brainchild" program of the 1930s; he received his M.S. in Educational Philosophy from the same institution. Founding editor of *The Tar Baby,* he has taught at Galapagos Junior College since 1941, where he is currently Bret Harte Professor of the Rhetorical Arts and Sciences. He has published monographs on David Hume, the grammar of Ernest Hemingway, and the prose style of Anatole Waxman-Weissman. He lives in Sonoma County and is unmarried.

Who was Benno Waxman-Weissman? Had that brilliant, tortured little man who juggled whole dictionaries in his head not left Vienna abruptly in 1934 and found his way to Sonoma County, there would be nothing to say about Anatole or any of the Waxman-Weissmans. Why did he come to America? Was it because he carried that curious misnomer about with him: "of Jewish descent"? Benno had never been inside a synagog. His

paltry knowledge of phylacteries and such could only
have come from his own lexicographical obligations and
probings. Benno's father was an atheist; and his father's
father, a merchant who dealt in crystal, had scorned his
faith to marry the daughter of a solid Catholic burgher.
This I got from Anatole, who knew less about Jews than
I did. Thus, I find it difficult to believe that Benno's position at the Nationalbibliothek was immediately threatened by the Nazi mushroom that had begun to tickle
Austria. A man of real talent, on the periphery of the
famed Vienna Circle of philosophers, why didn't Benno
pick Paris, London, or New York over Galapagos? And
once in America, why did he fall silent, when Marcuse,
Adorno, Arendt, Schlosswinkel,* Brecht, Moholy-Nagy,
Mann, and other German-speaking émigrés remained
productive? Galapagos. Galapagos. The truth is, there
was something suicidal in this very choice. Benno will-
ingly allowed his half brother Ulrich, who neither loved
him nor respected him, to turn him into a carpenter. "I
would see my father come home from the Mill six days
a week, his face, trunk, and shoes tagged with a fine,
even layer of sawdust," Anatole told me. "Sawdust on
his eyebrows, in his nostrils, his mouth, between his
fingers, under his nails, in the flaps of his ears. Only the
area around his eyes was clear, because of the goggles he
wore while working Ulrich's power blades. My father,
painted red, but no Geronimo. . . ." [Anatole was ten

* I have since discovered that Helmut Schlosswinkel fared little better
than Benno Waxman-Weissman in the U.S. His pathfinding study in
metalinguistics, *All Language Is Foul,* was actually written while
Schlosswinkel toured Upper Austria in 1932–33, and remained in manu-
script for twelve years. Schlosswinkel poisoned himself in Denver,
Colorado, in 1954.

and a half when his father died.] Benno Waxman-Weissman, in Galapagos, preferred to eat sawdust than play with words. It would be easy to conjecture that Benno's exit from Vienna brought about his wreckage. But I do not think it is a simple case of geography. No one died of Galapagos alone. I suggest that Benno Waxman-Weissman was in exile *while* he lived in Vienna. Emile Klatch, in his diaries and sketchbooks on the Vienna Circle, informs us: "Perhaps once or twice in a six-month span, there sat, off in the background, silent, with a hand over his head, the lexicographer Benno Waxman-Weissman, who came out of his tomb at the Nationalbibliothek to hear a pinch or two of our discussions, then crawled back inside. His movements were slack, and the nails on his gray fingers were very long; I never saw him smile. Schlosswinkel says he suffers from migraines." I conclude that it was more than the Nazis that drove Benno out of Austria. Was it the restlessness, the internal conflicts and doubts, the morbid imagination and frustrations of neurasthenia? At any rate, a journey from Vienna to Galapagos, no matter under what trying circumstances, would not have permanently crippled and isolated a man with a healthier constitution.

Silent father, silent son. Given Benno's muteness in America, one need hardly wonder over Anatole's marked slothfulness and early repugnance for scholarship, viz., his neglect of the classics, his predilection for illustrated cowboy books of the Gene Autry variety, his poor showing at school. Says Joachim Fiske, Anatole's former junior and senior high school teacher* [now

---

* See Joachim's article on Anatole's juvenilia towards the middle of the issue.

Associate Professor of Business English at Galapagos JC]: "Anatole was an indifferent student at best. Though he had an excellent command of grammar and an infallible sense of logic, his spelling was atrocious and his handwriting was that of a six-year-old: half-cursive, half-script, his large meticulous letters hugged the lines of the page. When he bothered to show up, he would sit in the back with a Gene Autry in his lap, one hand obstructing his face, oblivious to the rest of us. Invariably he fell asleep while I diagrammed sentences on the board and stumped his classmates with difficult constructions or an elusive gerund. I would wake him with a slap of the dictionary against my desk, mutter his name, and he would open one eye craggily, absorb my scribbles and say, *Move the bottom clause up a space, and two steps to the left*."

His school record would be excusable if one could only point to any obsessions in the boy, or an overriding interest in something other than his wretched cowboy books. Galapagos did not neglect the range of hobbies, clubs, contests, and sporting events that might consume a rambunctious man-child. There is no indication that Anatole entered the photography contest sponsored since 1939 by Penn Gemeinhardt and our Merchants Association; he shunned yoyo tournaments, fishing expeditions, Kite Day, and softball games. Once, it seems, and only once, he put together a model airplane for our Biennial Aviators' Fair [discontinued in 1947], but it was a flimsy thing, without proper cockpit or tail strut, its propeller wound with old, stretched rubber bands, and it fell apart before it climbed ten feet; unfortunately, this happened prior to my arrival in Galapagos, but Joachim Fiske and others assure me the story is not apocryphal. One failure, and Anatole returned to a life of sloth.

How then are we to account for Anatole's conversion at the relatively late age of twenty-two? That is, his consuming passion for the philosophical affairs of Ludwig Wittgenstein, his burrowing into the modest collections of our College library, his transformation into a lexicographer and logomachist of no small note. Fiske and Nina Spear [Business Manager of *The Tar Baby*] might interject elements of mystery or even pathology into Anatole's behavior; I choose otherwise. In becoming a scholar in his twenties, Anatole was attempting to relive his father's past; not the woodcutter of Galapagos, but the word-tumbler of the Nationalbibliothek and the student of philosophy at the borders of the *Wien Krug*. True, we cannot certify that Benno Waxman-Weissman ever met Wittgenstein at the Vienna Circle, since his attendance was so erratic: in fact, Anatole swore his father never talked about Wittgenstein. But what better subject for Anatole than a displaced Austrian isolate who seemed to feel more comfortable as a kindergarten teacher than an English don? It would be ridiculous to compare the local tremors of Anatole's work [though he does have a small but devoted following among French metalinguists] with the force of Wittgenstein's intellect, but whatever the difference between the two men, Wittgenstein touched Anatole's vitals, diffused himself throughout Anatole's colon, until one might justly say that Anatole was Wittgenstein "in miniature," as all things in Galapagos are likely to be.

Here we should turn to Sophie, who of the three transplanted Waxman-Weissmans suffered the most.

Caught between her mummed, neurasthenic husband and
a son who was a solitary at heart, she nevertheless came
to grips with the private temperatures, ambiances, and
odors of our Galapagonian life. Particularly, she registered at Galapagos evening high school a month after
the family settled in northern California, trained herself
to be a practical nurse, sewed mittens for American
servicemen once the war began, and learned English
well enough to speak in front of the Galapagos Businesswomen's Bureau about the wonders of Vienna and
Lower Austria. [This, I am told, occurred in 1936,
when all foreigners were curios in Galapagos, and before anti-German feeling peaked in Sonoma County; if
Joachim Fiske is correct, Adolf Hitler was admired in
certain areas of the County up to 1943.] The daughter
of a Russified German who had earned a respectable
sum supervising the candling of eggs and other things
for an army garrison in Lithuania Major, Sophie was a
toughminded girl who could fend for herself. But in the
face of Benno's intransigence and Ulrich's inconsistent
behavior toward the family,* Sophie backslid, became
an alcoholic, developed a fierce temper, went about in
rags, and ended up stone dead in a bungalow attached
to Yuba City's Northern Lights Motel. Drexel Fingers,
who found her and brought her body back to Galapagos,
wrote in his official report: "The deceased, widow of a
German cabinetmaker formerly employed at Wax's

---

* Her husband's half brother flirted with her at first, then grew increasingly distant, and finally took every opportunity to humiliate Benno
and herself. In return for bringing the Waxman-Weissmans to America,
did Ulrich expect that certain favors would be bestowed on him, that
Sophie would volunteer to become his mistress? We shall never know.

Mill, in her early fifties, but prematurely aged due to heavy alcohol consumption, lay sprawled in the dark shack where the Northern Lights stored its linen. She was in a state of dishevelment, being only partly dressed, her bra cups down to her belly, her blouse between her feet, but her underpants were firmly in place. There were scratch marks on her arms, neck, and face: I could not ascertain whether these superficial wounds were self-inflicted. Her eyes were shot with purple, her lips were turning black, and the veins stood out on her forearms and wrists. Three empty quarts of Old Crow were propped on separate bundles of linen. Each bottle was evenly placed, with a slight tilt to its neck. The shack had a God-awful stink." Scribbled in the margins, probably as a note to himself, Drexel added: "I knew I would track poor Sophie down in Yuba City." Had Sophie been raped? Did she drink herself to death? Had someone shared those last hours with her in the bungalow? Did the marks on her arms indicate the extent to which she hated herself? And we should not forget the arrangement of the gin bottles—compulsive neatness while she lay dying. Am I cruel to suggest that this was Sophie's ultimate gesture? The need for one final token of order amid the shambles? Drexel must have sensed this. He could have capitalized on Sophie's death; perhaps even parlayed its sordidness into a judgeship for himself. One can imagine: Drexel rounding up a dozen winos, emphasizing the scratch marks and the sag of Sophie's brassiere, enlisting the help of local newspapers. Did the whiskey bottles afflict him with silence? In any event, Sophie's death was hushed up. A two-line obit in the *Galapagonian Eagle,* plus one more mention, several months later, in a feature article about ex-Austrians and

Hungarians living in Sonoma County.

I admit here that I despised Drexel while he was still alive. Racist, redneck Sheriff, grand deacon of the Native Sons, his one vision was to restore Galapagos to its pioneer grandeur. I accept his charity towards the dead Sophie, but why should he have befriended Anatole, especially when he must have had an inkling of the Jewish ghosts in Benno's family tree? It was Drexel who stepped between Anatole and his half uncle, smoothing out their relationship as best he could; Drexel who aroused Anatole's interest in the natural life of the County; Drexel who intimidated the administration of Galapagos JC into hiring Anatole as a security guard. Ironically enough, it would prove to be a wise gamble: during the Charter Day riots of 1970 Anatole opened communications between the students and the Native Sons.

I shouldn't stray from Drexel. What was it exactly that drew him to Anatole? Something sexual? I doubt it. Drexel was married, had two sons and a daughter of his own. He might have trafficked with whores and wives of the County, not with young boys. Allow me to paw through my own traces. Drexel's marginalia disturbs me—*knew I would track poor Sophie to Yuba City.* I do not propose to diagram this sentence, to pry it apart in the style of Dalton Chess: to my taste, it smacks of a familiarity that is not apparent from Drexel's official report. A mingle of tenderness and contempt. Sophie Waxman-Weissman was a beautiful woman when she arrived here. Did Drexel pursue her? After all, Sheriffs can arrange their own hours. He might have popped in and out of the Waxman-Weissman household while Benno choked on sawdust at the Mill. How much suspicion would he have aroused? From all reports Drexel was a ladykiller in his mustache and tan boots. We shouldn't ignore Sophie's sexual needs. In a new country with a neurasthenic husband on her hands, might she not have been fallible to Drexel's brutish charms? At least for a while. And wouldn't he have gotten to know Anatole, played with him, brought him a few toys, become his second father, so to speak? A minimal, catch-as-catch-can grip on the past, but it makes sense to me. Guilt at Sophie's death and a clinging devotion to the boy. Anyway, Drexel almost caught hold of his judge-ship. He got statewide attention tracking the Oregon desperado Turkey Semple through the woods behind Galapagos, but he didn't come out alive. Drexel's own hard luck contributed to Anatole's death. He had an anxiety attack at the time, lapsed into a deep depression from which he never fully recovered. (A less introspec-tive Anatole would not have walked into a moving bus.) What are we left with? Four deaths, each tipped with a kind of violence, either from an internal or external source; and my own speculations, which readers are asked to ignore if they fail to enlighten, and forgive if they offend the living *or* the dead.

THE GALAPAGOS TONG WAR OF 1858

In the early 1850s, disillusioned Chinese miners from the "gold country" (the Dogtowns, Whiskey Bars, Jackass and Lizard Flats, Nigger Slides, and the other camps of Placer, Nevada, and El Dorado Counties) poured into Galapagos. Soon a plethora of laundries, spice shops, opium dens, gambling houses, eating places, and one temple cropped up on F and G Streets, and the Chinese population of Galapagos grew into the low thousands. Enterprising merchants of this nationality established homes for themselves in balconied two-story wooden houses on Lightstone Street near G. Incense burned day and night, and the little community had a definite Oriental atmosphere. Havoc broke loose, however, in 1858. Members of two rival tongs (secret, fraternal societies) exchanged bitter words in a gambling house on a hot July night. Both clans ruptured all relations, and hired Caucasian blacksmiths to make pikes, daggers, swords, spears, and tridents for them. On August 24 almost 400 members of the popular Sam-Wo Tong engaged 600 of its rivals in Galapagos square. Neither the Sheriff nor any other Galapagonian declared himself against the war; no one thought to intervene. The battle, fought in the company of banners and gongs, was shrill, loud, and messy; it lasted four weeks. The casualty list was quite high: 27 killed, 35 wounded or maimed. The Chinese community declined immediately thereafter. Today there are only about 100 Chinese in Galapagos; an Oriental restaurant flourishes on F Street, but it did not arrive here until 1947. Thankfully, Galapagos has not neglected the memory of its former Chinese inhabitants. An adobe house from old Chinatown, situated at 905 G Street, was restored by the Native Sons and our various women's clubs, at the insistence of Sheriff Drexel Fingers (d. 1959). Tended by unknown hands for many years, the Chinese burial grounds, near the old pioneer cemetery in Galapagos hills, has been looked after by the Native Sons since 1961. At the Drexel Fingers Museum of Galapagos Americana can be found swords, tridents, and spearheads from the unfortunate war between the tongs.

For news of other historic battles in or around Galapagos, consult GALAPAGA.

DALTON CHESS

Galapagos: A Topographical Sketch

Dalton Chess was born in Humboldt County, California, in 1939, and was reared in Siskiyou, Yolo, and Sutter Counties. An adopted son of our Junior College, he received the Associate of Arts degree with high honors from us in 1960, and was a Galapagos Fellow at Humboldt State. Assistant Professor of Sociology and California History at Galapagos, Dalton Chess is working on a demographic study of population shifts in the fifty-eight counties of California, and has contributed numerous articles on Western folklore, art, and politics to *The Tar Baby*. He is the grandnephew of the noted California authoress, Mimi Skedgell.

Tapping and measuring the square foot of road where Anatole was struck down would hardly provide us with any genuine clues to the man, but placing him in his habitat, without the easy temptations of numbers and statistics—what good would it do to know how many Christian Scientists there are in Galapagos, or where our tree surgeon lives?—and sketching Galapagos, in broad strokes, will, I feel, tell us something about Anatole; or at least reconstruct much of what he saw, as a boy, and as a man. Flathanded, no phrenologist or

master of psychology, all I can hope to show are
Galapagos' bumps and sprouts. Truthfully, in spite of
our flourishing College, we are a dying town. Founded
in the 1830s by a Portuguese-American fur trader who
arrived here from Salt Lake with a party of trappers,
whores, and convicts, looking for the Russian colony
at Bodega Bay, heard the water hissing in our Spring,
discovered a snap turtle in the vicinity, which, for reasons of his own, he thought miraculous, and sending the
trappers on to Bodega Bay, he remained with the whores
and the convicts, and built two cabins, the first real
estate in Galapagos Hot Spring. Within twenty years
we were the prime spa of the area. After the trapper
died, the whores, realtors now, ran the town; matrons
of the new Galapagonian society, they attracted bankers,
restauranteurs, and light industry. Millard Fillmore was
the first United States President to sleep here; Ulysses
S. Grant, Chester A. Arthur, and Grover Cleveland
bathed in our Spring; Rutherford B. Hayes took bottles
of our mineral water to the capital.

There were no paupers in Galapagos; it was the vacation ground of the rich and the near-rich, and the home
of those who catered to them. But our Spring began to
fizzle after the earthquake of 1894; other resorts became more popular, and our great hotels were scaled
down and revived as slaughterhouses, stables, lumber-
yards, and sawmills. The motor car eclipsed the stablers'
dream of building a pony empire, the slaughterhouses
eventually disappeared, and only one sawmill remained
until Stefan Wax, something of a cousin to Anatole,
abandoned Wax's Mill, and chose Orange County over
us, leaving Galapagos to the dogs.

The landscape has changed little during Anatole's

years: failed businesses, an occasional fire, one or two additions to the College, but the buildings and streets essentially intact. A boy of three, from Austria, boulevards, water, and a favored bridge in his head, his world of stone wrenched away by our two miles of rotting wood, dry air, and a low, sluggish skyline, this is the impression I have of Anatole's earliest encounters with Galapagos. In place of the Vienna of his parents, a pony in the street, the punctured bunting from last year's rodeo, a steamroller flattening the hot tar on Coronado Road, the Native Sons parading in their monkish capes, the smell of pine sap in your nose, the buzzing from Wax's Sawmill that worms into your consciousness, slips over your syntax and tightens your paunch, glues itself to the monotones we speak and write in Galapagos. Soon he would hear the plop of an air rifle, have beebees in his ass, the mark of a native.

I have evidence of Anatole's quick acclimation. At five he owned a Daisy one-shot, and must have sniped back at the other boys, either from a tree or his father's roof. The gun still exists. His initials burned into the stock and dated 1936; the blueing worn off the barrel, rust eating away the trigger mechanism. At seven he must have sat on the itchy grass around the Spring and watched Mr. Henry, our bullfrog, leap a good fifteen feet into the air, crippled leg and all. Other frogs were fair game, but not even the spoiled and arrogant Stefan Wax, two years older than Anatole, pigtail-snipper, leg-pincher, and Daisy marksman, would have dared take pot shots at Mr. Henry.*

---

* A curious oversight. Dalton should have known that Mr. Henry was later found in the same grass with a swollen belly and bloody eyes, his spine shattered by a beebee. Perhaps there were several Mr. Henrys,

I can feel the impatience of *Tar Baby* subscribers.
Now that you've swashed your toes in Anatole's habitat,
you want a direct plunge into town. Fine. What better
way of giving you Galapagos than tracing Anatole's
route to school? He lived in a house that his father
rented from Ulrich Wax, a cottage really, at the point
where South Spain Street empties into Coronado Road.
Ulrich owned most of the cottages on South Spain: clap-
board boxes put together in a week, with poor ventila-
tion and little protection from our frequent hailstorms,
insulated with a mangy rock wool, perfect for the mice
who chewed through the walls to get at it. Most of
Ulrich's mill hands lived in the cottages, and South
Spain from T Street to Coronado came to be known as
"Ulrich's Row."

Weekdays at seven in the morning Anatole shook himself out of the Row, turned left on Coronado, and
walked the two blocks to Sonora Indian Mound. From
all available reports school was barely on his mind; he
would earn demerit after demerit for dreaming in class,
although his topographer's map of Sonora Mound—
with its primitive contours and faulty hill shading—was
superior enough to hang in the principal's office. Anatole
must have stopped at the old Indian burial ground a few
minutes past seven, stashed his books, and looked for
trinkets and bones. In those days no one took an active
interest in Sonora Mound; it was a playpen for the
children of the town and an emergency garbage dump;
whole skeletons were unearthed and tossed away; skulls

and their identities became confused in the boys' minds. Thus the legend-
ary "Mr. Henry" passed on from one generation of boys to the next. But
how many extraordinary leapers could there have been with a crippled
leg? —Editor's Note. W.W. KORN

were bashed in; teeth given to a baby sister. It was only during Drexel Finger's second term as Sheriff of Galapagos, somewhere in the mid-forties, that the Native Sons declared Sonora Mound "an historic sight," became extremely possessive about "bracelets, jaw bones, and other such treasure found therein" (see *Galapaga*, 1944 edition), and offered to store the relics in the old College museum.

Anatole's devotions to the Mound were much more private. The smell of garbage didn't bother him. He knew the rat holes, the sharp cuts of rock, the areas where one would be likely to find wet condoms, beer bottles, and lace underpants stiff with purple blood, and he could ferret out the nesting places of old bones and arrowheads; he valued the arrowheads in particular, using them as pumice stones to erase the corns on his feet. Anatole was no mean pragmatist. He didn't ignore the archeological impact of his finds. With the help of his mother's Britannica, he catalogued the bones, arrowheads, and trinkets, and kept them in coffee tins, which he later turned over to Sheriff Fingers, when the Mound became sacrosanct and the College acquired its permanent Indian collection through the Native Sons. But consider Anatole on the Mound during its garbage dump years, his shoes filling with sand, in view of Galapagonians on their way to work.

—The German brat, what's his name?

—Black as a nigger with that mud and sand on him.

—Hear the little Jew can piece together a skeleton with wire and string.

—He'd better keep them walking bones off my porch.

—Oddest thing I ever saw! Boy at home in an Indian cemetery. Spooks you to think about it.

—Wonder if he ever goes to school?

—Snot all over him. Nobody taught him to wipe his nose.

A few of the townsmen might have chased him off the Mound, but they were grumpy in the morning, and they didn't want to dirty their shoes; why should they have risked antagonizing Ulrich Wax on account of a German nigger boy? Anatole traipsed, nose down, nudging the rocks with a toe, ignorant of the Galapagonians peeping at him, stooping to decide if the shape between his legs was a bit of glass or an Indian bead, until the bleat from Wax's Mill gripped the Mound and he could feel the tremors beneath him. His sides ached immediately; it wasn't the fear of a rock slide. He wouldn't have minded snuggling up to a jaw bone underground.

The bleat brought home to him the mundane concerns of Galapagos, and specifically, the boredom of school. It was a ten-minute run to Galapagos Elementary on J Street and Bear Flag Plaza. He would kick his knees and ride down the Mound, grab at his books in a panic, dart between our citizens, but his determination always broke after the second or third minute, and then he stumbled along Coronado, his eyes fixed on the spikes in a telephone pole, his hands rubbing the bones in his pocket. Cuckoo. Nigger baby. The citizens avoided him, frowned at the sand leaking out of his shoes and the dirt on his hands. Can smell him a mile away. Sticking to Coronado, Anatole came to the driveway and outer gate of Galapagos JC. Perhaps our quadrangle distracted him, and he counted the red tiles on the old Administration Building, followed the gush of water from the automatic sprinklers, craning for an overview of the arboretum at the back of the Inner Quad. Or did he just pass us by?

In any event, crossing Coronado he turned up Oxnard Street and encountered the Redwood Motel, its cabins glutting the corner of Oxnard and D. Had the town council given in to Mother Margaret Chace, her cabin train would have meandered up to F Street and over Tollhouse Bridge; she might have even asked for chunks of Bitter Water Creek. You wouldn't have guessed about our own decline from Mother Margaret's lust to tear up earth and build her cabins. *Galapaga,* the official guide to Galapagos, glosses over the Redwood Motel and Mother Margaret's career. It fails to mention her illegitimate daughter Cynthia, born in 1950, and would have you believe she was called "Mother" because of her shrewd business sense and the felicity with which her cabins multiplied. Shame on Seth Birdwistell and the other editors of *Galapaga.* None of us need cover up for Mother Margaret. I don't foresee any harm to Galapagos in admitting that the cabins of the Redwood Motel contained a whorehouse piecemeal, and that Margaret was a munificent mother to her girls. A widow in her mid- and late twenties during Anatole's years at Galapagos Elementary, she would sit for hours on her front porch, shotgun in her lap to protect the girls from stray, nonpaying customers.

She couldn't have missed Anatole on his morning walks. She must have cooed at him, offered him lemonade, played checkers with him. Wasn't this the reason for Anatole's chronic lateness at school? Several of Margaret's contemporaries, reliable Galapagonians, remember seeing them together on the porch, both of them in a fury, squabbling over the checkerboard, spilling lemonade, the stairs mottled with crunched debris from their all-day suckers, fat whores in midriffs lounging behind the cabins. For the benefit of *The Tar Baby* I reconstruct the essentials of one conversation between Anatole and Mother Margaret.

"King me, you runt."

"Stop cheating, Auntie."

"Don't butter up to me with that Auntie business. Just king me, runt, and be quick about it." She waggles the shotgun. "You wouldn't look too great without a face."

Her threat only serves to harden Anatole, increasing the temper of their argument. "You put a dead checker back on the board. I had you eight to three. Brush your teeth, Auntie. Your breath is sour."

Furious, she topples the board with the blunt nose of her shotgun. "I don't play with a whiner who makes false accusations about his friends and has little respect for his elders."

"Eight to three, Auntie. You can't erase that."

"Call me Margaret, runt. I'm not your aunt and I never was." She turns around, glares at the whores who snap the elastic bands of their midriffs with a giggle. "Quiet! Fat shits, can't a human being buy a little peace any more?" She hears a clump on the stairs, finds Anatole at the bottom of the porch. "Where are you going, runt?" she says, climbing down to him. "Stay."

"School," he frowns.

"It's only a quarter to ten. Stay. You don't have to king me, runt. Here. I'll put up the board. Eight to three? I'll take your word." She grabs a leg of his pants, tightening his crotch. "Be a sport. Stay. We haven't gone through half a lollipop."

The intensity of his frown frightens her; she lets him go.

He says, "Have to, Margaret," and runs.

Dolores, the fattest of the whores, chides her. "Won't

do to hug that boy, Mother. You'll only spoil him."

Not-so-fat Anita and Stephanie bunch against Dolores.

"You're jealous, Dolly. You want to rub him in your fur."

"Swallow him head first."

"Shut up," Margaret says. "I don't want you talking about friends of mine. Where'd he go? He forgot his books."

Out of Mother Margaret's range, Anatole chuffs up Oxnard in a panicky, lopsided run. Reaching E Street he talks to himself. "Spotteswood'll murder me." Must be his third-grade teacher. He doesn't have time to puzzle over the ideograms on the windows of F Street, Galapagos' minuscule Chinatown, or peek through the doors of the sweatshops, a nasty pile of blackwashed store fronts which spill into G Street, but do not appear in *Galapaga,* even though they are financed by our own Penn Gemeinhardt and his Galapagos Merchants Bank. Penn, who sits on *Galapaga*'s editorial board, would prefer to purge that little guide of all vestigial color. No whores or Chinamen wolfing noodles and ordering seamstresses about. We have to remain crystal pure for the tourists. Luckily, Anatole, as a boy, did not have to confront Gemeinhardt's sugarloafed Galapagos. He had a good whiff of noodles, muck, and whoresweat.

Following the boy's run, we move from the partial slum of G Street to H's mock suburban grass. Then the outcrop of a legitimate residential area on I Street, including a swimming pool or two, a mini-mall, a grocery store, and a smatter of lawns, flowered and unflowered, square, round, or crescent. Between I and J, our Spring, dry part of the year but wet enough to be featured in *Galapaga* as "The Home of Sonoma County's Leaping

Bullfrogs, True Rivals to the Celebrated Calaveras County Frog and Any Other Frog in America." Seth Birdwistell's wording, I presume. Coming off I Street, Anatole must have felt an appreciable dread. Between the stubbed pickets of the Spring he can see Galapagos Elementary, squatting in Bear Flag Plaza.

His soles chafe on J Street's gravel walk. Each step leaves a hazy print. The prints get deeper near the school. He raises his knees to soften his tread. But the evidence sticks to him. He's making holes in the walk. He can't move without defacing the ground under him. No point in going any further under the circumstances. He sits on his shanks measuring distances in holes. Ten holes to the school door. Fifty holes to K Street. A hundred and some back to the Spring. How many holes to Ulrich's Row? He closes his eyes to consider the specific bends and twists of the trip. He has ruts in his eyebrows from concentrating so hard. J Street————I Street ————H Street————G Street————He doesn't hear the eleven o'clock bell. The entire school moves up to the roof gymnasium for exercise hour. Faces plunk at him from an open stairwell window. A classmate risks a slew of demerits in order to shout, "Waxy-Weissy, Waxy-Weissy, get up before you shit in your pants." Satisfied, he proceeds to the roof. Anatole's sleeve is wet. Nothing unusual. He frequently drools on himself when he's solving a complicated problem. The hand rubbing his head doesn't startle him.

"Runt. What's wrong?"

He growls.

"I'm thinking, Auntie. Go away."

"People don't crouch in the middle of J Street without something being wrong. Why aren't you in school? Do I have to follow you everywhere? Go on."

"Can't. I keep interfering with the gravel. See those holes?"

"Holes?" she says, tugging her muumuu. "Act your age, runt. What do you think gravel is? You can't walk on it without marking it up. That's why the school sends the custodian out at five with a rake."

She sticks his books under his arm and carries him into school.

"Move your rump up them stairs. There's no gravel here."

She stops at Duckert's Creamery on M Street and orders a tub of sweet butter for her girls. "Put it on my bill," she tells young Duckert, husband, whoremonger, and father of six.

"Dad's clamping down, Mother. He appreciates doing business with you, long as your bills are paid by the fifteenth."

"I'm short of cash, Freddy. It's my slow season. You wouldn't want me to lay off Dolores, would you?"

"I sympathize with you, Mother, having to feed a truckload of fat women. I know their appetites. Dolores isn't fit company until she gets her butter and strawberry tarts. But the old man never met Dolores. Besides, I caught the scabbies at your place last week."

Margaret reaches over the counter, clawing the buttons on Freddy's shirt. "Who says my girls aint clean?"

Freddy stays there grinning, Margaret's fingers on his chest. "Whoa, Mother. Slow down. You don't want to alienate your best customer."

Margaret opens her fists, drops back; she finds a button stuck to her palm. "Mother," Freddy says, walking towards the gate at the end of the counter with the same grin. "Your girls are infected. Dolores got crabs in her teeth. I've been picking the buggers off my groin

for days." He flicks the latch on the gate, comes out.
"Be smart, Mother, and douse that slut with turpentine." Without a change of expression or a warning
grunt Freddy bashes Margaret on the lip. "Come in
here mooching grub from Dad and me for an establishment that's overrun with crabs," he says, watching Margaret squirm on his floor. "Control yourself, Mother.
Somebody might get the wrong idea seeing you on your
ass in Dad's Creamery." He grabs at her, shoves her
out the door.

"Fuck your wormy butter, Freddy Duckert."

She crosses the street and enters Galapagos Merchants Bank. The tellers and lower-echelon bankers
peek at her muumuu and her bruised lip. Penn Gemeinhardt, handing out souvenir feather pens to a group of
touring farmers, excuses himself and takes Margaret
into his office.

"Don't you squeeze my arm. I've had enough male
contact today, thank you."

"We wear street clothes in my bank, Mrs. Chace.
You visit me again with your nipples poking out I'll have
my sergeant deliver you home in a sack."

"My nipples don't seem to worry you, Mr. Penn
Gemeinhardt, when you bite into them every other
night."

"Not so loud, Margaret. Couldn't this wait?"

"No. I need two hundred dollars. Until rodeo time.
The cowboys'll get me through the year."

"Margaret, you can't expect Galapagos Merchants to
piss away money grubbing whores."

"I'm not asking for a bank loan. A personal loan is
what I'm after. How much am I supposed to put by if
you own ten percent of my hump, and Drexel owns another five?"

"Hush, Mother. My secretary is right outside the door. Bank's no place to discuss country business."

"Two hundred," Margaret says, and she covers the side of her mouth. "Oh, my God."

"What's the matter with you? You come in here without a brassiere begging for money, then you decide to have a fit in my office."

"So long," she says, and she runs out, her breasts jiggling at the tellers. Young Duckert sees her swish past the Creamery. He shrugs his head. She reaches L Street willy-nilly, frightening dogs and old women, scattering delivery carts. Sweat on her nose, muumuu hiked above her knees, she sends K Street merchants back into their stores. "A body's not safe with that horseface galloping around." Her flesh quakes in Bear Flag Plaza. Huffing, she opens the school door, hears the walls thrash. "You cost me two hundred dollars, runt. I had a dream about you in the bank. Knew you wouldn't climb up the stairs. Spend all day with your thumb in your mouth. What's that noise?"

"Gym, Auntie. Teacher must be throwing the medicine ball."

"Come with me, runt. We'll have toddies in my cabin. You write a note to school and I'll forge your mother's name. I got envelopes and a stamp. But no more checkers. Watching you jump over my men gives me heartburn."

Anatole follows her outside, ignoring the booms from the gym. She flattens his hair with her palm. "It'll be the old Indian rub for you if you don't move faster. Suppose your principal catches us sneaking away. How many truants can Drexel's jail hold?"

"Shut up, Auntie. I'm going as fast as I can."

Margaret frowns and pushes him towards I Street.

BEAR FLAG PLAZA

In 1839 Zachariah George, the first alcalde of Galapagos, reckoned the economic potential of our Spring, and built a public square adjacent to it, using convicts and Indians who were under contract to him. On the northwest corner of the square stood George's own home, an adobe mansion with iron shutters and iron doors. Five years later Colonel Benito Cambón of the Mexican Army, suspicious of the American settlers in Galapagos, occupied the alcalde's house, and the square was turned into a drilling ground for his men. A certain controversy has surrounded the person of Colonel Cambón. Unquestionably a loyal soldier, he was also an idler who fell in love with our waters and who took more of an interest in miracle baths and sulfur cures than in the upkeep of his garrison. The Colonel's lapses did not go unnoticed. Sometime in June 1846, during the Bear Flag Revolt (the historic uprising of American settlers against the Mexican rule of California), a war party of 32, instigated by that indomitable pathfinder Christopher ("Kit") Carson, seized the garrison and destroyed Colonel Cambón's men. Kit Carson's role in the massacre has never been determined. He was not with the actual war party, having spent the day in the foothills mapping trails. Meanwhile, Colonel Cambón, unable to face the ignominy of a decimated garrison, elected to drown himself in Galapagos Spring, thus giving rise to the legend

that the "Spanish blood" in our waters has amorous powers. Kit Carson lingered in Galapagos. Hoping to entertain him and to occupy his mind, the town gave him permission to re-name several of our streets. Carson could neither read nor write, but having been entranced by the letters of the alpha-bet, taught to him by an Indian girl, he decided to run Galapagos through the ABCs, even though the town, in 1846, ended abruptly at M Street. Shortly after Carson left Galapagos, townsmen would refer to the square as "Bear Flag Plaza," in honor of the June war party, and gradually the name began to stick. In the early 1860s the Episcopalian minister, Lysander Jones, placed a bell in the middle of the square, which was used to call out the Native Sons when-ever a rowdy appeared in Galapagos. The bell was no longer in service by the end of the decade. In 1871 Zachariah George's "Alcalde House" became the first home of the Galapagos Military Academy; the structure was razed in 1926 to make room for a new elementary school. A bronze replica of Lysander Jones' bell still exists; unfortunately, it was vandalized from our Plaza a few years back.

For news of other historic spots, consult GALAPAGA.

CYNTHIA WAXMAN-
WEISSMAN "STOKIE"

Remembrance of a Dead Husband

The following is an unabridged monologue by
Cindy W.-W. "Stokie," Anatole's widow, and now
"common-law" wife of the young China Lake
plumber Millard Stokie. At the time Cindy sub-
mitted to a session with my tape recorder she was
literally on the run, her new husband having been
fired from his job at the nearby United States
Naval Ordnance Test Station and told to vacate
his Navy-owned bungalow on China Lake. I trust
readers will excuse the broken syntax and inter-
ruptions in the text. No attempt has been made to
tinker with the thrust of Cindy's recollections, or
to impose my own logic upon her grammar and
sentence structure. Any such refinement would
have been cruel and reductive, and could only serve
to suck under the eccentric charm of Cindy's voice.
Readers are cautioned to remain attentive to my
system of markings throughout. In transcribing
the Cindy W.-W. "Stokie" tape, I supply a long
dash wherever the sound trails off or Cindy's words
become indecipherable. I avoid paragraphing and
minimize punctuation—Cindy was not preparing a
schoolgirl's composition. I indicate the relative
duration of her pauses by scaling the space between
sentences, and between clusters of words. Short
pauses naturally have short spaces. My own com-

ments can be found between brackets in the text. The title of the monologue is my own. *The Tar Baby* paid Cindy fifty dollars for the session, partly because of her reluctance to talk about Anatole and her fear of tape recorders, but also because of her husband's financial difficulties.

—The Editor

————Anatole. What do I think? He's a fish is what.   Or was. Husband ha. Booby hatch philosopher is better.   That crazy had a hundred and one jobs and couldn't support himself. I was old enough to marry him and suck him off but I couldn't sign him into Minerva State or get him out. My mother had to drive him to the hospital. Doctor says he's suffering from Cyclops fever. First he's jolly and can't keep his hands off me   then he's blue   and won't touch me for a week.   A case of walking Cyclops fever. Half-man husband.   Honey, am I right? [Stokie, in his undershirt, sitting on a broken rocker near the bungalow's only window, swigging beer from a quart bottle, belched at this point and said, "Tell the motherfucker to shove his talk machine up his smelly hole."] Millard   can't you be polite? Guess what I've been doing since I got clear of Galapy High? Moving from one idiot to the next. Men keep spooking me. That's my history. I caught the disease at home. My mother can tell the size and shape of every cock in town.   Millard, take that bottle out of your mouth and offer Woody some. ["Fuck off," Stokie said, gurgling the beer and spitting it back into the bottle.] While we're on the subject of men, how about dragging my father in? Margaret doesn't know who he is. That's what she pretends. Woody, you know? ["Sure he knows," Stokie said. "Everybody in Galapy knows. It's the old waxhead Anatole. Mr. Woodrow Wilson Korn, that girl's depraved. Ought to be arrested, putting out for her natural father and having a child with him. Little Bruno's got himself one hell of a handicap. Daddy who can't cross a road without being kissed by a bus, grandma who's diseased and a whore, and a mama who happens to be his half sister too. A mess of family in my estimation."] Shut up, Millard. You shut up. Always needling me. Telling lies about Anatole. I was happier when Drexel was alive. Drexel wouldn't have let me marry Anatole or you. Drexel would have sent me to beauy and etiquette school so I could have gotten an invitation to Dallas for the Miss Teen-age America pageant instead of being disqualified in Yuba City. ["Bullshit," Stokie said. "Lucky thing Drexel got himself killed before you was ten. He would have been squatting over your hole in a few more years."] Would not. Would not. Would not. Drexel carried me to the rodeo on his shoulder. Drexel combed my hair. Drexel brought me dresses and gave me pocket money. Drexel wouldn't allow Margaret to spank me. And he'd wipe you out for saying what you just said. [Stokie tipped the bottle and rinsed his face with beer. "Drexel's dust and clay and melted bones."] Big man. Stealing toilet pipes from the Navy. [Stokie sprang up, slapped her, and walked out sneering at my tape recorder.] ————didn't ask him to drive me to Yuba City I wouldn't be with him now. Why couldn't Margaret do it herself? It's not my fault if Anatole was

afraid to sit in a car. Millard got me high   and I
watched the little muscles in his forearms.   I started
thinking how his body must look when he's installing a
sink or threading pipes   and he took the roach out of
his mouth   and tried to kiss me.   I pushed him away.
'I'm married, stupid.'   I was in such a state by the time
we got to Yuba City I stuttered on the platform
and a girl from nowhere   with sugar cones instead of
boobs   won the talent show. I was the most beautiful
cheerleader Galapy ever had. You remember, Woody.
People in the stands paid to see Cindy not ten sloppy
boys with a basketball.   A lot it did for me.   I got the
biggest shock in my life before I graduated. I came running back from the marriage bureau with the license in
my hand and cornered Margaret. I screamed until she
had to lock the door.   'The clerk at the bureau says my
entry in the town register is *Galapagos, Cynthia.* You
said my name was same as yours.   Liar. Mother, you
ever meet any Galapagos, Shirleys around? Galapagos,
Brenda?   Or Brenda Galapagos?   How can I get
married if I have no name?'   She patted my neck like
I was a dumb cow.   'Honey, it's only a small point. The
town was afraid the State agency for bastards   and
bitches would poke into its affairs and find out you was
missing one parent   so it adopted you outright   then
gave you back to me.'   Wouldn't you think   that man
Gemeinhardt handled the paper work. Hustled the State
into believing Galapagos is my father. So Cindy No-
name married Anatole.   That's what Mother wanted
for years. Been bringing us together since I was thirteen.
Made me clean his cabin. Serve him breakfast in bed.
Shoved me right up to his nose.   Only it took a while
for Anatole to sniff. Maybe that's why I liked him.

Everybody at school was chasing me.   Teachers, janitors, football players. But Anatole had me worried. In
his reach every damn day   cleaning   cooking   getting
used to the hair on his belly   and his bald spot. Furious why he hasn't done any pinching   or grabbing   and
growing sick from wondering so much. Can't eat. Can't
sleep.   Can't ———— I'm vacuuming his cabin   sucking in pencils and paper clips   having to shake them
out of the bag   and he comes in wearing his College
cop shirt. He scowls   which is usual for Anatole   and
I jump on him, catch him around the belly with both
legs. 'Anatole,' I say,   'if you don't undress me this
minute, I'll squeeze the putty out of you.'   He
laughs, scoops his hands under me   so he's got a
grip on my bottom   and he rides me all over the cabin
my fingers stuck in his neck.   'Anatole, Anatole,
I'm so dizzy I could die.'   Then he puts me under the
covers and says, 'You can stay in my bed. But no more.'
Well.   I collect the vacuum and march out. No man's
going to take me to bed with my clothes on.   I stay
away two days. Margaret says there's black smoke over
my head from cursing so much. 'Mother, a girl my age
has the right to ask for some affection.'   Anatole's
got me freaked, because I'm back next day slapping dust
and lying under the covers stiff as a mummy. This goes
on for months. Anatole on his chair asking questions
Cindy afraid to move   or he'll think I'm scheming to
molest him.   'Long as you asked, Anatole, I do
feel spelling and grammar are holy   because if everybody broke the rules and wrote whatever he pleased,
you'd have a scratchy vocabulary that nobody could
use.'   We're yapping back and forth, about the yes
and noes of grammar   the spitefulness of paper money

and the Indian city under Galapagos. Meanwhile I've
got crotch ache   and nipple ache   and any ache you
care to mention.   Once, after policing the College all
afternoon, he falls asleep in his chair. I throw off the
covers, pull down my pants   sit on him   strip the buttons on his fly   grind him into the ground. First he
won't acknowledge a thing.   Then I see the changes in
his face. His mouth opens, his eyebrows move closer   he
crunches his nose. There's noises but I can't separate his
moans from mine. His throat rattles when he comes and it
confuses me   and gets me crazy because all I ever heard
before was the squeak of high school boys. Anatole kept
his eyes closed but he couldn't have minded it. We were
married soon as I was seventeen.   Mother put us in a
bigger cabin. I showed Tessie Karandash my diamond.
She was captain of the cheerleaders   and my best
friend at Galapy High. She said the diamond wasn't
worth a bat if Anatole came with it. Only she called him
Waxy.   'You're talking about my husband,' I said.
'Watch out.'   I told her she stinks   and threw off a
few of Anatole's   titles.   'He's a professor, a philosopher, and a law enforcer.'   'A baldie too,' she said.
'Fat and close to forty.   He's unglued.   He walks
into lampposts and spends his vacations at Minerva
State.'   'You're jealous,' I said.   'Nobody ever offered you a diamond, Tessie Karandash.'   We split
up over that.   Forever ———— [Here she had a minor
fit. Mumbling, squinting at me, she sat with her legs far
apart and slapped her forehead. The *thok, thok* of her
slaps caused my machine to flutter. I had to stop the
tape. Gambling coldly with myself, I played back a part
of the tape, aware that her voice might add to her panic
or shake her out of her fit. The sounds shamanized her.

She was utterly absorbed in them. "That me, Woody?"
Taking full advantage of her recovery, I stroked the
mike, rewound the tape, and plunked the machine on
record. She mumbled something about "talking too
big."] Woody, what topic was I on? [I mouthed "Tessie
Karandash."] Yeah, I'm the one who couldn't wiggle
free. Maybe I only got a general diploma but Anatole
taught me a lot about physics and radio waves. Words
leave a hook in your brain. I couldn't stop myself from
considering what Tessie said.   Most of it was true.
About Anatole being unglued. I'm not talking about his
lows. I could live with them. I'd wrap him in a blanket
feed him a toddy with basil and apple butter   and
sweat the meanness out of him. It was the other side of
his Cyclops fever that bothered me. He's sitting calm
and loose in a shirt from the laundry, eating a pork
chop, asking for apple sauce, and he says, 'Cindy, we'll
be rich by November or January.' I'm wrangling with
my pork chop   worrying about whether to steal al-
monds from Margaret for dessert or make do without
it   when that word   that low-sounding *rich* gnaws
through my gizzard until I'm ready to puke.   'Anatole,
what have you boxed us into this time?' He rolls the
chop in the apple sauce.   'I bought a piece of the College bookstore. In your name.'   The bank won't
trust him with a credit card because of his stopovers at
Minerva State   so he buys what he wants and signs my
name. Mother's wickedness is behind it. She's the one
who taught him to forge people's signatures.   'Cindy,
I'm expanding the paperback department. It's undigni-
fied for a bookstore to truck sweatshirts, lamps, and
shaving cream. Now *The Tar Baby* can have a separate
shelf.'   No point in screaming at him. You have

to fight Anatole's logic with some of your own. 'Honey, are you planning to get rich selling *Tar Baby*s? It's sweatshirts that keep the book business afloat.' Anatole must have been impressed   because his pork chop sank   and I brushed my teeth, powdered the slope between my boobs   and rushed off to Isaac Meskill that bookstore man who loved to connive with Anatole and freak him out of his wits. It was pulling Anatole up from his debts and seesawing with Isaac and the other Galapagos sharps that convinced me I could get along without a father   and showed the town Cindy Waxman-Weissman wasn't no ordinary child bride. 'Isaac, who cleared the sweatshirts off your shelves?'   He smiled his Isaac smile, which is two parts fraud and one part filth.   'I can't keep track of bought merchandise, *Missy*,' he says.   'I'm Mrs. Waxman-Weissman. And you remember that.'   He behaves better now.   'Mrs. Weissman, there's a gross of sweatshirts bundled in the shed.   Waiting for Anatole.' 'How much did he pay for them, Isaac Meskill?' 'Three hundred flat,   and two hundred in addition for shelf space to keep his *Tar Baby*s on.'   Woody, no offense to you, but *The Tar Baby* has brought an awful lot of trouble into my life.   'Isaac Meskill, you ought to be aware that I've got to countersign anything my husband buys. The family credit card's *in my name*.' 'Credit card?' he says, looking scornful.   'I got Anatole's promissory note.'   'I suppose if he bought the Merchants Bank, you'd believe him too.'   'I'm not worried,' he says.   'Mother Chace will make good on anything Anatole buys.'   'You leave Mother out of this, Isaac Meskill.'   Isaac juggles his smile. Filth pushes fraud to the side.   'Of course,' he says,   'you

can always pay me back bit by bit. Say, twelve to fifteen
bargaining sessions in the shed.' Growing up in a
whorehouse motel has some advantages. I can smell a
reckless man man who lets his crotch draw him into
the open, away from his safety zone. I smile my Cindy
Boom-Boom smile, leftover from my cheerleader days.
Sweet and thick. Then I lay into him.   'Isaac Meskill
what would the trustees of the College think if they
found you making indecent proposals to a professor's
wife. And prying promissory notes from Minerva patients? I'll have you running to the County court house
twice a day answering summonses for speculating with
a crazy man   and attempting to fuck his wife.'
He stumbled up against his shelves.   'Nobody's
renting space for *Tar Baby*s, Mr. Isaac. You put those
sweatshirts back where they belong.'   And I gave
him a clean view of me, front and rear, to eat out his
heart. I had my fun scuffling with Isaac and them other
pirates.   Gemeinhardt.   And that clothing man
Mulholland who sold Anatole three dozen seersuckers
so he could outfit the attendants at Minerva State. What
happens? I trade Galapagos for a water-shy lake.
It was Millard.   He turned me against Anatole.
'You want to saddle yourself to a sickie your whole
life? You can't win no beauty contests sitting in Galapagos.'   He promised to take me to Dallas and
Miami for the pageants. He said it's nobody's business
if I'm a married woman. Dallas ha.   Miami. Millard's
parked his ass in the State. We're on the California
hurdy-gurdy. He can't scare up a dime. 'Baby,' he
says, 'everybody needs a plumber. I'll do a little fixing
and we'll move on.'   He did so much fixing with his
wrenches, I can't name the quantity of Sheriffs who are
after us. Aside from being a crook, he's a rotten

plumber.   Woody, I don't feel so good. I'll talk to the machine again tomorrow. [She watched me pack up, suspicious of my felt pen. "What are you writing on the reel, Woody?"

"Only your name. So some fool won't erase the tape."

She peered shrewdly at the check I gave her, snapping the paper, slanting it with pinched fingers. "Beats me, Woody. All the time I was married to Anatole I never knew *The Tar Baby* had its own checks."

"I can pay you the fifty in cash if you want."

"No, no," she said. "I prefer a *Tar Baby* check. To-morrow, Woody. I think better in the mornings. And I'll be less shy with the machine."

Millard collared me outside. He offered to carry the tape recorder up to my hotel. "I'll see you to your room, Mr. W.W." I told him I'd look after my own things, thank you, and he followed me up the road.

"Don't be cross, Woodrow."

I couldn't abide his wheedlings or his shuffle. I wanted to wring his neck. Gratitude to Cindy and my obligations to Anatole and *The Tar Baby* kept me civil.

"Ol' Woody Wilson, come on back to the bungalow. Cindy's dying to entertain. She likes you. Don't you concern yourself about me. I'll sleep in the woods. I'm not afraid of Turkey Semple. He only strangles people in the north. Never heard of him hanging out in China Lake. You can have her for fifty dollars, W.W. Twenty-five? She goes round the world, Woodrow. You'll get more wizardry out of her than anybody at Mother's. Come on. Ten dollars? *Five.* That's my last offer . . . Ah, you. Should have known you wouldn't be inter-ested."

The crinkled paper on the walls of the China View had a fish-and-bird motif. A pesky fan blew hot air at me from the ceiling. It had a crack in its housing and couldn't be switched off. I stared out the window at the stunted vegetation on the dry bed of China Lake. I'm a man who ordinarily relaxes in his underwear and socks, but I stripped off everything at the China View. Even the bed clothes scratched. I sat in a tub of rusty water and played back the Cindy W.-W. Stokie tape, scribbling notes to myself on a pad. *Skirts two obvious areas: abandonment of little Bruno and A.'s death. Random omissions? Might be freer if Stokie were gone for the day. Pay him his fifty? Expensive operation for one tape.* The felt pen worked fine in the tub. My splashings blotched the page. I can't conceive what was on the proprietor's mind. He sent up the house prostitute, a distressing woman with gaps in her teeth, who was amused by my naked body, the pen in my hand, and the tape recorder on the toilet seat. "Sweetie, you don't need me. You got your voices." Nothing to gain by shouting at her. She left of her own accord.

Avoiding breakfasters downstairs, I ran to the cottage around eight, more fond of Cindy than ever, but nagged by the tape. Stokie's pick-up truck was nowhere. The porch rails had been broken off. I looked inside. Cindy shouldn't have demeaned Stokie's capabilities. He'd gutted the cottage overnight; smashed the furniture and carried off the plumping; ripped out window frames, light fixtures, and wall sockets; and painted WOODROW WILSON on the floor, in baby blue. Had Cindy gone with him reluctantly? Humoring myself, I imagined her waiting for me among the wreckage, eager to talk.

Having no desire to win the day clerk over to *The Tar Baby,* I simply crammed the hotel's magazine rack with our back numbers, and left China Lake.]

A BRIEF HISTORY OF THE NATIVE SONS

Visitors to our County might be tempted to consider the Native Sons a prettified philanthropic society that exists solely to congratulate itself and bungle into County affairs. This is an unfortunate appraisal. The Native Sons arose over one hundred years ago to meet an immediate need. In 1861 Galapagos was given over to a veritable reign of terror: failed gold prospectors from El Dorado County, licentious itinerant farmers, and the Mexican bandit, Joaquín Tiburcio, ruled the town. Unlike its neighbors, Galapagos did not have the benefit of a vigilance committee. Many of its officials, and certainly its Sheriff, were in league with its lower elements. Oddly enough, help against the riffraff came not from the California militia, but from the Episcopalian church, which established itself in Galapagos in 1857 on the block bounded by Espinosa, Fawn, C and D streets. The Rev. Lysander Jones, minister of the new parish, understood the rude facts of Galapagos life. In 1860 alone he conducted 389 funerals and only 2 marriages and 1 baptism. Relying on his most active parishioners, Father Jones organized the Native Sons, which promptly decamped the prospectors and the licentious farmers, together with the Sheriff, and tarred the bandit Tiburcio. For the next five or six years, the Sons themselves policed the town, relinquishing their power only after they brought in another Sheriff. Since that time the

(*Turn over for GALAPAGA*)

Sons have had a working relationship with all Galapagos Sheriffs, though in recent years this relationship has corroded somewhat. In 1863 Father Jones, now retired, was elected the first grand deacon of the Native Sons of Galapagos. The deaconship, it should be noted, is only a semi-official position. The grand deacon cannot enjoin his brother deacons to act; he may only petition them; he does not control the finances of the organization; nor does he enjoy the right to expel wayward deacons. But in spite of the office's limitations, the very best grand deacons have always managed to exercise a profound moral grip over the organization. The honor roll of Galapagos grand deacons is comprised of the following names and dates of service:

Rev. Lysander Jones, 1861–1889
Sheriff Pete Sloughs, 1890–1899
Captain Newbold H. (Harry) Chilton, 1900–1917
Stillman Brewster, 1918–1921
Murray Duckert, 1922–1929
Tom Lick, 1930–1937
Penn Gemeinhardt, 1938–1942 (resigned to serve
    with U.S. military)
Sheriff Drexel Fingers, 1942–1959 (killed in office)
Penn Gemeinhardt, 1959–1962
Frederick Duckert, 1963
Penn Gemeinhardt, 1964–to present

JOACHIM FISKE

Anatole's Juvenilia

The child of a German wet nurse and a California
berry farmer, native Galapagonian Joachim Fiske
earned his teaching certificate at the former Lam-
bourne Normal School of Yolo County. Twice
the recipient of a Sterling Teacher Award, this
veteran of twenty-years service in the Galapagos
public school system joined our faculty in 1959.
Associate Professor of Business English and subdirector of our School of Pragmatic Letters and
Philosophies, Fiske is also a poet, an amateur crim-
inologist, and *The Tar Baby*'s regular film re-
viewer.

Anatole: a near genius who couldn't spell, a lazy boy,
an unruly boy, a boy under Mother Margaret's wing,
who couldn't memorize a word of French but knew the
argot of whores and petty crooks, a boy without friends,
painfully shy, a boy with an instinct for grammar, who
snored in class and ruined my days, a boy obsessed with
the Indians of Sonora Mound, who wouldn't plot *The
Last of the Mohicans* but could fabulate inventories for
the Mound Indians from a few broken relics and pull
their history out of the air. Because he was disgruntled
over the "unadventurous spread" of my report topic

list and hence a nuisance during business letter practice,
I gave him the singular opportunity of picking his own
topic. If it is shocking to admit I hoped Anatole would
mire himself in an impossible project that would keep
him out of my scalp for the entire winter term, I beg
The Tar Baby not to eye me with too much disfavor. I
wanted to protect my students' sanity, as well as my
own. Armed with *Ethnology in a Nutshell,* which he
borrowed from the class library, the twelve-year-old
Anatole set out to investigate the biodynamics of the
Sonora Mound and the epiculture of the defunct Indians
buried underneath. Here, then, for *The Tar Baby,* an
extract from Anatole's "Report on the Pitfaces":

The Pitfaces were gruesome and pitiless. They never achieved
the hegemoney[sic] of an actual tribe, since they had no leaders,
no hunters, no priests, no slaves, no carvers, no clans, no weavers,
no cooks. Each Pitface fended for himself. Children were vicious
by the time they were six. Old women had to whittle their own
branches for a crutch. Fornication was rife among the Pitfaces.
A man crept in with the nearest unoccupied woman or girl.
Husband and Wife aren't part of the Pitface vocabulary. No
baby could tell his own father. Although their tramping ground
was practically on the ocean, the Pitfaces didn't have the sense
to hunt for sea lions, crabs, or snails. They picked berries instead, ate grubs and worms. Up to the smallpox epidemic of 1813,
these Indians were filthy, nameless, and poor. The epidemic
dessicated[?] the Pitfaces and got them a name. The other coastal
Indians shunned them all the more. Ugly now and itchy, with
scabs on their noses, their testicles, their thighs, the Pitfaces kept
to themselves. They lost their appetite for berries and grubs.
They forgot how to fornicate. They occupied themselves exclu-
sively with their burial mound. This mound was the single great
curiosity of the Pitfaces. They must have been necromaniacs in

their hearts. Alive, a Pitface meant nothing to himself or his Pitface brothers. But once he was a rotting corpse, his value went up considerable[sic]. The Pitfaces let go their gruesomeness and almost became a clan when they worried and moaned over the dead. They put mud cakes on the corpse to discourage the worms and the flies. But they left the forehead clean. Every Pitface bumped heads with the corpse before it was buried. Head bumping joggled the Pitfaces[sic] nerves. In their mourning clothes they trampled berries and grubs and picked up rocks and branches and the bones of dead animals. They strolled the woods pelting birds and clubbing rabbits and baby deer. Once they butchered every living thing within sight of the mound they ate a few berries to keep alive and sat still until the next Pitface died. The tribes north of the Pitfaces grew rich trapping salmon and candlefish and harpooning whales. They carved pictures of their sumtuous[sic] life on their harpoons, on their arrows, on their canoes, on the rattles belonging to their priests, on the bodies of their enemies, and other places. They hoped to remind their neighbors and the world of their superiority over all men. The Pitfaces continued to scratch themselves. They died off looking into each other's ugly face. More than one anthropologist feels the Pitfaces were an ecological mistake. It would have been better for everybody, including themselves, if they had never been born.

The class's initial reaction to Anatole's report was one of horror and amazement. We were disturbed by his description of the Pitfaces. Their habits appalled us: wanton copulation; avoidance of parental responsibility; orgies of bloodletting after rubbing heads with a corpse. However distasteful the Pitfaces were, these bleak fumblers affected us sorely, and we pitied the trickling out of their lives. Still, I could only give Anatole a B for his efforts. I closed my eyes to his atrocious spelling, but I had to penalize him for abusing his imagination.

Anatole's "Report on the Pitfaces" was a shameless
coupling of fact and fiction. What evidence had he
amassed for the existence of the Pitfaces? True, no
trained archeologist had examined the Sonora Mound
at the time of Antaole's report. A few years later Seth
Birdwistell's students would prove that the Mound
Indians were an integral portion of the Skwakamish
chiefdom. The Skwakamish developed a sophisticated
procedure for the division of labor. The Mound Indians
inhabited the southernmost sector of the chiefdom. They
did, indeed, specialize in berry picking [Anatole's report
wasn't completely fanciful]. And they were caretakers
of the Skwakamish dead; though the northern fractions
of the Skwakamish, which consisted primarily of har-
pooners and tradesmen, practiced their own method of
interment. Anatole, of course, could not have known
about the complicated interplay of Skwakamish society.
But he should have been more modest in presenting his
facts. Lucian Bonnefroy, the class scientist, flayed Anatole because of this.

An alert boy from Canada, Lucian nibbled the edges
of his chapstick during Anatole's delivery. He pulled
on his lip while Alana Kent, a girl who never washed
her neck, asked a gratuitous and disjointed question,
typical for her [I have always believed there is an exact
relationship between clumsy language and body dirt.]*
"Anatole, why, if the Pitfaces built it, is the mound
called Sonora?"

Patient with her, Anatole said, "Because the earliest
settlers of Galapagos assumed it was the work of Indians up from Mexico, they gave it a Mexican name.

---

* Joachim, Joachim, are you aware of your own musty smell? —The
Editor

Or perhaps they were just fond of Mexican names."

Lucian stood up, bowed, drubbed the chapstick against his palm, and announced: "Too many pits, Anatole, much too many pits. Follow me:

(a)   Smallpox? No! An outbreak of cholera killed the Indians in 1813. Cholera attacks the bowels; it doesn't scar the face.

(b)   You swear the Pitfaces weren't artisans or warriors; but my brother Martin owns an arrowhead he dug out of the mound. I can bring it in as evidence.

(c)   How could anybody 'forget how to fornicate'?

(d)   Which anthropologists specifically called the Pitfaces 'an ecological mistake'? Name four. Name three. Name two.

(e)   Who was the first Pitface?

(f)   When did the last one die?

(g)   Without smallpox, where did the pits come from?

(h)   Did Pitface women ever lie down with white men?

(i)   Were the Pitfaces destroyed by a different kind of pox?

(j)   Did the Pitfaces keep pets?

(k)   Do Indians have dandruff you suppose? If you think I'm digressing, don't answer.

(l)   How many berries could an average Pitface pick in an hour?

(m)   Did the berries give him diarrhea?

(n)   Can you name another worm-eating tribe?

(o)   If a Pitface baby wasn't weaned, who taught it to pee?"

Anatole was skunked by the questions; he dandled against Lucian's ineluctable logic and Lucian's ineluc-

table wit. The girls in the class admired question "o."
The thought of an Indian baby passing water pleased
them. Questions "h" and "i" interested a number of
boys. Stupid, unwashed Alana worried about the Pitfaces' diarrhea.

"Arrowhead," Anatole muttered. "Pitfaces put the
weapons of their enemies in with the corpses. They
didn't have arrows of their own. The pits came from
smallpox."

"Cholera," Lucian said, sniffing the chapstick. He
walked behind Anatole, plucked Magruder's *History of
California* from our library shelf, balanced it on his
knee; we listened to the pages thrash. Settling on a page
near the end of Magruder, he read in a smirk: "The
cholera pandemic of 1812–14 began in the Ganges
delta, spread by land to Russia, via Mongolia, and by
sea to the Philippines, reaching North America in the
fall of 1813, giving rise to the fabled *Indian crash* of
that year, which narrowed the population of the Haida,
the Makah, the Chinook, the Tsimshian, the Skwakamish, and the Tinglit by sixty percent."

"What's a pandemic?" Alana asked.

Daniel Budwing, medium bright, wanted to know if
Magruder's figures were exact.

Lucian slammed the book. Two girls trembled, one
coughed, another sneezed. Anatole slept with his chin
in the inkwell. An auspicious sign, I thought. Smallpox
out of the way, the class could return to its doughy comforts: Alana drawing grime to herself, Anatole breaking wind in the middle of a dream, Lucian concentrating
on the etiology of bitter rot.

I blame Mother Margaret for prolonging the Pitface
issue. Do twelve-year-old boys travel to Yuba City all

by themselves and find native informants in a brothel? Margaret had ties with the Northern Lights Motel. She took him there. He brought that disgusting person into class: a pockmarked, beshitted Indian who claimed to be the last Pitface alive. Coached, bribed, sodomized, and fed by Margaret, he came prepared. Lucian couldn't shake him. The girls up front nosed the tar on his shirt and the ordure in his underpants. Gaggling, pointing at his warts, his rags, his blotched palms, the filth on his ankles, the knots in his hair, the snot in the brim of his hat, they soon turned morose. He garbled his name in Pitface: it meant He-who-belches-in-the-face-of-his-enemy. He preferred Nicholas St. Justin, his Christian name.

Lucian put on airs with Anatole's informant.

"Sir, can you account for the kinks in your personal and tribal history?"

"No kinks, Mr. Bonnefroy," Nicholas St. Justin said. The ordure notwithstanding, he had an even disposition.

"Let's pretend there was an unknown smallpox epidemic, an epidemic Magruder forgot about. Are you ready to tell me that your pockmarks are inherited? that the Pitfaces passed on their complexion from generation to generation?"

"Not at all, Mr. Bonnefroy. The name 'Pitface' was only figurative. The bird shot on my face comes from a severe eruption of the chicken pox."

Lucian, in a furor, boggled his chapstick and retrogressed to his old habit of picking dead skin off his lip.

"What do you mean figurative?"

"Oh, mother," Nicholas St. Justin said. [An Indian expletive, or was he calling for Mother Margaret?] "Ask me what I know. My aunties gave granddad his black spots. They sprinkled coal dust on a melted candle, and daubed him with it."

Anatole stood mum during this exchange. Licentious neglecter of my own students, I passively observed shit-clinging Nicholas. He swabbed toilets, I believe; ran errands for the bawds at the Northern Lights. But he had his appeal. I had never seen a tar-shirted man use language effectively before.

"It's a lie about the candles," Lucian squealed. "We'll have to deodorize the school. You stinkpot. Go home."

Lucian got support from his classmates. The boys had tired of Nicholas and Pitface talk; the girls were indignant over the ordure. Except for Daniel Budwing, who was in awe of anything anthropological, and Alana Kent, who liked the smell of shit, the class echoed Lucian's complaint. "Stinkpot. Go home."

I was about to swoop through the room, extracting apologies; Nicholas prevented me. He bowed, the snot shingling on his hat, and left.

The aftermath is obvious: Lucian turned the class against Anatole. He was excluded from the volleyball games on the roof. His report was discredited. Scatological stories about him, Nicholas, and Margaret were told to his face. A dollop of pigeon dung was left in his inkwell. But the harassment leveled off in a month. Gradually the Pitfaces came into favor again. I take no credit for it. Lucian had turned the class around. His devotion to science pricked him into vindicating Anatole. "There's factual truths and mythical truths," Lucian declared with his customary pith. "The Pitfaces are short on one and long on the other. Nothing further has to be said."

We've all gone on to new careers. My move was the

simplest. Ten blocks east by southeast, from grammar school to our Junior College. What about the graduating class of Galapagos Elementary, 1943? Half the boys are farmers or mechanics in the Sonoma area. Alana's neck didn't impede her nubility: she has two sets of twins, to date. Harry "Butch" Wooser is a Sacramento policeman; Wayne Strotter owns his father's brokerage; Daniel Budwing, more ambitious than the others, is interviewing pygmies in Malaya; he lives on a houseboat and has no intention of returning to the States. Lucian Bonnefroy, our most famous living graduate, is earning plaudits in the West for his work as a computer scientist. Lucian's built a computerized California data and literature bank, called "Kit Carson." He's been pampering the computer with detective stories to pep up its vocabulary and plot-sensitivity, though he hopes Kit Carson will one day write a lucid, factual, nonsmutty novel of the Old West in the electromagnetic language of "feed-speak." Kit Carson has met with a large share of hostility. Seth Birdwistell wrote a scathing denunciation of "feed-speak" in the Spring, 1970 number of *The Tar Baby*: "Punch Card Babylon." Birdwistell's article has split the faculty at Galapagos JC, the older professors siding with him mainly, and the younger ones, drummed on by Nina Spear, attacking him at lectures and in print. Though personally sympathetic to Provost Birdwistell's views, I have remained neutral, owing to my feeling for Lucian. Were Anatole alive today, would he approve of Kit Carson? I wonder.

TAR BABY PERSONALS

Cripple, age 30, would like to meet generous person any age to teach him to dance socially. Small gratuity. Only serious need apply.
Tar Baby Box 11

FLEA MARKET
N Street Park
Bargain in the Sun
With Together People
Through the Week

WAXMAN-WEISSMAN
1931–1972
Peace, Anatole

March 12, 1972
Dear Patrons,
We want to apologize for the dreadful conditions at the Royal Sponge Burn-Out last February. As producers of the Burn-Out, we have to assume the majority of blame, but we did not know beforehand that the Sponge's own security force would be selling tickets illegally at the side entrances and ripping off members of the audience. Needless to say, we will never again be duped by the Sponge.
Sincerely,
The Management
M. Bogart's
Electric Teet
Yuba City

Six mothers and six children urgently need 15 rooms in Galapagos. Can pay up to $300.
Tar Baby Box 3

Young baker with no kitchen wants to make bread in your home. Guaranteed not to leave a mess. Will accept other tasks. Sorry. Can't groove on anything far out. Walter. Reach me at the College bookstore.

GIRLS 5–9
(slight 10's will also be considered)
for one-hour live photo sessions. Discreet. Parental approval a must. Go to N Street. Ask for Jay.

20 stall horse farm, 31 acs., 10 room farm house. Dirt cheap. Must relocate. Can no longer bear to live in Galapagos.
Contact Tar Creek Realtors.

PATCHQUILT PRESS
has the following position open: Super-sharp Girl Fri. Must have an ear for native literature. Should not be computer-freaked. Good vibes. Good pay. Write us c/o The Tar Baby, Galapagos.

ATTRACTIVE GRANDMOTHER
seeks companionable mate, 40+. Must be proficient conversationalist. Bald man w/belly okay. Rodeo hands will not be considered.
Tar Baby Box 1

BRANDO FREAKS
Free showing of *One Eyed Jacks,* any time, any place. "The sweetest Western ever made."
—Joachim Fiske.
TB Box 2

Margie, we know you're with the Royal Sponge. Come home. Mom, Dad, & Uncle Nauls.

GALAPAGOS HOUSEWIVES
Crave variety? How about a brunch date? I'm a mature W/M college professor, clean & generous, who desires hard contact w/ occasional attractive nooners.
Tar Baby Box 1

LARGE REWARD offered for missing Border terrier. Grey markings. Weight 15 lbs. 3 yrs. old. Only answers to Honeydog. Heartbroken.
Tar Baby Box 9

Talk & Slide Show: Seth Birdwistell, "California Diggins,"
Galapagos Country Church
4 p.m. Thur. June 8 (free)

TAR BABY PERSONALS

STREET PEDDLERS
Earn 30% commission selling fast-moving magazine. Easy work. Okay bread. For full details, contact Nina. TB Box 1

"RUBBER SOUFFLÉ"
seeks two (2) dynamite chick guitarists. Must be dedicated and have some bread. Leave your name with Jay at the Flea Market. We'll find you.

ONE SUPERGIRL to sell specialized products to housewives in Galapagos area. Must enjoy indoor work. Aboveboard, reliable firm. TB Box 11. Send snapshot!

JOACHIM FISKE
Poetry readings at our Flea Market every second Sunday. Come celebrate Galapagos with me.

TURKEY SEMPLE DAY
Honor the exploits of this internationally known provo on May 12 at the N Street Park. Grab this: We have been denied use of the campus mall, and the Sheriff's Office is hassling us about a park permit, but the celebration will go on in spite of them all. Will Turkey show? Come and find out.

FEMALE IMPERSONATOR
(traveling thru Galap. area w/daughter) needs feminine companionship. All races welcome. French love available upon request. Gay is out of the question. Look for me on Sundays at the Flea Market. I cruise from 9 to 9.

GALAPAGOS JR. COLLEGE
Join the growing field of American Education. Opportunities for:
Secretaries
(w/without steno)
Janitors
(handicapped acceptable)
Security Guards (1)
(will train)
Our staff enjoys
•Free tuition
•Scenic campus
•Use of College computer
•Boating on Deadman's Creek during Winter
•Opportunity to work with top faculty
•Vacation, health, and other benefits.
Tar Baby Box 3

Businessman needs jack-of-all-trades for lots of things. No steno, lite typg, some suckg. Animal lovers preferred. Knowledge of German desirable.
Tar Baby Box 11

TAR BABY SPECIAL
Snot-green hearse. Looks like German command car. Special rate to movement women. Also have antique roach clips, decals, and heated toilet seats. See our man at the Flea Market. Ask for Mel, Irv, or Jay.

Doing time in Idaho. 15–life. Would like stimulating intellectual pen pal. Male . . . or female. Not interested in smut. Write McNabb, TB Box 12. All mail will be forwarded to me.

GALAPAGOS SWINGLE
Newly matriculated, seeks same. Have firm, hairy bod. Excellent profile. No bad odors. No birthmarks or unsightly blemishes. Look for me at the College mall. Smokers, alcoholics, drug users, bi-men, fatties, senior citizens, please leave me alone.

ATTENTION! ARTISTS & PENCIL FREAKS!
Need caricaturist for good spot at Galapagos Flea Market. You dabble, we supply the customers & the stall. Tremendous potential for crafty sort of guy. Can also use 10 popcorn vendors. See Irv, Mel, or Jay.

SETH BIRDWISTELL

Auguries of Futility: The Misinventions of Anatole Waxman-Weissman

Born in Blue Nile, Texas, on January 11, 1907, naturalist, grammarian, and practical anthropologist Seth Birdwistell was educated abroad. He is provost of Galapagos Junior College and founding director of the Galapagos School of Pragmatic Letters and Philosophies. The only nonnative with full membership privileges in the Native Sons of Galapagos, Provost Birdwistell is also a member of the Pi Club; the Sonoma Beautification Council; the National League of Ornithologists; the Rubber Horn; Far Western Bailiffs; the Society of Angry Grammarians; Spade and Dye; Friends of Northern California Drum Majorettes; and the Wholesome Revelers. His stubborn ten-year economy drive brought the College its new Life Sciences Building, which houses the School of Pragmatic Letters and Philosophies, the Drexel Fingers Museum of Galapagos Americana, and *The Tar Baby*. Provost Birdwistell lives alone in the cliffs overlooking Galapagos; his winterized cabin can only be approached via a funicular railway; three generations of students have ridden in the Provost's hand-cranked funicular car. Without question the most popular teacher-administrator at the College, Birdwistell expects to step down from his provostship next fall and devote himself to a comprehensive study of California's past.

Tar Baby buffs, I have no intention of profaning the dead.

Those five hundred and thirty-seven of us* addicted to *The Tar Baby*'s querulous nature must have followed my running feud with the writings of Anatole Waxman-Weissman in these pages. But my vitriol towards Anatole's work has not eaten into my impressions of the man. A *homo illiteratus* by his own admission, Waxman-Weissman was nevertheless a gifted teacher, a competent security guard, and a gentle, though eccentric, creature. It was his misfortune to have become the darling of certain obscure, evil-minded French critics. A spate of misplaced and useless activity has surrounded the man and begun to destroy what minimal authenticity his work did have. In the past year alone I count no less than nine articles and monographs: *Waxman-Weissman, sa Vie, son Caractère, et ses Idées avant 1970; Les Débuts Littéraires de Anatole Waxman-Weissman; Oeuvres Posthumes; Souvenirs de l'Année 1971; Waxman-Weissman et ses Projets Inédits; Les Fantômes de Galápagos; L'Expression Figurée dans l'Oeuvre de Waxman-Weiss-*

---

* If my distinguished colleague is poking fun at the shortness of *The Tar Baby*'s subscription list, he should be reminded that we can also be found on magazine racks in nineteen cities and eleven States, without even considering Vancouver, and that newstand sales push our circulation well over a thousand. —The Editor

man; Les Jours d' «Anatole»; and *L'Essai Fantastique en Amérique de «Wittgenstein Among the Redwoods» à Waxman-Weissman.* For this I blame *The Tar Baby.*

To discuss the "*œuvre*" of a man whose lifework consisted of a trunkful of notes, an aborted biography, and one elliptical essay endlessly revised is laughable and criminal. Had *The Tar Baby* not indulged Anatole by publishing six versions of "Wittgenstein Among the Redwoods," it might have saved his sanity* and quashed the controversy between myself and Nina Spear. Unless I am mistaken, W.W. Korn is planning to bring out a variorum edition of "Wittgenstein Among the Redwoods" as a *Tar Baby* special. Madness is the only word one can use in describing such a project.

Anatole juggles paragraphs, hacks away whole incidents, changes the names of minor characters, but the facts and the setting in each published version of his "Wittgenstein" are quite compatible: Ludwig Josef Johann Wittgenstein, alive and flourishing in America in the 1960s, is a teacher at a suburban Kindergarten for aphasics located in the Galapagos foothills; furthermore, he is separated from his wife Agnes, lives in a grimy hut, and rarely changes his underwear. Now, it is obvious to most of us that the actual Wittgenstein died in 1951, in England; he never visited California; he had no wife; his person and his possessions were invariably clean; he was a kindergarten teacher in Austria during one of his periodic retreats from philosophy, but there is no record that he ever taught at a school for aphasics.

---

* Is Seth Birdwistell implying that *The Tar Baby* did Anatole in?
—The Editor

"Wittgenstein" advocates would be wrong in assuming I am eager to smash Anatole's props. I am well aware of the connection between aphasia and the pessimism of Wittgensteinian philosophy. Casting his semifictional Wittgenstein as a man who attempts to restore the power of speech to brain-damaged children seems a remarkably poignant invention. "Ludwig stared contemptuously at his zond [a wire apparatus inserted in the patient's mouth to keep the tongue in place for a given sound], twisted it out of shape, threw it in the basket, and smiled at Maria, Bruce, Manfred, Kingman, and Jane [aphasic children at the Galapagos Hills Defectology Clinic]. Taking off his shoes, exposing his pathetic, twisted socks, he climbed on the desk, barked, crawled about, scratched himself, and wiped the drool from his lips. Maria, Bruce, and Kingman laughed. Jane shrieked. Manfred imitated Ludwig's motions and his noises. Ludwig hunched over the desk and answered Manfred bark for bark. Then Maria, Bruce, and Kingman barked. Jane stopped shrieking and gazed at the others. Moses Dessart [the addlebrained, pinchbacked director of the Kindergarten clinic who undergoes several mutations in the six published versions of "Wittgenstein"] heard the barks, opened the peephole in Ludwig's door, humphed something, and walked on. Ludwig jumped down, clutched his chalk, and drew the ears, nose, and mouth of a wolfhound on the board. 'Dog,' he said, turning to Maria, Bruce, Manfred, Kingman, and Jane. 'Dog. Dog. Dog.' Kingman picked his nose. 'Dug,' Maria said. Bruce growled at Ludwig's wolfhound. Manfred said 'Wuf.' Jane sat agape. Ludwig stuck his fingers in her mouth. She immediately said 'Dog, dog, dog' " ["Wittgenstein Among the Redwoods," first published version, *The Tar Baby,* Summer, 1961.] Doesn't the nonfictional Wittgenstein suggest in his *Tractatus Logico-Philosophicus* that we are all aphasics, children struggling with words, walled in by the accumulated dross of our ornamental, metaphysical, falsely humanistic language? (We must all learn to say "Dog, dog, dog.")

Had Anatole kept his Wittgenstein (whom we shall henceforth call "Ludwig" for the sake of clarity) inside the classroom, I would have fewer complaints, in spite of the absurd California setting. But the moment Ludwig strays from the Kindergarten, he is weighed down by Anatole's misinventions, and "Wittgenstein Among the Redwoods" disintegrates. We see Ludwig empty his bowels at the side of a road; hear him recite a filthy limerick while he masturbates; watch him rut with a whorish cashier in the ticket booth of a Galapagos movie house; follow him up to his mountain hut, where he defecates again, chews moldy corn flakes, crashes into spider webs, dreams of murdering his absent wife. To what purpose? Show the world that Wittgenstein was a satyr with loose bowels? Nonsense! Anatole's scatological props and paradigms reveal nothing about Wittgenstein's *Sprachspiele* [language games] or about his austere and secluded life. In fact, the quality of Ludwig's thinking is dismal throughout. Supposedly at work on a grammar for the word "cunt," he mutters "*nichts wert*" [worthless] on the road and delivers banal speculations on the "putrefaction of time" to Betty, the cashier, moments before coitus. In my opinion Betty is perfectly justified in padlocking her ticket office and screaming, "Ludwig, you're a lousy lay." (Under similar circumstances I would have behaved no differently.)

"Wittgenstein Among the Redwoods" is the work of a melancholic. Without question it prefigures Anatole Waxman-Weissman's madness and collapse. W.W. Korn should have been the first to read the signs of Anatole's futile life in Ludwig's absurd behavior and misshapen, rambling thoughts. Why did he ever encourage Anatole to revise the "Wittgenstein"?* One version would have been sufficient, more than enough.

Not even a "heartless old neuter"† such as myself could deny Anatole's gift for caricature or the playful energy of his prose. But the humor seems a bit ingrown, even incestuous, to me; almost as if the "Wittgenstein" were a private joke written for the benefit of the faculty and brighter students at the School of Pragmatic Letters and Philosophies. Moses Dessart, who dissolves into Maurice Quim, Myron Muncion, and Matthew Asquith [depending on which version of the "Wittgenstein" you dig into], but remains the director of the Defectology Kindergarten, a man with a spotty head, who builds funicular railroads in his spare time and rides in them, is obviously modeled after me. (*Tar Baby* buffs, don't think for a moment that venegeance is on my mind; I rather like Moses-Matthew-Myron-Maurice. There is little malice to Anatole's parody: in spite of his bumblings, Moses Dessart is the gentlest character in the "Wittgenstein.") Jane Blade, the aphasic child who learns to utter brittle sentences with Ludwig's fingers in

---

* I don't propose to defend my conduct at the bottom of Birdwistell's pages. Readers are invited to inspect my article, "The Other Anatole," which appears at the end of the issue. —The Editor

† I did refer to Birdwistell as "that sexless old man," but it was in another context entirely. —Nina Spear, Business Manager

her mouth, bears a striking resemblance to Nina Spear, in name, personality, and sentence style. Manfred Drake, the oldest aphasic, who is nine in one version, twelve in another, and barks with a Southern accent, whose parents are missing and lives with a recreant uncle [not unlike the dead Ulrich Wax], loves to chew on "nigger babies" and sketch cartoons on butcher paper, could only be Woodrow Wilson Korn.*

One shouldn't ignore the variants in Ludwig and his family. Ludwig is childless in the first three versions of the "Wittgenstein"; in the fourth version [1965], Anatole provides him with a daughter, Bonita, who lives with her mother in Santa Fe and is afflicted with alexia and agraphia: she cannot read or write. She is perfectly normal in version number five, and may or may not be illegitimate, since Ludwig has a dream in his hut that Turkey Semple is her father.† In the sixth and final

---

* Birdwistell's reading of the "Wittgenstein" is simplistic and ironbound. In his attempt to impose one-to-one relationships on Ludwig's world (i.e., Dessart = Birdwistell, Drake = Korn, and so forth), he shows little understanding of transfiguration psychology. If anything, Anatole's personæ are composite portraits. Manfred Drake could just as well be Stefan Wax, who *is* a cartoonist. Or Anatole himself. And, I admit, Woodrow Wilson Korn. *Or* all three, and more. The Provost's mention of "nigger babies" seems a calculated and shoddy gambit to turn me into a racist by inference. He chooses to forget that I am no less a Galapagonian than he is; that I escaped from the South at an early age; that I detest all things chocolate and have *never* chewed a "nigger baby" in my life. —The Editor

† Curiously, Provost Birdwistell slides over the fact of Turkey Semple's historicity. Apart from Ludwig himself, Turkey Semple is the only *real* figure in the "Wittgenstein"; doesn't it suggest that Semple, the desperado-rapist who attacked and killed Sheriff Drexel Fingers, was very much on Anatole's mind during the writing of the "Wittgenstein"? I mention this because of my own active interest in Semple, who is still at large, and was last seen skunking two old fishermen, robbing them of

published version [1971], Bonita is alexic but not agraphic, and Anatole is convinced that Agnes, his wife, who screens his letters to Bonita, is distorting their meaning, so he includes visual material—keyless diagrams, balloonless comic strips—in the hope of entertaining Bonita without the plague of words. He fails. His diagrams and comic strips only serve to confuse Bonita, to mystify and torture her, and she nearly dies of brain fever. In despair Ludwig loses complete control of his anal sphincter, leaves a "river of shit" wherever he goes, and becomes a coprophiliac: he sees feces in his sleep, conceives of a magic bull who can exchange his penis for a turd, etc., etc. What are we to make of Ludwig's cloacal musings? A feisty aphrodisiac (love and fundament caught in the same barrel)? A profound endorsement of "la vision excrémentielle"? An indictment of the American craze for sophisticated indoor plumbing? *Nichts wert.* Anatole would have been better off had he chucked the "Wittgenstein" and stood on the southeast corner of G Street and Bushel Road, watching the migrant apple pickers inside Lapham's Beanery eat with piss and cow dung on their sleeves; the women nursing their brats, the men fondling their daughters, without regard for Lapham's short-order cooks.* Then he might have been able to tell us something substantial about perversion, filth, and coprophagy.

Again, I blame the entire *Tar Baby* staff. The fourth,

shirts, boots, and social security checks, outside a remote Nevada bordello. —Joachim Fiske

* I'm sorry to say that Provost Birdwistell's geography is wrong. Lapham's Beanery is situated near the *southwest* corner of G Street and Bushel Road. —Dalton Chess

fifth, and sixth published versions of the "Wittgenstein" underscore in crude fashion the progressive deterioration of Anatole's mind. Towards the end of his
life Anatole himself suffered from periodic attacks of
alexia. He was unable to read written material of any
sort for days at a time. His mother-in-law, Margaret
Chace, had to correct student papers for him. (The comments of this unschooled woman, when decipherable,
were earthy, humane, and much to the point, in spite of
the erratic punctuation, the faulty grammar, and an
epidemic of run-on sentences). I'll be blunt. Isn't it possible that Waxman-Weissman, who wandered in and out
of Margaret Chace's "motel" for over thirty years, and
must have had some contact with her employees, might
have been in an advanced stage of neurosyphilis while he
reworked the "Wittgenstein"?* † ‡ A preoccupation
with feces is, I believe, a frequent sign of syphilis. How
many syphilitics (including Maupassant, Voltaire, Al
Capone, and perhaps George III) have strangled on
their own excreta? And, it seems to me, the linguistical
quirks of the sixth "Wittgenstein"—the lack of connectives, the plucking out of essential adjectives, the
utterly barren style—is further evidence of a diseased
mind.

Nor should we blind ourselves to the arbitrary nature
of Anatole's protagonist. Why Wittgenstein? Couldn't
Anatole have burdened someone else with his misinventions? Here Harvey Gimbel's excellent story, "Benya

---

* Rubbish. —The Editor.
† A cruel and flatulent speculation. —Joachim Fiske
‡ Where did this brainstorm come from? —Nina Spear

Krik in Boston,"* comes to mind. In transporting the
King of the Moldavanka from Odessa to Dorchester in
order to handle the Irish crooks of South Boston [the
Jewish merchants of Dorchester have paid for his pas-
sage], Gimbel, a graduate of Harvard, plays up Krik's
inadequacies in the New World. What better subject for
a study of the prostitution of American morals than an
orthodox bandit with an Old World innocence and
charm who ends his days floating face down in the
Charles? I wish one could find an equivalent merit to
Anatole's choice of Wittgenstein. I'm afraid no such
thing exists.

Nina Spear may tintype me as senile and meddle-
some, but I am not "dawdling in the shadows," as she
says. *Tar Baby* buffs, remember this: I was the one who
hired Anatole Waxman-Weissman to teach pragmatic
philosophy at Galapagos. I knew the man. I respected
his primitive intelligence. I could see him from my windows at the Life Science Building, jogging around the
inner quad in sweat pants borrowed from our Athletics
Department, his badge in place, fists against his chest,
staring past students who avoided colliding with him
only because they were familiar with his route; you could
follow the plunge of his belly or keep an eye on his
fat cheeks; his bald spot was a different matter: either
it got lost in the stucco or it gaped at you from a crackle
of light.

My friends at *The Tar Baby* would have been much
the wiser had they left off correcting copy in their warrens

---

* A pretentious piece of dreck, which attempts to exploit the chauvinism
of the American Jewish reading public, and is not fit to be mentioned
with Anatole's "Wittgenstein" in the same paragraph. —Nina Spear

and alerted themselves to Anatole's quadrangular run. True, Nina might have dismissed it as simple exercise. If she's right, why didn't it burn off the fat, put color in his face, affect his slouch? No, Anatole's "exercise" was futile. Buildings crabbing at him from four sides, a face, an arm, a stripe of cloth drifting in and out of his field of vision, the whole of the "Wittgenstein" locked in his head (in all probability he composed his sentences, made word changes, during these jogs), Anatole running, running, running, and going nowhere.

Instead of typemarking the latest version of the "Wittgenstein," *Tar Baby* staffers should have come out of their warrens and pulled Anatole away from the inner quad. Then there would have been less jabber about *Oeuvres Posthumes* and *Les Jours d' «Anatole»*; divorced from his "Wittgenstein," no longer subsumed by language, Anatole might be with us today, sick perhaps, but alive in Galapagos.

STEPCHILDS OF GALAPAGOS

Presents Its Construction Fair
(formerly ROYAL SPONGE BURN-OUT)
for Home-Town Justice

Dedicated to Our Peace Magnate
Sheriff JAROLD HAWES

FOUR COLOSSAL ROUND-THE-CLOCK PROJECTS:

- Build Straw Duplicates of Sheriff Hawes: perfect play toy; you can burn it, pluck it, or fuck it

- Resurrect Anatole: prove to the world that Galapagos saints and poets don't go dead

- Construct Your Own Red Light District: screw free sex; help bring the lovely whores back

- Action Kit: instructions on how to liberate a bank, a data processing center, a Lincoln-Mercury dealer (Music & Guerilla Theatre supplied by the Sponge)

FEATURING:

THE TAR BABY
LITTLE BARLOW
ANATOLE MEMORIAL COMMITTEE
SHERIFF'S FUND
COMMITTEE TO TURN KIT CARSON GAY
GALAPAGOS BAIL BARGE
THE ROYAL SPONGE

SUNDAY, June 10 · N Street Park
FREE! FREE! FREE!

from GALAPAGA, *the official handbook to Galapagos*

OLD GALAPAGOS, PART I

Five shallow, nearly empty arroyos, or creeks, meander through Galapagos: Arroyo de Armargosa (Bitter Water Creek); Arroyo de Zapato Chino (Chinese Shoe); Arroyo de los Muertos (Deadman's Creek); Arroyo de las Ranas (Froggy Bottom Creek); and Arroyo de la Brea (Tar Creek). The historical, cultural, and geographical significance of the five creeks is difficult to measure; all have contributed to the shaping of Galapagos in one way or another. ¶ Froggy Bottom Creek was the hideout of the Galapagos bandit Joachín Tiburcio (flourished here in the 1850s); from his perch on the west bank Tiburcio would maraud women and children who came to wash their clothes; in order to discourage further visitors, Tiburcio's men took to croaking, and they spread reports that the creek was infested with bullfrogs, hence the name Arroyo de las Ranas. ¶ The site of a former Indian encampment, Deadman's Creek is famous for its petroglyphs (rock carvings). The Galapagos petroglyphs, with their crude depictions of human handprints, curling snakes, many-legged beetles, a rabbit, bear tracks, and the like, could once be found in abundance on the rocks along the creek; in 1939 these rocks were moved to the College museum at great expense. A kitchen midden, or Indian refuse heap, was located near the east fork of this arroyo; rich in organic material, the soil here is exceedingly dark; quite a few skeletons and artifacts, including arrow points and flint chips, have been plowed up. The original name of Arroyo de los Muertos was Dunghill Creek. ¶ Mostly submerged, Chinese Shoe trickles under Galapagos. Early settlers believed that

Galapagos' crazy Chinese, ensconced in F and G streets, had tunneled through the floors of their shacks and were mining the underground creek for gold. After an old shoe was discovered in the slough behind G Street, a band of suspicious Galapagonians raided the shacks of Chinatown; they could find no extraordinary tunnels, but the name Chinese Shoe had already stuck. ¶ Crude oil, or *brea*, once oozed out of the ground near Tar Creek. Indians may have used the *brea* to secure their arrowheads and caulk their tiny boats. The earthquake of 1865 evidently sucked most of the crude oil out of Tar Creek, though an occasional black spot can still be found in the old channel of this arroyo. Prehistoric animals trapped themselves in the *brea*. Bones of great interest, including those of the giant ground sloth and the prehistoric bear, have been exhumed from Tar Creek by ambitious students at Galapagos Junior College; these bones are currently housed in the Drexel Fingers Museum of Galapagos Americana. ¶ Bitter Water Creek furnished the power for Galapagos' earliest sawmills and gristmills; in 1849 no less than six mills operated on the west bank of the creek. Four of the mills have since disappeared. The fifth one was reroofed in 1873 and used as a bottling shed by the owners of Galapagos Spring; it is now attached to the Wayneflete Electrical Company. The sixth mill, disused for many years, fell into the creek in 1898; its water wheel (Galapagos Registered Landmark #4), covered with beetles and a thatch of moss, sits there undisturbed.

MORRIS S[EMPLE]* PLOTCH

Some Preliminary Notes Towards a Morphological Survey of "Wittgenstein Among the Redwoods" (Including an Account of My Relations with The Tar Baby)

Literature scientist Morris S. Plotch was born in Philadelphia in 1935 and raised in White Plains. Part-time lecturer at The Teachers College of Eastern Arizona, Plotch was once a handyman, a stocks and bonds runner, and a female impersonator. He is the father of two girls, Ava and Gloriann.

CHARACTER CHART (prepared by Nina Spear for inclusion in *The Tar Baby*)

MORRIS: author of "Plotch's Notes"; see biographical sketch above

JULIA: Plotch's scrubby wife

AVA: Plotch's younger daughter; a naggy three-year-old; possesses a phantasmagorical vocabulary; seems to disapprove of Plotch

GLORIANN: Plotch's older daughter; five; suffers from

---

* Not to be confused with Turkey Semple. —The Editor

a curious ill-defined speech impediment; considered to be Plotch's favorite

SHEPPARD: laundromat owner; once Plotch's friend

IVA JANE: Plotch's wayward mistress; known to have a bad temper and an evil mouth

DELOS: Plotch's scummy boss; Julia's paramour; quack linguist; half Jew; has been performing freakish experiments on little Ava; like Plotch, a refugee from White Plains

At Sheppard's Wash & Dry for Julia. Lazy bitch says she can only paint her toes at home. Ava and Gloriann were fighting behind the soap dispenser. Ava called Gloriann "Miss Cream Crotch." The other launderers —a scatter of Arizona bachelors, schoolmarms, asthma sufferers, and menopausal housewives—sniped at me from their laundry carts. "Ava. Say something nice about your sister." She stuck her fingers inside the soap dispenser, pulled out clumps of free soap. "Shouldn't steal from a machine that can't defend itself, Ava." She licked the soap, played up to the bachelors and the marms. "My old man's unzipped." I collected Gloriann. Together we fumbled open the door of the washer, stuffed in corduroys, pillowcases, underthings, and Glori's controversial rubber doll with the articulated vulva and the crumbling belly button that the schoolmarms object to. Grown women fussing over a maimed doll! (Ava chewed off its wrists.) The marms would complain less if the doll wore something in the washer; am I supposed to punish Glori because she prefers to rinse its cotton dress at home, in the toilet bowl? This time I wrapped the doll in corduroy before I chucked it in.

"No bleach, Glori. Just a bibble of soap. Call me if you hear gurgling behind the door." I sat her on a bench, her feet a safe distance from the washer's moorings, and she sucked her thumbs with my instructions in mind, her face intent, an eye fixed hard on the little door. She didn't have Ava's pitch, Ava's flair, Ava's seductability, but she was reliable, tender, and her concentration was perfect. No unpropitious knock or agitation inside the washer would have gotten past her. I retired to Sheppard's magazine basket, in search of the Miss America coloring book; seems a randy old man among Sheppard's steady customers mucks up the Miss Americas, and I wanted to tear out a sample page for Julia, prove to her that art can thrive in a laundromat. Shuffled the home and gardening mags, the technical journals, police gazettes, the rotting pamphlets on Arizona lore, and all I came up with was a raggy blue cover with bleeding type; a homespun quarterly, no less, sitting in Sheppard's basket. I dangled the contents page. "Wittgenstein" stopped me cold. I hugged the mag, walked between the benches, reading. The marms squawked at me. Glori's doll had unloosed itself from the corduroy during a shift in the washing cycle; its soapy vulva bobbed against the door. "Disgusting," one of the marms said. Gloriann put her nose against the door. Ava pushed her away. "I told you. I told you." She jumped up to snatch the magazine. "Crazy Morris. He spits words."

Munching cornflakes, the four of us, Ava with her face in the bowl, asking for seconds, Julia stirring the pitcher of sour milk, me with the mag splayed on the table, feeding Gloriann and turning pages.

"I liked you better in drag."

Julia's hostile because I haven't humped her in months; she's been dating my boss, Delos Malkin, chairman of language arts at E. Arizona.

"I said I liked you better in drag."

"Julia, shouldn't be lubricious in front of the girls."

"You superior bastard. If you sold a few of your books maybe I could buy fresh milk. What's that?"

"*The Tar Baby*."

"Oh my God," Julia said. "Don't tell me you and Delos are working on a new experimental grammar?"

"No. *Tar Baby*'s nothing like that."

Ava emerged from her bowl, mush on her lips. "It's a dirty book, Mama. It's got a naked man in it."

"I wouldn't be surprised. That's what your Daddy's linguistics is all about."

Glori's mouth was open. Julia swiped my spoon. "You want to stuff her to death?"

She burgled the pockets of my denim jacket, found my last dollar bill, and went off to the supermarket with Ava. "You'll have to come up with your own supper tonight. I've only got enough for me and the girls."

Julia gone, I began to thrive. I combed Glori's hair, washed her hands, read words to her out of *The Tar Baby*.

DEAR TAR BABY,

YOUR SPRING '69 NUMBER HAS SHATTERED MY LIFE. "WITTGENSTEIN AMONG THE REDWOODS" IS BOTH NIGHTMARE AND

DESIDERATUM, A SEMIOLOGICAL "STEAL." BUT I WON'T BORE
YOU WITH PROFESSIONAL JARGON. I AM INTRIGUED BY ITS
AUTHOR'S DOUBLE-BARRELED NAME. WAXMAN-WEISSMAN, DOES
SUCH A PERSON ACTUALLY EXIST? (MISS?) NINA SPEAR IS ALSO
TO BE COMMENDED FOR HER VIGOROUS ARTICLE, "GUILLOTINING
PRESCRIPTIVE GRAMMARIANS, PART II." I AM ENCLOSING TWELVE
DOLLARS FOR A LIFETIME SUBSCRIPTION. PLEASE DO NOT CASH
MY CHECK UNTIL THE SUMMER, SINCE I AM SHORT OF FUNDS
AT THE MOMENT, YET DO NOT WANT TO BE DEPRIVED OF THE
TAR BABY.

HOW CAN I MEET WAXMAN-WEISSMAN?

M. SEMPLE PLOTCH

Julia in cucumber tights, trundling Ava off to the
nursery (dance classes and day care, courtesy of E.
Arizona T.C.); Ava collects her water colors and jar of
paste; Julia crosses her mirror, leaving a sad face (pre-
view of a sour afternoon? Delos fumbling with her
tights during sex at the drive-in). Glori waves goodbye.
Ava warns me from the porch. "Watch out, Dad. Make
sure sissy pees in the bowl, not on the seat."

I shut the window, slick down my hair, pluck the wig
off Julia's bald hairdresser's dummy. "Hungry yet,
Gloriann?" I comb out the wig, squeeze it over my skull.
Glori smiles: soon, she knows, it will be time for the
makeup bag. Wig secure, I get undressed, put on Julia's
French bra and diamond-patterned panty hose. Taping
my flaccid calves, I squirm into Julia's boots, hobble out
of her closet in body sweater and midiskirt. Short of
breath, I mutter, "Glori, now." She softens the eye-
liner cake, hands me blush and mascara, wets the eye-

shadow brush with her tongue. "Glossy olive today?" I paint Glori too. Dollish image of her old man? Not in the least. The make-up is more becoming to her; warms the interior mold of her face; makes her less of a thinker. Julia ought to take a harder look at her daughters. Ava clubs you with her sentences, but Glori's the true voluptuary. Calculating and brittle, Ava's only a tease.

We clutch hands, walk into the crisp sun, my wallet stuffed in Glori's pocketbook. Sheppard catches us, miles from his laundromat. He wouldn't have strayed this far unless he were perturbed. Fellow graduate student, in philosophy, roughly my age, Sheppard's secured himself with a ten-year lease on his Wash & Dry. He lives in the back room, among the water pipes, an air duct knocking over his head. But he's less of an anchorite than you might think; his room has a comfortable kitchen area and a shower wide enough for two. Perfect for Julia (quick scrubdowns between dates with Delos while Sheppard attends the coffee pot?), but she has the sense to stay away from him. Delos, at least, is beholden to Ava. Out to get the drop on all of us, Malkin's been analyzing Ava's morphemes for over a year, with hopes of compiling a universal grammar for speakers of American English between the ages of zero and six. Sheppard is closer to me; he'd rather nuzzle Glori's silences than the cluttered wonderland of Ava's speech.

"Morris, you stole my *Tar Baby*. Give it back."

"Sheppard, I've been shaking your magazine basket since the fall of sixty-five. There was never a *Tar Baby* underneath."

"Malkin put it there."

"Delos is into Waxman-Weissman?"

I walk off with Glori, twitching, gagging in Julia's

clothes. She leads me to the restaurant, sits me at Ivey Jane's counter, puts a menu in my hands. Exemplary student-waitress, Ivey is a broadcast major and lives above the restaurant.

"Morris Semple," Ivey whispers. "Fix yourself. Your mascara's dribbling."

"French fries for Glori," I say. "Nothing for me."

I take the ketchup bottle and salt cellar up to Ivey's rooms; Glori sucks her French fries near the window. "Jesus," Ivey says. "Drop the blinds. You want the whole world to know?"

She undresses before I do; I untape my calves and have Ivey sponge them in alcohol. We hear the plip of the ketchup. "M. Semple, can't she sit in the other room? It's harder to come with her around."

"Impossible! Glori doesn't like to be alone."

We wallow in Ivey's bed. She knuckles my scalp, her fist under the wig lining, and harps on Glori again. "M. Semple, she's a dumdum. What girl of five can't speak?"

"Why the rush? She takes it all in."

Ivey pokes her face over the bed. She's itching to draw sounds out of Glori. "Say *ah*, Gloriann. *Ah-ah-ah-ah-ah-ah-ah.*"

"Don't crowd her, Ivey Jane. She'll speak when she has something to say."

"Know why she's quiet, M. Semple? You've freaked her. Eating pussy in front of her eyes. . . . Semple come back."

We clomp down the stairs.

"Perverts," she screams at us. "Who you making up here, M.—me or Gloriann?"

✲

***THE TAR BABY* of GALAPAGOS**
BUSINESS MANAGER'S OFFICE
from the desk of Nina Spear

Dear Morris S. Plotch,

Grateful acknowledgement for your lifetime subscription to
The Tar Baby. We are not uptight over your financial straits
and shall, without fail, hang on to your generous $12 check until
midsummer. Thank you also for your kind words about my
article on the idiocies of prescriptive grammar and its vicious
attempts to hackle our language. For your information, Mr.
Anatole Waxman-Weissman does exist and is faring well at the
moment. He lives in Galapagos and can be reached at *The Tar
Baby* or c/o Mother Margaret, Redwood Motel. I should caution you beforehand. Anatole is a shy person and may not
answer your letters. However, if you have anything specific to
ask about "Wittgenstein," you might address your inquiries to me.

Hoping you enjoy our future numbers,

Humbly,

N.S.

for THE TAR BABY
April 3, 1971

Flak from Julia.

"You're warping my boots with your fat toes. Buy
your own."

"Who picked them out and paid for them?"

"Can I help it if you're a lousy boot fetishist? And
you're stinking up my sweaters. I told you to shave your
armpits."

Ava rushes in, quieting us with her seriousness and
agitation. "Mother, sissy's brushing Tou-Tou's teeth

again. Her toothbrush is drowning in pee."

"Shouldn't squeal on Glori, Ava. I'll rescue Tou-Tou and the toothbrush."

"Stop patronizing her," Julia says. "I'm sick of it. Do you expect her to close her eyes while her big sister falls in love with piss in a bowl?"

Both of them glaring at me, I step between them and into the bathroom to confer with Gloriann. I take her doll out of the toilet, rinse her toothbrush in clear water, scrubbing the bristles with soap in my palm, and flush the bowl. Neither of us minds the flecks of pee in Tou-Tou's worn rubber mouth. "Ava's a snitch, Glori. Mustn't play with Tou-Tou unless you put the latch on and lock yourself in. See . . ."

Julia pounds on the door.

"You piss-loving bastard, bring Glori out. All her bad habits come from you. I swear, I'll get Delos' crowbar and claw you out."

I catch him in his office.

Sly one, he gives me his pitch before I can get in a word. And I'd spent the week crafting a resignation speech, to be delivered with bites. "Tell me, Plotch, when you're humping Ivey with your wig on, do you pretend you're a woman . . . or a man?"

"Delos, admit, you planted *The Tar Baby* in Sheppard's basket. It was a deliberate ploy. To aggravate my colon, give me worms."

Pocketed behind his desk, smug with me, his dictionary and papers between us, he says, "*Tar Baby, whose Tar Baby?*"

With short deft blows I chop away his dictionary, his lamps, his sheath of notes, to get at him. A vein pops over his eye, and I let him go. His tongue flounders in his mouth. I wait for his speech to come back.

"Citybilly, you were a lousy stripper in a gay bar. A ten-dollar-a-night man. Your ass was open to the universe. I picked you off the street, handed you a career, fed you teaching assistantships and research grants."

"And exploited my little girl, fucked my wife."

"Get away from me. You're fired."

"Remember, Malkin, there'll be no more cunny from Julia, no experiments with Ava."

Mentions of Ava key him up; toadlike, he hops around his desk, beats me to the door. "Plotch, be reasonable."

"Skunk, you've been photographing Ava in the nude."

"It was strictly scientific, I swear. We shot her with a pinhead, a microcephalic dwarf. My assistants were there."

"That makes it worse."

"Morris, we blacked out her eyes. No one will recognize her."

"You send that photograph through the mail and I'll rupture you."

"Don't worry, Morris. It stays in my grammar. It's attached to a diagram. I compare Ava's brain-weight/ body-weight ratio with the dwarf's. Plotch, the girl's phenomenal."

"I don't want to hear about it."

"Morris, you couldn't believe the storage facilities she has in a brain that size. She puts the average college student to shame. Imagine what she'll be uttering at five or six."

"Malkin, why don't you study Gloriann?"

His eyes glaze over, his features squash with disgust. "Plotch, this isn't a zero-degree grammar. I need sounds, sounds."

"Glori has output problems, I admit, but if you could track her thoughts, you'd be swimming in morphemes."

"Please," he says. "One daughter at a time."

From *A Syntactical chart of* "Wittgenstein Among the Redwoods" (*The Tar Baby,* Spring 1969) *for Children Seven Through Ten,* compiled by M. Semple Plotch and Delos Malkin, and funded by the Department of Defense, U.S.A., as part of its "English Grammar for Americans Abroad" series:

PART III:	Lexical Counts
CLASSIFICATION V:	Waxman-Weissman's Use of Common and Non-Common Nouns
COMMON:	dog, rat, men, titmouse, toads, town, elks, trout, girl, frog, boys, curs, leopards
PROPER:	Mr. Wayneflete, Mr. Spotteswood, Ludwig, Agnes, Bonita, Moses Quim, Betty, Royal Crown Cola, Tiresias, Yvon, Manfred, Jarold, Maria, Barry, Galapagos, Kingman, Clive, Jane, Chevrolet, Uncle Satch, BVDs, Mugwamp Republican Party, Drexel Fingers, Sister Murray, Boraxo, Vivian, Corregidor
COLLECTIVE:	family, knot (of toads), country, confabulation (of twits), flock (of pimples, of men, of geese), murmuration (of starlings, of idiots, of shrews), unkind-

ness (of ravens, of toads), jury, gang (of convicts, of women, of elks, of fools), nation (of piss-a-beds)

CONCRETE: john, zond, pomegranate, condum, seed, coil, pimple, crack, chrysanthemums, pudenda, costermonger, hand, book, knee, fart(?), rice, pap, cuff, condiment, wen, desk, whimple, shrike, pencil, ruler, chalk, cockle, yogurt, blanket, testicle, sweat

ABSTRACT: pity, lust, simplicity, attitude, taboo

COMPOUND: ice cream, treehouse, cocklebur, dingleberry, shoehorn, carbon monoxide, tracing paper, tinfoil

VERBAL: ululating, swimming, fibrillating, fucking (as in, *Fucking* over and under the cashbox, Betty and Ludwig bruised their toes)

COCKAMANIE:* swuzzling, crooch, tuckboot, waterwink, cockziggler, thap, hulp, criuler, dispickapear, thrumposis, crawadaddy, solepap, thanatoosis, toothpost, hilp, gemeincraft, mindblubber, fatherfood, vestigments, penispoppuh, holp

Ivey's exposed me on high-frequency radio. Delos is behind it. He gave her a spot, a two-minute talk show, on E. Arizona's Megacycle Theater. "Friends, watch

---

* I gather that "cockamanie" refers to neologisms, portmanteaus, and other noun blends. —The Editor

for that married teaching assistant, thirty plus, who masquerades in woman's clothes to charge up his shrunken sex, befriends girls twenty and under, holds their hands, talks big, puts down language while he gets into their pants. This creep has a giveaway. He goes nowhere without his daughter, a husky five-year-old who can be recognized by her idiotic stares and perpetually closed mouth."

Shut ourselves in my studio. Heard a whimpering through the door. The staccato gasps flushed me out of my hiding place. "Can't be Ava. The articulation is much too poor. And Ava doesn't cry." Glori and I peeked outside.

"Delos dropped us," Julia said.

"What about his grammar? His experiments? His allophone charts?"

"*Vagitus uterinus*," she said. "His new interest is fetal crying. Sounds before birth."

Ava's wails scragged her syntax, disfigured the crystalline shape of her words. "Maaaama, Maaaama, Mooooma . . . Unca Malkin doesn't like me."

Caught Gloriann teaching herself how to whisper.

"Stop that! If you're ready to speak, shout it out. There's too much fragmentation in this house. Do you want your lips to harden into a pucker? *Shout*."

She ran to her mother. Sulky Julia had little sympathy for my theories. "Screw," she said, and I saw Glori's smile behind Julia's hip. Wouldn't want to meddle with that smile. Glori thrives in chaos. Ava may have collected the phonemes from my fights with Julia, but Glori took the rancor in. Told you, Delos, you've been interviewing the wrong girl. Ava's the one who worries me. Her morphological structures have collapsed. Suffering a syntactical breakdown, she babbles meaningless combinations of words. "Grocery peepoo mama."

I put on my coat.

I barreled past nurses and Malkin's assistants at E. Arizona's shanty hospital. He was in a smock and surgeon's mask, outside the delivery room, crooning to his oscilloscope. I ripped his mask away.

His assistants pulled me to the ground.

"Delos, you hear? You'd better integrate yourself into my family life. Julia's getting shingles. Ava's a mess."

"Schmuck," he said, playing up to his assistants, squinting at the mask in his hand. "I'm discovering phylogenic speech patterns, and he bugs me with domestic squabbles. Moron. Ontogeny means shit. I waste myself scoring every human sound from birth to death, when I should have been sticking my fingers in uterine water. How can Ava's morphemes compare with a talking fetus? Plotch, listen, in one delivery out of fifty, the water bag breaks, and the baby breathes air and screams before it's born. That's why I'm waiting. I want to record the scream."

"Why?" I shout from the ground. "It'll only scratch your equipment."

His assistants fling me out of the hospital.

Ava's deterioration is nearly complete; she no longer bothers with words. She runs through the house yawling random strings of sound. "Yehhhhhhhyooooooeeeeeee-hhhhhumpoooopaaaa." Wherever Ava is, under my desk, in Julia's closet, staring at the water level in the toilet box, I'm not far behind, wiping her nose, putting fresh rags on her boiling throat. "Ava, don't you want to hear the calliope, have your own horse at the merry-go-round? We'll ride in Daddy's old Ford. Come with me, baby." She breaks away, the rags unwinding, dropping under her feet, and I won't be able to track her without listening to her yawls. Selfish father, I haven't been blind to the damage: Ava's stretched vowels have stained my face, left a permanent scowl. I'd have my pick of hair pie if it weren't for that. Co-eds line up to peek at me because of Ivey's broadcast, but they scramble off when they see the cuts in my head. Got my eye on Glori. Off in the background, shifting for herself, she smiles and whispers to Tou-Tou. The doll has a rotten odor; Glori doesn't wash its dress in the toilet any more. The household chores have fallen on me. Julia sits in her room, wearing last week's underclothes, absorbed in her five gray hairs. I knock, enter. "Julia, I'm doing the laundry." Yawning, she cooperates, raises one arm, gives me a thigh. I unclip her bra, roll down her stinky pants, drop them in my sack. Her thigh against my knee doesn't sway me. But there's crust in her eye sockets, dirt around her belly. How else can you explain away desire? Does it come and go with a hanky wipe?

She moans, the dirt rubs off, my hand twitches, she pulls me into her musty bed. Glaaaaaa. Urrrrrrrr. Ooooooooop. I'm jealous of Malkin, for the first time. He's heard the stress signs in Julia's moans. Caught the highs and the lows. Screwed her while his assistants read her vibes in the window of his oscilloscope. What electrical device did he use on Ava? He went too far with her. Are her babblings in the other room a proto-orgasm, induced by memories of Malkin's electronic touch? I cried on Julia's belly. "Morris, what's wrong?"

"Nothing," I said. "Your come startled me. I'd forgotten the sound."

She stares at her big toe.

"Morris, I'm sorry."

The toe wags in my eye.

"I faked it. I didn't come. I couldn't."

She brings the toe over my head.

"Because of her."

In the crack between Julia's elbow and left nipple, Gloriann, smiling, fondling Tou-Tou, watching us.

Vagitus uterinus has flopped. "Bubba Morris," Delos cries, fouling my life. He knows I detest telephone bells. "Delos, catch me at the laundry, wire me, but don't call," I say, my tongue flicking the mouthpiece. The phone is dotted with earwax and other leakage. My fingers hurt.

"Bubba, we find a water-bag baby, a classic example of the fetal wail, and what happens?"

"The baby farted at you."

"No. The oscilloscope fell asleep. The beam didn't even shiver. Bubba, let me come over. I'm shaky."

"Only at your own risk. Julia may scatch your eyes out, and Ava is capable of anything."

"Bubba, what are we doing in Arizona? I miss White Plains..."

He arrives in a string tie, Western boots, and a bone-white suit. He has cabbage roses for Julia, charlotte russe for Ava, thatch of moss for Glori, balls for me. Cream on her chin, Ava intones "Unca Malkin." Julia warms up to him. Malkin sidles past me, boots crackling. They stare at one another, Ava, Malkin, and Julia; eye-beams jell over Julia's moisture machine. (Arizona air spots her skin, she says.) Grabbing hands, they run out to Malkin's Volvo. I switch off the machine. Glori and I smother ourselves in the drying air. She sticks a finger in the moss.

PUNCTUATION PROFILE FOR 11 AUTHORS
(Malkin, Plotch, 1971)

Table 1. Punctuation distribution per 300 words of text, randomly selected by the profilers

	,	.	;	—	()	...	?	!	:
Swift, Jonathan *A Tale of the Tub*	21	12	8	0	0	0	1	0	1
Austen, Jane *Emma*	26	10	6	0	0	0	3	0	0
Dickens, Charles *The Mystery of Edwin Drood*	16	13	4	2	1	0	2	0	2
Melville, Herman *Bartleby the Scrivener*	35	8	1	4	0	0	2	1	1

PUNCTUATION PROFILE FOR 11 AUTHORS (CONT.)

	,	.	;	—	()	...	?	!	:
James, Henry *The Beast in the Jungle*	21	7	2	4	0	0	1	0	0
Kafka, Franz *The Hunger Artist*	18	22	3	0	0	0	2	0	0
West, Nathanael *The Dream Life of Balso Snell*	12	18	2	0	0	1	1	0	1
Wouk, Herman *Marjorie Morningstar*	22	15	5	1	1	1	1	1	1
Nabokov, Vladimir *Pnin*	17	17	2	0	0	0	3	0	1
Roth, Philip *Portnoy's Complaint*	36	6	8	1	2	3	7	7	1
Waxman-Weissman, Anatole *Wittgenstein Among the Redwoods*	13	25	0	0	0	0	0	0	0

To be distributed free of charge at the Literature Scientists Convention, Galapagos, 1972.

Under optimum conditions, Ava has found her tongue. She shines for Unca Malkin. Her sentences "bristle" with morphemes, as the saying goes. Malkin's assistants claim his oscilloscope is in heat: the window fogs whenever Ava burps. Her week of babbling must have juiced her up. Whirring from room to room, with dust rag, furniture polish, and chlorine crystals for the toilet, she makes supernumaries of Glori and me. "Mother, tell Dad to tell sissy that Tou-Tou's dress is discoloring the bowl. Can't they play in the street? How can I accomplish anything if I'm surrounded by pests? Mother, Dad ought to keep Tou-Tou out of the laundromat. Dolly has sores on her arms from bumping around in the washer. If he doesn't dress the sores, attend to them properly, they'll get gangrenous and Tou-Tou may die. Must I be responsible for everything? Lord!"

Dear Mr. Waxman-Weissman, would you mind it terribly if my daughter and I visited you at the Redwood Motel? I swear I won't mention Wittgenstein, stylistics, or your preference for concrete nouns. My daughter is well-mannered and never talks above a whisper. As for myself, I'm an only child, about thirty-four (my birth certificate is smudged, and my parents used up so much of their energy in feeding me, they lost track of my chronological age), I can chop wood, mend socks, play a woman if you catch me in the right mood. Nina Spear has cautioned me about your retiring habits, and you needn't feel any obligation whatsoever towards me, my daughter, or this letter. I don't expect a reply. With warm regards for the Tar Baby, I remain M. Semple Plotch.

Malkin has rid himself of his White Plains jitters: with Ava and Julia he's on a four-day junket to petrified forests, prehistoric cities and caves, sloshing in the arcana of his adopted State. The sun bakes my roof, the moisture machine wheezes in the sitting room; abandoning Tou-Tou, me and Gloriann twaddle near the wall.

I'll gut the fool who says I'm not a researcher!
"Metalinguistics is that science which pukes on law-
givers, prescribers, censors, and refiners, which loves
dirty old men and prepubescent girls (preferably under
eight), which values the hairy, veiny materiality of
speech, its interplay with all other human functions."
(Plotch, 1971) "Die Sprache ist ein Teil unseres
Organismus und nicht weiniger kompliziert als dieser."
"Language is part of our body and no less complicated
than this." (Wittgenstein, 1915, Plotch translation)

Sheppard's pronouncement upon reading "Wittgenstein Among the Redwoods": *Wörtergemisch.* A confusion of words. Refers to Waxman-Weissman as "that
sad case." Did he shove first? We wrestle in the Wash
& Dry, knocking over benches, crushing laundry baskets,
chewing plaster chips; Glori joins the shindy, rides Sheppard's head. His best customers pull us off. "Idiots. Pigs.
Stay out of here." He throws our wash into the gutter.
Glori crunches her eyes. We dumbfound Sheppard, walk
off. Surprises for Ava and Julia when they get back from
the caves. No underclothes. No towels. No Tou-Tou.
No pillowcases. No sheets.

"Wittgenstein Among the Redwoods" = *minima sen-
sibilia* + black ink + flesh on a noun

A-n-a-t-o-l-e scrambled and smashed, yields:

> anal + toe
> ala + tone
> ale + NATO
> ate + loan
> oat + lean
> alate + no

Anatole, have I violated your name? Am I wrong to push for a Waxman-Weissman reader? Sentences from "Wittgenstein Among the Redwoods" recited by every fourth-grader in Arizona between deep breaths, though it's true that your vital capacity (the amount of air forced out of your lungs) has little to do with the quality of your voice, as any phonetician knows. Should I inform the State Legislature of my addition to the curricula, while Delos is away? But who will we get to illustrate *The Tar Baby Sampler?*

We're ready. "No wigs, Glori. A fresh start for both of us. We'll buy underthings on the road. Without Tou-Tou, who will you whisper to? I'll have you shouting before we cross the State line." With a grease pencil swiped from the language arts department I draw thick, uneradicable lines from here to Galapagos, ruining my Shell map. We sit in the car. I squeeze the gnarled choke, our paper valise up against the back seat. "Gala-pagos, Glori." The old Ford rattles, coughs gas. Glori, you want to drive? Smoke spots the windshield, pours through the windows. Glori removes my fingers from the steering wheel, pinkies first, pushes me out of the car. She cuts the motor, bats the smoke with her fists, drags the valise into the house. "Scared," I say. "What if Anatole doesn't want to see us?" Glori rubs each of my paws, warming them. "Tomorrow. We'll start again tomorrow. When the smoke clears out. Glori, bring me your comb. There's a bug in your hair."

[N.B., we have cut, added to, edited, and sparingly re-vised Mr. Plotch's notes in order to standardize them and match the high critical tone of our special "Anatole" number.—*The Tar Baby*]

OLD GALAPAGOS, PART II

Galapagos' boundaries in 1850 were Coronado road on the east, P Street on the west, Hardscrabble Street on the north, and De la Guerra Street on the south. Traffic over Coronado Road was considerable even for this day, and a way station was established near Gerónimo Bridge at the confluence of Bitter Water, Tar, and Deadman's creeks. According to a check made by Bayard ("Saturnino") Goodeschill, Galapagos' first tycoon, 617 horsemen, 1,003 footmen, 867 stage passengers, and 98 mule trains passed by Saturnino's tollhouse during the two middle weeks of February, 1850. Though most of the travelers pushed towards gold country, quite a few stopped in Galapagos for a "soda bath." Situated at the foot of Bitter Water Creek, where the arroyo sinks into dry sand, our Hot Spring was already a favorite pioneer spa. By the end of 1849 the Spring had been made an important station on the Sonoma-Sacramento stage line, and Galapagos Spring Station became much more than a quaint and pleasant water hole. Three barns, four hotels, a butcher shop, a laundry, and two saloons stood next to the Spring. The barns, the hotels, and the larger saloon, with its spindle-rail balcony, were owned by Saturnino Goodeschill. Perhaps the most peculiar citizen Galapagos has ever known, and certainly the richest, Goodeschill, a native of Connecticut, arrived around 1837 with forged papers from the Yale Divinity School. Evidently, the alcalde at Galapagos interpreted Goodeschill's papers as a medical diploma, and in 1840 he began to practice medicine here. Charging a modest fee,

Goodeschill would bathe his patients in our Spring, and then have them swim in Bitter Water Creek. Goodeschill's fees increased with the success and fame of his water cure, but in 1843 he gave up his practice and dedicated himself to the economic and social well being of Galapagos. During the following year he founded the Merchants Bank, and became our alcalde, coroner, treasurer, surveyor, and judge. His Mexican and Indian retainers made soap, blankets, and shoes at his ranchería in the foothills. Hardly a carouser, Goodeschill spent his leisure hours with his Mexicans and Indians (who called him "Saturnino" with much affection), teaching them to read music. Soon Goodeschill's frontier orchestra, with imported flutes, Spanish trumpets, and a native drum, performed on Sundays in the town square. During the Mexican War Goodeschill grew increasingly disenchanted with the American occupation of California. (Ten to fifteen U.S. troops were billeted in Galapagos from 1847 to 1849.) In 1850, after California entered the Union, Goodeschill organized a "cholo" army from his retainers and a group of former Mexican convicts. He declared Galapagos "a separate and independent State and Country." He did not have the backing of our citizens, however, and the Country of Galapagos failed to get off the ground. Disgruntled after his army was taken away, Goodeschill abandoned all his Galapagonian projects, and retired to his ranchería, where he succumbed during the smallpox epidemic of 1854. No permanent site in Galapagos bears Goodeschill's name.

MONTE FALKES

At the JC: W.-W. as Teacher, Cop, and Rodeo Dog

Twenty-three-year-old Monte Falkes has been the
road secretary of the Cummerbund Stampede for
the past five seasons. A special student at Galapagos
Junior College, Falkes audited Anatole's course in
pragmatic philosophy during the spring of 1970.

Ever run with a maverick rodeo? Shit in your britches,
rosin in your teeth. Riding with cripples and blacklisted
cowboys, because nobody else would have us. Ol' Cummerbund Stampede may have goosed the world in 1937,
but it couldn't fit into Walla Walla this season, and got
shoved out of Yuba City season before. Can't afford a
legitimate clown or a full-time announcer, so I get to
prod the bulls with a hotshot, roll in a wet barrel, croon
to the dinks in the grandstand, and keep the Cummerbund's shifty books. You blame me for wanting an education? I'm tired of whore baths in a gas station sink.
I'm tired of bedding down with horse doctors, wiping
the muzzles of pampered stock, selling dung to the
farmers before we move on. When I read that word in
the Galapagos catalog, p-r-a-g-m-a-t-i-c-s, I knew what
it was all about. Pragmatics means sending your shirts to

the Chinaman and kissing laundry soap goodby. Buzzer Carmody, owner, stock manager, and chute boss of the Stampede, and seventy-year-old poop, bothered himself over my connections with the JC. "That miserable cow school," he said. "Aint no College." He tore the pages out of my catalog. "I wouldn't waste my time pissing in Galapagos."

"Old man, you got cowshit inside your brain."

I can take liberties with Carmody; it's my clowning and managerial abilities that's been holding the Stampede together. I brought the Sponge over to the Cummerbund, and Buzzer half hates me for it. He'll never be able to tolerate the idea of a rock band on the rodeo circuit. We'd be hustling in the streets without the Royal Sponge. Scrubby bronc riders and chickened bulls don't fill arenas any more. I snatched the mess of paper away from Buzzer's hand. "Why'd you ruin my catalog?"

He grabbed at me. "Galapagos. Had to beg me to park here in '35, Mr. Monte Falkes."

" '35 is long gone, Buzzer. If we didn't hit Galapagos, Humboldt, or Colusa, you'd be sitting on the porch of a San Jose nursing home, talking about your '35 and your '36 with all them other old boogers. We got to pray that man from the Merchants Bank stays alive another year so he can remember your name, or they wouldn't have us in Galapagos."

"Penny Gemeinhardt? He's nothing but a whore trader. Next thing you'll be telling me the Redwood Motel underwrites rodeos."

"Stop badmouthing Galapagos and the JC."

I explained myself to the College dean.

"Mr. Birdwistell, now it may be true I'm deficient in arithmetic and English basics, dogging rodeos since I was eleven, and roping pigs, but if you let me into the JC to study pragmatics, I might prove my worth to you. I promise to be in Galapagos at least three months a year, and I'm thinking about quitting the circuit."

The dean must have liked my talk, because after I paid the seventy-five-dollar fee, he told me to shop around for courses. Buzzer's cowboys razzed me about the interview. "College boy," they said, pulling my corduroy coat. You won't catch me paying mind to gimpy bull riders.

"Clay?" I banged on the rear of the Sponge's hearse.

The blinds crackled. He popped his head out, Clay S. from Portland, the Sponge's lead singer, plucker, and composer. "I'm in, Clay. The JC took me. For a flat seventy-five, any course I want, and no examinations either."

"What kind of degree are you getting?"

"I didn't discuss degrees with the dean."

"I'll bet you didn't." He started riffling the blinds, and the slats snipped away his face.

"Clay Spielholtz," I said. He hates people using his family name. He let go of the blinds. "Who got you this gig? You couldn't afford insurance on your hearse when I picked you up. Groveling in Bolinas."

"Gig yourself," he muttered through a warp in the blinds. "I'm carrying the Cummerbund. You want to push me off, Monte Falkes, just knock on my door. I can get along without your wiggy cowboys."

Think I was going to let any Portland Spielholtz hurt my feelings about the JC? I sat in my trailer circling words from the catalog, wondering whether I should study practical English, practical geography, practical history, or practical philosophy. Next thing, I talcumed my ass, stole a ringed notebook from the Galapagos Five and Dime, and showed up at the introductory lecture of Philo Naught-Naught-One. The JC couldn't have put much stock in a lecture that was held in a tin shed touching the Galapagos cesspool, a mile from Birdwistell's office. I counted faces in the shed. Chicano in a paratrooper's shirt, two bloods, five of the ugliest girls in America, a dozen Sonoma boys in JC sweatshirts or buckskin coats, with pink eyes and Buffalo Bill mustaches, and a campus cop. Chew on that, Portland Clay. Philo Naught-Naught-One was such a mindfucker, Birdwistell had to send in the fuzz to cool it down. Only this fuzz was bald and fat, and liked to suck the rust off his handcuffs. "Where's the prof?" I said. The Sonoma boys played cat's cradle with the five ugly girls. "Where's the prof?" The Chicano stepped on my boot. He pointed to the cop with the rust on his chin. "W.-W.," he said. "Listen to him."

W.-W. clipped his badge off, and the class began. He shut his eyes, breathed through his nose, and let the air out in a hiss. "What books do we use in Naught-Naught-One?" All I heard for an answer was hisses around the shed. He had the whole class breathing.

"No books in this course," one of the bloods grumbled at the end of a hiss, both eyes shut. "Follow the man and breathe." Damn class of boogers! Seventy-five dollars for the philosophy of calisthenics when I get enough exercise dodging bulls at the Cummerbund. But if I paid my money, I wasn't going to lose my chance to hiss.

"Hgggggggg.   Sssssssssssssssssssssssssssssssss-ssssss.   Hgggggggg.   Ssss—"

"The new boy is showing off, W.-W."

I brought my hisses down, blended myself into the

class's grubby drone. The static filled my neck, puffed inside my ears. Then the hissing stopped, and W.-W. lectured to us. What's the purpose of snatching note-books? Wasn't a damn thing to write. W.-W.'s lecture lacked common sense. All he could talk about was a dumpy television set and a baseball game that never took place. I nudged the Chicano. "Got a smoke?" He whacked me on the wrist.

"Nobody turns on in W.-W.'s class."

I decided to sit tight and listen. W.-W. couldn't lec-ture in one spot. He rubbed against the blackboard, put filth on his shirt, and crippled his boots with his pacing. "In our hypothetical World Series," he says, "the Giants are playing Oakland at home. The A's are down three games to one. You, *G,* a rabid Oakland fan, work for the Galapagos Post Office. Regrettably, your schedule at the PO is in conflict with the games. You sorted mail during the three Oakland losses, and were able to watch only a snatch of the one Oakland win. In the critical fifth game, the Giants ahead 11–10 you arrive home at the top of the ninth, switch on your old-fashioned black and white Motorola with its floppy aerial, cleft knobs, and minuscule screen, and use your pliers to jiggle the tuning knob as Reggie Jackson* ties the game with his second home run of the day. The team bats around with-out an out. Singles for Bando, Roof, Cater, Green, and Campaneris, doubles for Monday and Tartabull, a triple for Blue Moon Odom.† Crazied up by the rash of hits, you plip the aerial, cackle at the screen. Reggie clears the

---

* Formidable slugger of the Oakland Athletics for the first two-thirds of the 1969 baseball season (his home run production dwindled in Sep-tember). —The Editor
† Other, lesser Oakland players.

bases with a long bullet single. You jibber over the top-heavy score. Oakland 20, Frisco 11. The A's bat around again. A walk, five singles, two doubles, a homer for Bando, no outs. 27–11. The A's have chewed up six Giant pitchers. Reggie doubles to right center. You feel a slight twinge in your bowels. Your eyebrows notch as the A's bat around safely for the third time. You jiggle the fine tuner to the left. Reggie triples off the score-board. Your shoulders stiffen, your face settles into a rigid, quizzical stare. You remember that in the minute and a half of the other game you watched, Monday and Roof doubled back to back. The unavoidability of your reckoning jars you, sours in your mouth. *No* Oakland A can be put out while you, *G*, Galapagos postman, watch them on your Motorola. Absorbed in your power over the teams, you jiggle the tuner in both directions, turn the volume down. Reggie homers over the Folger's Coffee sign. Bando splits the webbing of the Giant third baseman's glove with a line single. Monday doubles him home. Prickles appear on your jaw. You notice them in the shine of the screen. You have an itch to snap off the aerial's twin ears, to wipe out the Motorola and free yourself from the obligations of the game. There's an easier way. Switch off the set. The pliers slacken in your hand. You visualize Odom, without you, swishing, Campaneris and Tartabull bobbling soft flies to center-field. The Giants have one more turn at bat. What's the meaning of 39–10? You force out a squeal. A lead of twenty-nine runs no longer seems absolute. Would 46–10 secure the game? 113–10? Should you wait until the A's clear a thousand? Considering your ignorance of this world, couldn't Frisco get every one of those runs back? Starting with an innocent bloop single over Campaneris' head. Your talents may not be reversible. Grunting at the screen won't stop the Giants. While your head drifts, Oakland bats around another time. The Giants send in a utility outfielder to pitch. Reggie confirms your gloom, singling through the pitcher's legs. Your face in the screen, you sit, knees together, pliers on the floor."

Spit hung on W.-W.'s lip from talking so hard. He brushed it aside, and threw the story of G to the class.

"The trouble with your Post Office cat, W.-W., is that he's time-freaked. Worrying that people will starve, kids won't go to sleep, schools will close, Penn Gemeinhardt will have to declare a banker's holiday, mail won't get delivered unless the game finishes. W.-W., Galapagos could hump itself, and the schools and the banks could stay closed, because if I was G, I'd sit there twisting knobs forever."

"I don't feature that, Michael Garcia."

"Baby, you want everything to shut down on account of one sick, boring game that's being played in W.-W.'s head?"

"Ask the new boy what he thinks, W.-W.?"

"I'm for G," I spluttered.

"Me too," four of the five ugly girls said.

W.-W. sucked his handcuffs.

I left the shed tearing the rings off my notebook. "Practical philosophy," I said. Buzzer Carmody caught up with me near my trailer.

"Get out of that corduroy, Monte Falkes. You're on in twenty minutes. If I don't see you in blackface and clown suit before I get back from the chutes, I'll shove you to Little without your barrel."

I set my hand mirror on the washstand, slapping at the moths around my curtain. Dug pins into my hair so I could fit the metal plate over my scalp and put on my stingy-brimmed barker's hat. Mummied myself with thirty feet of cheesecloth, because a barrel wasn't worth a lick against Little Barlow unless you were wound in from your ankles to the top of your neck. Strapped on my corset, stuck my fingers in the grease can, patted my cheeks, my eyes, and my forearms, picked out yellow galluses, attached them to my baggy Cummerbund jumpsuit, and got inside. Grabbed up my rubber teeth, my gloves, and my joke cards, and walked out with the barrel.

Damn hearse near run me down. A Viet Cong flag jutted over the bumper. Jason, Clay's backup harmonica, mechanic, and second guitar, stuck his fat head between two junior high babies who were riding in the hearse, then dropped his harmonica under his crotch, and aimed it at me. "Gonna let me piss in your barrel, Monte honey?"

The girls chuckled, and one of them stared hard and said, "Is he a rodeo nigger, Jay?"

"That's Buzzer's suckabelly. Ignore the gunk on his face. He's a country boy. Sits in his barrel when the bulls are up, so he can play with his dingle."

I walked around Jason and shouted to Clay.

"You were right about the JC. Gypped me out of seventy-five."

Only I couldn't keep up with him because the barrel was knocking my shins. I fell in behind Mr. Maggles, Buzzer's one-eyed strawberry roan, an ancient bucking horse with swollen knees. I had to shellack his withers before every performance to hide the scabs. We marched to the grandstand on O Street, with the Sponge up front. Buzzer sat on his roan, holding the Stampede's colors near the tail of the procession. Maybe he hated Clay

Spielholtz, but he didn't fool himself about who the crowd was paying to see. Half the junior high school population of the County must have been in the O Street stands. The hearse freaked their minds. "Sponge, Sponge, Sponge." I put down the barrel and climbed the catwalk behind the portable bucking chutes to the announcer's platform. Penn Gemeinhardt and four of his Native Sons collected near the microphone, hunched in navy blue capes, their skinny legs rocking on the wood. Below us, in the band box, Jason was testing the Sponge's amps. Gemeinhardt trained his binoculars on the hearse. His jowls tightened on him. "Do I see an enemy flag in this arena, Mr. Falkes?"

"Pay it no mind, Deacon Gemeinhardt. Them boys are veterans, every one. They served in Nam. That flag's a souvenir. Clay Spielholtz uses it for a nose rag." I shuffled past him, eased between two of the Sons, tipped my stingy brim, and jabbered into the microphone. "Ladies, gents, cowboys and cowgirls of Sonoma, children of Galapagos, seat of the ol' JC, welcome all to the thirty-ninth consecutive appearance of the Cummerbund Stampede, the grandest little show on earth." At Fresno or Marysville, I would have rode the microphone across the platform, hooking my galluses onto it, pretending it was a stickhorse, but this was Galapagos, and the teeny-boppers were screaming for the Sponge. The bronc riders, with numbered oilcloth squares stuck between their shoulders for the bareback go-rounds, were scrounging behind the chutes, spitting at the hearse. Gemeinhardt tussled my elbow. "Falkes, never heard of a Grand Entry without a salute to the flag."

"You'll get all the flags you want, Deacon. Only don't you cramp me now. You hear them girls in the stands.

They'll eat us alive if I don't give them the Sponge."
And I huggled the mike. "Folks, this is your own Monte
Falkes, known on the circuit as Bull-Hazing Monte, the
original Man In The Barrel. On my left is Mr. Galapagos himself, Penn Gemeinhardt, deacon of the Native
Sons, who's been bringing you the Cummerbund for
more years than a poor boy like me can remember. A
hand for the Deacon."

The Sons in the audience flipped their capes, a few
old women yapped with their hands and teeth, Buzzer's
stock bellered and mooed beyond the catwalk, Mr.
Maggles grinned sleeping on his feet, but the girls
crunched up sounds, colors, looks, dirt, and wood on O
Street with their begging for the Royal Sponge. I jigged
over to the edge of the platform, dragging the mike.
"Making their honeymoon appearance in the O Street
arena, the latest addition to the Cummerbund, the pride
of Buzzer Carmody, a rock group from Portland that's
been tearing up the circuit, laying down music that can
quiet Little Barlow, the meanest bull in America, Melvin, Jason, Clay, and Ron, formerly the Stepchilds, and
now the Royal Sponge." The platform shook under us,
and I thought we'd be crashing in with the bulls, but all
I had to do was shout, "Stick it in, Clay," and them girls
shut up. They weren't going to risk losing a word out of
Portland Spielholtz's mouth. That first bloodshit scream
of Melvin's guitar zipped up Gemeinhardt's face, and
the Native Sons stood bundled inside their capes, afraid
the music might contaminate them. Spielholtz climbed
the band box rail in his high-water britches, his tie tack,
dabbled with gold, burning into his neck, his boot points
winking on the rail, and put it to us.

Manure dust in your fingernails
Rock rosin on your head
I'm a lonesome, groansome cowboy
Hustling for some bread.

I'm fucked out, my friend
Trouble when I urinate
I think I got the claps
Can't handle any freight.

I'd retire in a minute
Leave this frontier day jackpot
But the Government's into me
With its outcome taxes and the lot.

So I'll remain a scumsucking bull yoker
Carry rope and rosin bag, leather jumper and bell
And if I draw Little Barlow
Ride the sombitch out to Hell.

Brothers, don't you pity me
I'll survive the blisters on my ass
Cause I'm a double-rank cowboy
Too tough for my day to pass.

But you can bury me in dipshit
With my jumper and my bell
And I'll dream of Little Barlow
As I'm bucking into Hell.*

The girls wouldn't let Clay off the rail. The bronc riders, the steer wrestlers, the calf ropers, and the chute hands, who despised Spielholtz previous to this, had hankies in their eyes. Buzzer cried into Mr. Maggles' bumpy withers, ruining the dye job I did on him, and

---

* "Cummerbund Exploitation Boogy," by Melvin Ritter and Clay S. (with additional lyrics by Monte Falkes), Copyright © 1969, Big Tenn Whirlybird Weather Station Early Warning Systems Propaganda Music Co. & The Stepchilds.

shouted "Again, again, again," along with the rest of us. But the Deacon wasn't satisfied. "There's no profanity clause in the contract I signed, Mr. Falkes. Get them boys out of the box."

I whistled to Clay, pointed to the exit, and said, "Folks, due to circumstances beyond the Cummerbund's control, circumstances quoted to me by Deacon Gemeinhardt and the Sons, the Royal Sponge will be shipping out. Clive, Jerry, Sam, run in the broncs, if you please."

Jason stalked through the band box plucking wires, Melvin scratched his prick, Clay gave me the fingeroo from his window. The hearse drove out of the arena, and the girls, moaning and stamping, followed behind. Couldn't have been more than twenty people left in the stands, half of them Native Sons. The cowboys cinched up their broncs, then slicked down the pieces of oilcloth on their backs, had their last smokes, and straddled the chutes. I snuck mean looks at Gemeinhardt and prepared my spiel for the faithful. "Since we're down to a friendly circle of rodeo dogs, I'm going to bring on the saddle broncs without the usual popgun explosions of the Cummerbund rifle team. Out of chute number five, Weldon Bowdocker from Pill Station, Texas, on a fearsome horse called Battle Scar. Stick it on him, Weldon!" Weldon Piss-in-pants Bowdocker was a near-sixty rail-road porter on loan from the Southern Pacific because of a touchy bladder. Naturally he'd wet a bronc before he had the chance to spur him. Piss-in-pants would have had trouble hanging on to a stickhorse. With Battle Scar it didn't mean a thing. Mangy, toothless roan couldn't spill a sack of beans. I might have learned from Mr. Maggles and slept on my feet, if Deacon Gemeinhardt didn't pinch my ribs. "Stampede's half over, Mr. Falkes, and I haven't witnessed any deference to the flag."

I cranked the record machine, had a chutehand wake Mr. Maggles, and we sang "The Star Spangled Banner." I rushed the bareback riders and the steer wrestlers, left the calf ropers high and dry, and called for the bulls. "Ladies and gents, the final attraction of the Cummerbund Stampede. Buzzer Carmody's hand-picked bull riders on savage brahmas, featuring that amazing chute rattler, the previously mentioned Little Barlow."

"Never seen bulls with such runty horns," the Deacon said. "I'll lay a dollar Buzzer manicures 'em every night."

"You care to sit in my barrel with Barlow over you, let me know." Shut the sombitch up with that one, and I went on. "Coming out of number three, Shorty Holland, the human cannonball, on a brute from Texarkana, Panhandle Babs. Careful now, folks. Shorty might be flying into your seats." Babs is in love with that ruptured mulatto, and they've been working up an act for the boogers. Soon as Shorty settles on, Babs shakes his dewlap, blows air through his nose, and Shorty leans hard and somersaults over Babs's rump. Say this for Gemeinhardt. He caught Babs's phony grinds and the unnaturalness, the too-perfect gesturing of Shorty's leap. I introduced three more bulls, eyeing Barlow meantime in number four, his hump curving over the chute gate, and Wylie Dubler, Buzzer's pro, squatting behind him in a padded jumper. Little's sucking nostrils and rumpled poll let you know he wasn't going to tolerate a cowboy on his back, or 'low any bull bell to clap under him.

"Wylie Dubler out of chute number four, high on Little Barlow." I put in my rubber teeth, and stuck Gemeinhardt with my joke cards and the microphone. "Clean jokes are on the blue cards, smutty ones on the green. Keep the boogers happy."

"You're mumbling, Falkes. Take that stinking rubber out of your mouth."

"Need it for Barlow," I said. And I stomped down the catwalk, hoping the vibrations would bug the Deacon, and speculating how raw my knees would get after a roll in the barrel. Can't call yourself a bull-baiter without owning supernatural side vision. Saw that blue sleeve near the edge of the catwalk, then the badge, shirt and bald face, without moving my neck. W.-W. a rodeo dog! Trucking with the Cummerbund. Expect he didn't care for my announcing. If I knew you'd be calling, W.-W., would have varied my routines. Made it a green card day, even if old man Gemeinhardt shucked me off the platform for violating the Galapagos language codes. Thinking about W.-W. crippled my stride, made me see-saw in my galluses when I had work to do. Piss-in-pants socked my hat, his knuckles bamming into the metal plate on my head. "Quit crooning on the catwalk. No girls in the stands. Just fools in capes and widowwomen. Want to leave Wylie sitting under Little?"

We rolled the barrel out to the middle of the arena. "Stop her there, Weldon." I could have wrote you a handbook on Little Barlow's jabs and kicks once he broke from the chute. He'd take Wylie to the left, fake a spin with Wylie hugging the bull rope and leaning too far, then go left again, and whip him over his hump. Wylie'd be on top three seconds at the most. He did land with his leg twisted, his jumper over his ears, ten feet from the barrel. "Little, fittle," I yelled, waving my hat to get that mother's attention. Otherwise he would have gone for Wylie's head. I crawled in, chin against my knees, rubber teeth secure, so Piss-in-pants could roll me over to Little Barlow and leg it to the stands with Wylie crooked under his arm. The arena clear, nothing but dust balls and bilge wood between me and Barlow, I let out my amazing, shit-curdling bull call. "Little? Booger-booger-bugger-boo." You warble at him, you practice pinching your throat, and you can freak a bull. How else could I drive Barlow insane the past year and a half? It's the sounds coming from the barrel. "Little? Booger-booger-bugger-boo. Kiss a clown's wooden ass, Barlow brother." And don't expect much affection either. Because the first bump, the twisting and hooking with both his horns, is going to lose your hat for you, spindle through your body, crease that dish protecting your brains, put a split in your rubber teeth maybe, and you're lucky you don't strangle on your galluses. So if it's got to be Barlow vs. the original Man In The Barrel, you can guess who's getting greased. Think anybody in Gala-pagos would quarrel over how long I sit with my knee caps squashing my face? Barlow putting shivers in the wood, I fancied navy capes swarming from the microphone, grandmas approaching the P Street exit, Shorty yelling into Buzzer's ear about how ol' Monte's been barreling half hour, and Buzzer avoiding him, his drool on Maggles' neck, W.-W. the last man in the stands, working Barlow and me into his next lecture, something about the Man In The Barrel's ability to sustain himself chewing on his galluses before Little breaks his horns diving and hooking or starves to death. I had the perfect chance to reconsider pragmatical philosophy. Because living alone, under Barlow, I could appreciate W.-W.'s postman with the wiggy television knobs. Brothers, roll up the arena, carry the chutes away, I'll pull through. "Little? Booger-booger-bugger-boo. Booger-booger-bugger-boo *from* GALAPAGA, *the official handbook to Galapagos*

ULRICH WAX

High-minded critics at our College and elsewhere have accused us of being a walled-in, brittle community that feeds off its own offal and can only tolerate the viscera of Native Galapagonians; corrupted from within, we have no possibility of energizing ourselves from without. The late Ulrich Wax belies this little country formula. An Austrian by birth, Ulrich wandered through Prague, Hamburg, Amsterdam, Buenos Aires, Guatemala City, Mazatlan, and San Jose, before settling in Galapagos. Having no time for formal schooling, Ulrich taught himself English by memorizing early editions of *Galapaga* and a child's version of King James. He busheled workmen's trousers, tanned Galapagos hides, picked our lettuce, and purchased the Brandy House, a disused luxury hotel off Coronado Road. With a shrewd eye for business, Ulrich brought in machinery, resurrected the Brandy House as Wax's Mill (sawmill, lumberyard, and carpentry shop), and became the second or third richest man in Sonoma County. Though his own life demanded a strict frugality, Ulrich was quite generous to those less fortunate than himself: he provided modern housing for his employees, installed toilet facilities for our migrant farmers, and rescued three of his distant relatives from a Hitlerized Europe. Nor should we forget Ulrich Wax's passionate involvement in the affairs of Galapagos. He supported only reform candidates for public office; he donated large sums for the restoration of historic buildings and sites; and most important, he gave his advice, his time, and his money to our numerous charitable, educational, and commercial organizations. When he passed away in 1970 (over 1000 of our citizens attended his funeral), these same charitable, educational, and commercial organizations purchased a memorial lite for his gravestone; last May hooligans from within our own County pirated the memorial lite and overturned Ulrich Wax's stone; the Native Sons of Galapagos hope to repair the damage, and have offered a reward of $100 for information leading to the identification and arrest of the hooligans.

For news of other distinguished natives and non-natives, consult GALAPAGA.

ANATOLE WAXMAN-WEISSMAN

Scrapings

The following pages have a circuitous history. They originally appeared in *Magie,* a Paris journal of metalinguistics, and were lent to *The Tar Baby* by Professor Claude Chardin, director of studies at the Centre National de Lexicologie Pratique and chief editor of *Magie*. An admirer of "Wittgenstein Among the Redwoods," Professor Chardin commissioned Anatole to write these pages. Anatole worked on them during the last year of his life. Unfortunately, Professor Chardin, who translated "Scrapings" into French, misplaced the English text, and because Anatole seldom kept carbon copies (we searched through his papers with the help of his mother-in-law), our Business Manager, Nina Spear, was forced to "untranslate" the French version in an attempt to reconstruct Anatole's prose. Miss Spear asks me to assure *Tar Baby* readers that any limpings in the text are most likely her own and Professor Chardin's. "Anatole," she said, "always wrote with a fluid hand." We thank the editors of *Magie* for their kind permission to reprint "Scrapings." Miss Spear and I should be held responsible for the title; the French version has none. —The Editor

§

§§§ 1 §§§

For him, all things begin and end with families . . .

How could he ever step outside mother, father, dead sister Helene?* He didn't remember her crib. She lived two months and died before he was three. Mother stored her swaddles in a trunk. A shedding blanket. A dark green nightgown. She put eggs in father's lunch bucket, rubbed his goggles in her spit, packed him off, so she could drag out the trunk, sit in the back room with a hand stuck in Helene's nightie. Who says children aren't resourceful? He had a stable of fetishisms at five. To soak up the twitch in mother's shoulder, her croodling attentions to the nightie, he conceived of a strict, unswerving process for peeling father's eggs. Shog the bucket, grab an egg, peck at the shell for weak spots, smack it once against the bucket, get under the splinters with a nail, pull off the ragged skin, palm it, smother it, master its cold, slippery feel, smudge it with your dirty fingers, bite into the crown until you taste yolk, then gobble it. Shog the bucket again. Repeat the process. Watch for blood clots and gray, rubbery yolks. Signs of an unhealthy chicken. Where's Bruno? Down J Street with his grandmother? Shifting for himself in the grass? I wouldn't want to outlive my son. Margaret, take away my fatherhood. Tell him I'm his older brother. I won't terrify him that way. What's sibling rivalry compared to eggs in a lunch bucket and a father's crooked step?

---

* Helene Waxman-Weissman, b. and d. 1933; see Chronology, p. 5.
—The Editor.

§§§   2   §§§

Lazy mornings on Margaret's porch, afternoons
patrolling the quad. On campus he was Sergeant Sunshine: the officer with baggy eyes and broken handcuffs,
who never wore a hat. He nodded to students, but
nudged away from them, and avoided faculty. He didn't
want to talk about surds and irrational numbers, or
about the prevalency of zero in costumes, manners, and
speech. He was sunning himself, making good use of his
campus name. Bonney fell in with him, and they took
turns together, twice around the quad, Bonney respect-
ing his hermetic needs, remaining silent until they jogged
past Life Sciences for the third time. "Gadding about,
Anatole? Keeping the quad safe? You ought to be nicer
to me. I haven't annotated your lectures or mixed into
your affairs. Couldn't you visit me? Once?"

"Lucian, I'd prefer not to step indoors."

"Shabby of you, Anatole."

"Promise not to mention hardware or software?
Nothing alphabetic or numeric? You won't ask me to
sing for Kit Carson?"

"Anatole, don't be a hog."

They strolled behind Life Sciences, entered a tacky
lean-to, ducking their heads. He couldn't determine
whether the pricking odor around him came from
Bonney, the punch card operator, the hobblewood floor,
the keyboards, the helixes, the display screen, or the
interference of his own body with the doings in the
shack. The primitive conditions of Bonney's work life—
the cribbed space, the dwarfish consoles, the milk stains
on the screen, the gummy look in the eyes of the card
puncher—afflicted him, pushed him in Bonney's direc-

tion. It had taken him a year to pay his respects to Kit. Why? The computer was his exegete. Kit Carson had studied his sentences, contracted them, converted them into digits. A metal bulb pecked his hand: in his confusion, brushing against the keyboards, Bonney had slipped him a microphone. "Kit can mimic your style or play it straight, but he won't be able to get you, Anatole, unless he hears your voice."

He managed a few pips: an uneven thank-you, some gabbled advice for measuring the circumference of a bald spot with quarters, nickels, and blue ink, and a formal goodby. Then he tore out of the shack, Bonney grabbing after his clothes, shouting, "Waxy, Waxy," the card puncher sneezing, an ugly brown mole breaking loose on the display screen, which he chose to interpret as Kit's summary of him.

§§§ 3 §§§

In order to maintain his health and improve his carriage, he often did setting-up exercises at home. Margaret would kick in the legs of her table, wheel her bed into the hall, wrap Bruno in a blanket, snug him down on the drainboard, and broom off Anatole's exercise space. She discouraged callers and stray dogs, put the telephone bell on low, plugged the earphones into her little Japanese radio, worked without her shoes, to protect his breathing and guarantee him an uncluttered flow of air. Still, his exercises had minimum value. Whether squatting with a bench on his shoulders, dipping between two kitchen chairs, or hardening the fibers in his stomach with a simulated medicine ball, after a few pushes and grunts he lost his concentration and gave himself over to his past. Margaret would find him crumpled on the floor, his considerable belly under a chair, rasping his dead father's name, which he mentioned in no other context. Picking him up, dusting him, returning the chairs to the kitchen, collecting Bruno from the drainboard, she would say, "Tomorrow, Anatole. I'll count for you and hold your knees. We'll crack your breathing difficulties." And he would flop into her bed, leaving her to remove his satin exercise shirt, the one she made for him from a pattern in *Galapaga*.

§§§   4   §§§

On a Friday approaching his thirty-ninth birthday, he decided to map the whole of Galapagos, not for the town's benefit (the street guide in *Galapaga* was colorful and sufficient), but for his own immediate pleasure. It gave him the excuse to rewalk Galapagos, to sight down Coronado Road with a pencil up against his eye, to carry a sketchbook, to move out of his worded self and into the homey comforts of a picture, a directional arrow, a nonevocative street name. He tramped through backyards at odd hours, bungled against clotheslines, rope after rope, snapping clothespins and leaving impressions of his thumb on sheets and pillowcases, lost a heel off Sheriff's Bridge, and ended up with glaring deficiencies and disproportions because he disliked the tidy, shopkeeper's logic of the alphabeted streets and wouldn't touch them. On Anatole's map A Street led nowhere, and he created the illusion of a disjointed, spongy town without contours or a definite interior, which had little to do with the actual life, shapes, and street plan of Galapagos. Expecting relaxation, to free himself of analogies and systems, to sketch only those patches of Galapagos that appealed to him, he discovered the opposite: he was mapping the carbuncles on his own body. The ridge of fat around his navel resembled his drawing of Sonoma Mound; the irregular, hairy arrow where his eyebrows met could easily have been Sheriff's Bridge; the veins on his calf anticipated the windings of Coronado Road. He roosted on South Spain, gimletbrained, for almost three hours, determined to draw his father's house (now a watchman's shed attached to one of the College's parking lots) without imposing his anatomy on it. He dozed, erased, stared, and duplicated the furrows in his big toe. He ignored the watchman's imprecations. He didn't have the energy to explain his interest in the shed. He would have roosted three more hours, sketching and erasing, but the revolving blue bubble on top of the Sheriff's car affected his eyes. "Sheriff Hawes," he said, "mind parking inside the lot? You're obstructing my view. Can't sketch with supernatural light coming off your automobile."

"How's Margaret these days, An'tole? Business hurting? Nobody stopping at Mother's?"

"Wouldn't want to venture an opinion, Sheriff. I'm only a boarder."

"Knew your true mother, An'tole. Real well. I used to drive her to work. Lovely woman. Took her in my predecessor's wagon. You remember him, An'tole. The former Sheriff of Galapagos. The one who's got streets named after him. Hard on me occupying his chair. A hero like him, killed on the job. People might expect the same from me. He was fond of you, An'tole. Always talking about you and your mother."

"Click off the blue light, Sheriff, please."

"That's better. That's what I call politeness. Saying please. I mean, we shouldn't have trouble communicating. Two peace officers like us. What the hell you doing anyway crawling around in the dirt, drawing lines on paper? You been driving my switchboard girl crazy. Complaints coming in. *Ma'am, there's a deputy in my yard.* Can't you doodle in your civvies? What's that?"

"Street plan," he said. "I'm mapping the town."

"Shoot. Took the computer up at the College nineteen minutes to do a street plan. And you been on your gut over a week. Ever hear from your wife?"

"No," he said.

"Shouldn't call yourself a boarder, An'tole. Disrespectful to Margaret. Being how you're her son-in-law and all."

He had difficulties with Hawes' men, who ran him off the streets, broke his pencils, messed the pages in his sketchbook, dropped rumors about his family ("That your wife I saw, An'tole, in a Chinee Lake motel, soliciting Navy boys?"); the more the deputies goaded him, the harder Anatole mapped. He would return home, his ribs sore from sketching, dust in his nose, and catch the hiccups drinking ice water too fast. The noises frightened Bruno. He could never cure himself. Margaret had to lie him down, stand on his back, rock, pound with her feet, and squeeze the grumblings out of his chest.

"Penn Gemeinhardt wants to meet with you, Anatole."

"What about?"

"Your map, I suspect."

"How'm I going to get there?"

"Oh, I'll take you over. But I'm staying outside. Son-of-a-bitch hasn't visited me in fifteen years."

"You can climb off now, Margaret. My hiccups are gone."

Margaret drove him up into the hills, with Bruno in his lap. She wouldn't budge from the car. Gemeinhardt was on the shingled sun porch of his mountain house, soaking his feet, and wouldn't talk to Anatole unless he brought Margaret in. He stumbled out, banged on Margaret's fender, courted her for Gemeinhardt. "He won't have me without you, Margaret."

"Tell him to stick it," she growled through the window.

"Can't. He's got sores on his insteps, and bad news might make them worse."

"Hell on him." But she unlocked her door. She lost her bearings on Gemeinhardt's sharded footpath, shied up near the humped exterior of the sun porch, and Anatole had to lead her by the hand. "Aint been inside Penn's country house before. Disadvantage, Anatole, not being able to catch a man on his home ground. All I got to see was his galluses and his banker's vest. And I'm bitter about it, I suppose." Gemeinhardt dried his feet with paper towels. Bruno sat under him playing with a silent butler, fingers inside the hinged lid, drawing ashes and crumbs. "Fine child," Gemeinhardt said, tilting his neck and watching Margaret on the sly.

"Where's your wife, Penn?"

"In town. Buying buttermilk. Don't you fret, Mother. Marnie's got her social chores to do. She's raising cash for Sonoma orphans. Gives us an hour to kill."

"I aint fretting, Penn. Couldn't care less, your wife sees me or not. Where's your sense? Aggravating your foot blisters with paper. Don't you have a decent towel in this house?"

"Turn the corner, Mother. Linen closet's up three doors. Better not touch the ones with the gold stitch to them. Break Marnie's heart, waste her anniversary towels on my feet."

They heard Margaret paddle off, her wooden shoes clomping through doors at the back of the house. "That woman's taking over. Wouldn't surprise me any, she switches us to a different room. Friends of mine tell me the Sheriff's been dinking your tail in mud, Anatole. Seems I can't appreciate this Jarold Hawes. He's not my idea of a Sheriff. Sucking up to the College computer. Tracking criminals from a damn shed. Who's he caught lately? Some lowdown snake in the grass murders the best Sheriff we ever had, and Hawes lets twelve years go by. Sits on his ass, tickles his ear, and says, 'No cause to worry, Mr. Penn. Turkey's a dead man, he decides to visit in my territory.' Couldn't scatter a flea with that electronic fodder bag. Anatole, I don't know why you've been out scratching on a pad, and I don't care. But if I have to choose between a computer map with dots in it, and a map that's crooked and human, no question where I stand. Disregard my foot blisters. Nothing like that's going to idle me. A majority of deacons at the Native Sons are behind you, three of every four. Be a boon for the Sons, Anatole, if you allowed us to finance your project. We wouldn't hold you down. Interfere. Just a scribble at the bottom saying we sponsored you. Fair enough?" Gemeinhardt wrote a personal check for two hundred and seventy dollars with agitated, undisciplined strokes. Rare penmanship for a banker, Anatole mused. One would expect a softer hand. He had nothing eventful to say about his map. He accepted Gemeinhardt's check, and folded it lengthwise, mindful of the sum. "More if you need it, Anatole. You can start clean.

Hawes won't be a nuisance. He's promised you access to the streets, on our advice."

His pact with Anatole achieved, Gemeinhardt concentrated on the little noises of the house. He went to dab his toes with the crumpled paper, but stopped, intimidated by Margaret's shuffles. She came in, encumbered with biscuits, towels, and tea things. "Two men," she said, "two men with clinkers over their eyes," and she caught Bruno with the silent butler against his lips, taking ashes in. She spanked him, swabbed his mouth, and gave Anatole the biscuits to distribute. She threw the paper towels away. Staring up at Gemeinhardt, on her knees, she thrust his feet in thick, furry, gold-stamped towels.

Later, in the car, she smiled. "Anatole, I'm glad you brought me along."

"You did the bringing, Margaret. I can't drive."

"No matter. I'm satisfied. Had a terrible urge to spy in that bitch's pantry. She bakes with black flour, Anatole. And there's cockroaches in her breadbox. She's the sloppiest woman that ever lived. Had to dust her teacups before I could use them."

"Go anywhere in this County, Margaret, you'll find roaches and dust."

"She's sloppy, Anatole. You can't change my mind."

Anatole should have confirmed Margaret's image of Marnie Gemeinhardt's kitchen. Why did he squabble over dust in a teacup? He couldn't begrudge Gemeinhardt's slanty commune with Margaret. Was it the underbellied intimacy wedging through the sun porch that troubled him? An aging banker, the sachem of Galapagos, deserved to have his feet scratched by his one-time mistress.

Margaret nudged Anatole's hand. "That old man

aint all bad. Did you see how he took to Bruno?"

"I saw," Anatole said.

§§§   5   §§§

With the Sons squarely behind him ("three of every four"), the Sheriff staying out of his reach, people smiling on his sketchbook, Anatole stopped. "Lost my feel for mapping," he told Margaret. This wasn't entirely true. Arrows and pictures still delighted him, but he was frightened by the implications of his map. Galapagos, in his sketchbook, had assumed the wormy, coiling shape of an intestinal tract, presumably his own, and he had little desire to go on drawing his guts. He returned Gemeinhardt's check and continued walking the streets. He wanted to clear his head of taxonomies, to quit being a reader of griddles and signs. A taxicab dusted him near Bitter Water Creek. The windows unrolled, and he heard a crackle of shouts. "Can't you walk straight, you bowlegged cocksucker?" "What you expect from a baldie?" "Bunch of sleepwalkers in California." Instead of shouting back, he fell into old, meager habits; jogging along, he *analogized* the taxicab, and divided the world into pedestrians and motorists. So doing, he composed the essentials for a pedestrian's handbook:

1.01 People sitting and moving in metal shells are dangerous, malicious, nervous, and rather strange.

1.02 Pedestrians, on the whole, are charitable, sinuous, less excitable, and likely to have a better mental outlook.

1.03 The tensed, cramped position of the motorist has weakened the human spine, and is creating a race of frowning troglodytes.

1.04 It is unnatural for men and women to breathe in an atmosphere of metal, plastic, rubber, and glass.

1.05 At the first sign of an approaching vehicle, the pedestrian owes it to himself to scream and run . . .

§§§ 6 §§§

On the *third* Wednesday of the month Margaret cut his hair. He would circle the date on his wall calendar and write "scalp & nails." He refused telephone calls, saw absolutely no one that afternoon. Margaret sat him on a stool in her parlor, pulling a genuine barber's sheet, ripped in places, and with irregular peppermint stripes, over his shoulders. If he complained when she nicked his forehead with her thinning shears, she would say in her most matter-of-fact voice, "Used to be a professional, you know. Can't you sit without squinching?" And he would close his eyes, breathe to the crunch of her shears. The haircut lasted two hours, during which she tolerated no sounds from him. She swore that facial movements, neck twitches, and throat noises harmed her barbering. Sometimes Anatole's attention strayed and he would admire the thumb grip on her cutting scissors or think of his wife's naked body. She had to jolt him upright then, pinch a shoulder blade. "Don't slouch. Wish I had my hydraulic chair. Never would have sold it, Anatole, if you'd been sociable after you moved in."

"Time out," he muttered. "How come you can ramble, and I've got to keep quiet?"

"Barber's privilege," she said, snapping his head forward. She ate up both hours trimming his neck and the line behind his ears, tapping his bald spot (a method that was supposed to thresh new blood into the top layers of his scalp and stimulate hair growth), combing his

widow's peak, flecking off the clayey dandruff scales,
evening his sideburns, snipping the stubborn little nostril
hairs, massaging his shoulders, calves, and thighs with
the curved end of her Hoover vacuum wand, and blow-
ing hair off him with enormous huffs from her mouth.
But what relieved the agony of two hours on a stool,
and made him take note of "scalp & nails" day, was the
mixture of white, perfumed mustard that Margaret
smeared on his face before every haircut. "People used
to die for my mustard baths, Anatole. They'd line up
five deep. Couldn't get them out of the chair. Aint no
substitute for it. Nothing soothes the skin and washes
the pores like white mustard." Beyond the mustard's
medicinal value, its tingle, and its tight grip, he enjoyed
observing himself in whiteface, his ringed eyes staring
up at him from Margaret's low mirror, the mustard beginning to fissure at a nobby point along his forehead.
After Margaret scraped his face clean, and took the
stool away, he would thank her and remove himself to
the bedroom.

"Aint you going to ask me what I did to your pompa-
dour?"

Shuffling his calendar, with next month's mustard bath
in mind, he often forgot to answer her.

§§§   7   §§§

On May 4, 1970, between three and four in the afternoon, as he was lying in bed preparing a memorandum
to himself, he discovered that he could no longer deal
with written words. His hard-lead pencil refused to
stroke out *a* or connect the ligatures of *b*. He reduced
himself to tries at the alphabet. His *e*'s were eyeless;
his *r*'s had no ears; the crossbars of his *f*'s and *t*'s were

missing; he had trouble with his *h;* even his *l*'s were incomplete. He grabbed the nearest book; the letters washed together, making no sense at all. "I'm blind," he said. Then he screamed. Frowning at him, Margaret held two fingers before his nose.

"How many?"

"Two," he said.

"If you can read fingers, you can't be blind."

After watching the unsure angle of his pencil, his struggles with the book, her frown withdrew, and she provided him with an explanation. "It's alphabet disgust, Anatole, that's all. Happens to bookworms on occasion. Their bodies build up a hate against words. Sunshine will cure it. And hiking in the woods. You have to look hard, with both your eyes, at a bird, or a salamander on a rock, and not think about naming it. When you finish bleaching out the names, and snuff up the colors and the different folds, bake your system in it, maybe letters and stuff will come back natural. Meantime, I'll do your reading and your writing."

Hugging himself, he would pace the oilcloth floor in shabby socks, feel the nobs of his spine, handle his chin, and dictate to Margaret.

"For him, all things begin and end with families . . ."

§§§   8   §§§

Under Margaret's sway, he sought the companionship of salamanders and birds. He clawed into a lettuce, shredding down the rocks in Margaret's yard. He waited on his haunches. No salamanders came. He fisted stale soda crackers into the trees, and drew a mob of noisy jays. The jays took over the yard. They dove after Bruno, pecked a hole in one of Margaret's screens, shat

on his bald spot with delight, and irritated him more so
with their raucous love songs. He stopped feeding them.
They sat in the trees and squawked. He bought an air
pistol on the installment plan at the G Street hobby
shop, paying two dollars down and listing Margaret and
the Native Sons as credit references. He waved his
pistol at the jays. The squawking persisted. He shot into
the trees, his pellet shattering a leaf. Satisfied, he slept
into the middle of the next day, awakened by the jays.
He relieved his bowels, shattered a few more leaves, and
fell asleep. Margaret phoned in, advising the College
switchboard that her son-in-law, Waxman-Weissman,
lecturer and security guard, was temporarily indisposed.
Next morning a black-bordered card arrived with the
College's seal and "Condolences from the entire faculty
and staff." The words *computer-generated document*
were stamped on the back. She showed the card to
Anatole. He tore it up, yawned, and dropped pellets
into the nose of his gun. He might have clung to the
jays for another two weeks, eating, sleeping, shooting
(Margaret guarding his pellets, keeping them out of
Bruno's mouth), but an accident occurred. He aimed at
a tree, expecting nothing, and a bird plopped out. The
fluffed wings, the bald head, the body stuttering on the
ground amazed and debilitated him; without his wits
he'd bagged the loudest, meanest, and baldest of the
jays. It hopped once, screeched. The other jays abandoned Margaret's yard. Plagued with gloom he mea-
sured the bird's chances of recovery, and decided to
finish it off. He split a wing. His pellets thumped the
bird without effect. Blood dribbled off its beak. Margaret heard him crying. She took the gun out of his
hand, creased up her face, aimed over her left shoulder,

and killed the bird. She buried it after putting Anatole
to bed. He tried to ignore her scratchings in the yard.

§§§ 9 §§§

Testing his resources after the debacle with the jays,
Anatole sold his air pistol and decided to become a
huckster at the Galapagos Flea Market. He asked Margaret how he ought to go about obtaining a peddler's
license. She tore off a page from her receipt book,
scribbled something on it, put it in Anatole's hand, and
furnished him with sandals, sun cap, and three dollars
worth of change. He presented Margaret's page to the
surly young monitors at the check-in booth, assured
them he couldn't spell his name, and was given a sandwich board with leather pouches on both sides. The
monitors brushed his hair, looked inside his mouth,
fitted the sandwich board over his head, and sent him
off. Anatole resisted opening the pouches. He had no
idea what his wares were supposed to be. He tramped
across the market grounds, stopping long enough to
finger a lamp, a camera, a World War I helmet, at his
favorite stalls. He banged the sweat from the visor of
his cap. He shook his sandals free of twigs. The straps
of the sandwich board bit into his neck. He ignored the
bites. Gobbling sesame chips from the natural foods
stall, he gave in to the feel of the day. Bugs rolled on his
tongue. He refused to spit them out. Yellow jackets
floated past him, always at the level of his nose. He convinced himself that the thick, swarming air in N Street
Park could support his whole weight. Accordingly, he
gripped the rear board and leaped with his knees pointing out. The other vendors admired his kicks. An undersheriff waved to him. Anatole wondered if the Sheriff's

Office had its own stall. Children with greasy hair attacked the pouches over his thighs. Their mothers and fathers and other couples poked into his chest. He lost the desire to jump. Dollars were put into his hand. All his pouches had been opened. He squandered his change. Mothers were robbing him. He picked arms and wrists off him and ran to a different section of the park. People there were just as rude. They jockeyed into position to sample his wares, scratching him, stepping on his toes. The pain made him curious. He had no intention of relocating again. He cleared a circle for himself with a shake of the sandwich board, and began to inspect the pouches. From the pouch under his collarbone he withdrew a waterpipe, a retractable pencil, an opaque jar labeled "Miracle Spring Mud," a used clarinet reed, another opaque jar labeled the same, the hose and metal clip of a douche bag, the douche bag itself, mottled, with cracks in its skin, a soap eraser, a gimlet, a tube of vaginal jelly, a yellow pickup stick with one blunted end, a dish towel marked "College Cafeteria," a dildoe, a blue pickup stick in perfect condition, a baby's rubber sucking nipple, a second dildoe, larger than the first, a dysfunctional cartridge belt from the Sheriff's Office, a watchband, an ice pick. He stopped. The abundance and variety of articles disheartened him. If he persisted, he would compel himself to annotate his wares, play with the mud jars, sort the pickup sticks, compare dildoes, connect up the douche bag . . . He undid himself, stood the sandwich board against a tree, snapped the pouches shut, and went home.

§§§   10   §§§

When his reading and writing difficulties failed to clear up, Margaret proposed a curative trip to Idaho.

"We'll visit McNabb," she said. Anatole moaned. Mc-
Nabb was his *other* exegete, a withdrawn embezzler who
sent Anatole commentaries on his work from a prison
farm near Coeur d'Alene.

"Margaret, what will I say to him? He'll ask me
questions, and I'll have to shrug."

"Don't shit your britches," she said. "I've answered
all McNabb's letters for the last three years. I'll do
your talking."

Margaret baked a rhubarb pie for McNabb, and she
loaded her Packard down with bundles of comic books
and old clothes for McNabb's mates. She would have
had Anatole string the bundles, but sensing his nervous-
ness, his suspicions about McNabb, and his nausea before car rides, she put the spool in Bruno's lap, and
strung the bundles herself. Bruno and Anatole climbed
into the back, finding room among stale paper, vests,
jackets, and shoes. Anatole rummaged through the vests,
picking out loose buttons. "Whose clothes are these,
Margaret?"

"Can't swear," she said. "Collected them from the
Native Sons. They're partial to convicts, it seems, long
as they live in a different State."

Crawling from bundle to bundle, Bruno made his way
to the front. Margaret seized his pants, and handed him
over to Anatole. "Chain you up, Bruno, you don't stick
to your Daddy." She wouldn't allow Anatole or Bruno
to sit with her. "That's the deathtrap seat next to me.
Don't want no passengers up there."

"What about your seat, Margaret?"

"I can shake off any road problem with my blubber.
No harm to me. I aint the Daddy in this car. Sit where
you're at."

He settled in, tired of vests, a finger in Bruno's pants

to nip his climbing habit; watching men and women scuttle out from the crosswalks, he felt obliged to re-think his pedestrian's handbook. With their shoulders humped, the lips on their browned faces clutched in a snarl, their bellies wobbling, their arms and legs pad-dling with awkward, choppy strokes, they seemed as mean-spirited and ill-postured as any motorist. He put another finger in Bruno's pants, and slept on a bundle of comic books.

*   *   *

The pages break off here. Professor Chardin, who is fond of elisions and language tricks, offers no explana-tion. It may even be true that *Magie* prefers to see Anatole avoid McNabb. *The Tar Baby* belongs to a different school. Having no desire to frustrate our de-voted readership, we telephoned Mother Margaret Chace. Mother Chace informed *The Tar Baby* that the only things she could remember about the trip were the shyness of the convicts and McNabb's sneer. We wrote the prison farm next, anticipating a fuller report from McNabb, whose trenchant notes on Anatole's style in our "Cries" department have earned him a following among our readers. Perversely, McNabb's answer to *The Tar Baby* was garbled and curt, and largely un-printable. We volunteer the few relevant portions of this letter, kindly edited by our Business Manager, for whatever they are worth.

. . . Old sow. Her armpits stank. Maybe deodorants reached the cities after her time. We decided she was a Salvation Army general from the way she stuck hats on us and fed me pie. Baby snot in the rhubarb, I swear. She wiped the baby's nose and tore slices with the same hand. Peculiar child. It had her piggy eyes and his chin flab, and it wore a long shirt with shit in the crutch. That baby was so crudded up, couldn't tell the poundage it was carrying.

. . . Ought to warn a man before you visit. Would have washed my dungarees for Anatole. Slapped the potato beetles off my neck. Brushed my teeth. Smuggled root beers from the commissary. Put my bunk in order. I never asked his kid to chew my dirty socks. No chance to get out my *Tar Baby* collection and bone up. Anatole came in last. He counted light bulbs and wouldn't look at me straight. Scabby old sow of his must have figured I was a natural clothes tree. Kept making me try on shoes and hats. I got so disgusted I said, Brother, explain the word "cockziggler" to me. They don't carry dictionaries on this farm. She poked her nose in. Said the warden advised Anatole not to mention anything in *The Tar Baby*. Explaining words to a convict is against the Idaho sedition act. Crap, I said, and I threw them out with all their charity and moldy hats. Anatole, I can feed off your articles without adoring you.

from GALAPAGA, the official handbook to Galapagos

MARNIE GEMEINHARDT'S TURTLE PIE
(consummate hostess and wife of banker Penn Gemeinhardt)

1 pt. commercial turtle soup
1 onion, quartered
2 cups cubed potatoes
1 cup diced carrots
1 bay leaf
4 peppercorns
1 clove garlic
1 teaspoon powdered thyme
½ teaspoon rosemary

1 teaspoon salt
¼ cup flour
2 tablespoons sweet butter, melted
1 small sprig parsley
commercial pie crust
4 lbs. turtle meat, freshly killed, if possible

1. Cut up turtle meat and put into heavy pot; cover with cold water and commercial turtle soup. Add bay leaf, parsley, thyme, rosemary, garlic, onion, peppercorns, and salt. Cook over low heat about 2 hours. Allow meat to cool in turtle liquor.

2. Remove meat; strain liquor from pot and put back on high flame, boiling it down to 1½ cups.

3. Dip meat in flour mixed with salt, and roll into balls about the size of a walnut.

4. Put meat in a deep pie dish. Add potatoes and carrots. Pour in purified turtle liquor. Cover with pastry; cut slashes in center to allow for escape of steam. Brush well with butter.

5. Bake in medium oven for 2½ hours. After first hour cover crust with buttered paper to prevent overburning.

Yield: 8–10 portions, depending on hunger and affinity for turtle; leftover turtle liquor should be saved for other purposes.

For further recipes from distinguished
Galapagonians, all succulent, consult **GALAPAGA.**

NINA SPEAR

Conversations with Stefan Wax

Daughter of a wandering lieutenant general,
"Army brat" Nina Spear was born on a military
post in central Georgia, and raised in various parts
of the Southwest. She attended the Charleston
Music School ("I was expelled for copulating under a piano with the janitor's boy, but the school
had been dying to get rid of me because of my in-
volvements with the socio-sexual underground in
Charleston, which coalesced around the Fuck
America Club"); Savannah Arts & Agricultural
College ("A shitty school. I left after two
weeks."); Bennington of Vermont ("They took
me because of this ten-page application blank autobiography I wrote about my father's hang-up
over the areolas of prepubescent girls and boys, my
mother's dipsomania, and my six weeks of being a
dyke, all of which was a lie. I ran off with a visiting potter who dropped me in St. Louis"); and
earned her B.A. with distinction from the University of Nebraska ("I was tired, and wanted to
sit in one place."). She holds no graduate degree.
Brought to Galapagos Junior College by W.W.
Korn to manage *The Tar Baby,* Nina Spear is also
attached to our Pragmatic Letters and Philosophies Division. Her interests include metalan-
guages, female onanism, the writings of Anatole
Waxman-Weissman, and the computing machine's
potential for imprinting human speech.

Cartoonist Stefan Wax, Anatole Waxman-Weissman's half cousin and the subject of this interview,
was born in Galapagos, California, on July 5th,
1928. He moved to Laguna Beach in 1970.

INTERVIEWER

Stefan, much, perhaps too much, has been made of the
bad air between Anatole's father and your own. Can you
help us clarify the origins of this feud? Was there ever
a time when Ulrich and Benno were close? Why did your
father shorten his name to Wax? And why didn't he
promote Benno to a more respectable job once he
bothered to bring him to America? Was your father in
love with Sophie Waxman-Weissman? Was it his wish
to humiliate Benno by having him stay a lowly carpenter?

STEFAN WAX

A glut of questions, Nina. A true glut. I'm hungry.
Couldn't we eat and talk later?

INTERVIEWER

No. Tell us about the feud.

STEFAN WAX

Father seldom mentioned his other life. He came to
America, on his own, before he was sixteen. I think his
family drove him out. When he was drunk or blue about
something he'd mutter that Uncle Benno had a *Bandl-*

wurm in him. A tapeworm. That's the only word of German he ever used.

INTERVIEWER

Bandlwurm? Curious that your old man hit on such a word. What could it mean? Poor Benno hosting a live *Bandlwurm* with suckers and hooks and sex organs, bleeding him, shriveling his intestines. Possibly *Hymenolepis nana,* the dwarf flatworm, common to the Georgia of my childhood, which gutted Auntie Sara. Or was Benno's worm of a more elliptical, transubstantial variety?

STEFAN WAX

Nina, shut up. Do you have to blow things out of all proportion? As if I cared about your Auntie Sara. Poppa was nine years older than Benno. His mother died when he was five or six, his father remarried, and poof! he had a new brother in the house. Nina, feed your head a little. His stepmother must have despised him. She couldn't have been pleased about having a dark, skinny boy around to remind her of an earlier wife. She spoiled Benno, fattened him at Poppa's expense. There's your *Bandlwurm.* Nothing elliptical in it. Poppa displaced by his baby half brother.

INTERVIEWER

Half. Half brother. Ulrich halved by Benno. Made to feel half a boy. An exquisite paradigm. But if your father closed you out of his past, how do you know so much about this *Bandlwurm* business?

STEFAN WAX

Guesses. Picking up his drunken slurs. And you fault Poppa for streamlining his name, for becoming Ulrich Wax? It was his way of sludging off his father, Benno, and his prickly Austrian skin. Where do you think his lust for being an American came from? Nina, why are you such a dumdum? After slaving his ass off in a tannery, living like a grunge so he could buy into an old hotel, piece by piece, and convert it into the hottest sawmill north of Petaluma, after settling in, having me, you expect him to welcome Benno, his wife, and his brat?

INTERVIEWER

Stefan, didn't you pass over something? What happened to your mother?

STEFAN WAX

Nina, don't you get delicate with me. I'm a bastard, and you know it. I've had a stretch of nurses, housekeepers, sleep-in maids, but no mothers. And I'm glad of it. For all I care the woman who mothered me could still be working for Mrs. Chace. Poppa imported a slut from Yuba right after I was born, showed her around, played at being married, and dumped her a few months later. You got a nose for smelling psychological shit. Use it. Here's a man who learns about women from his stepmother. Why shouldn't he end up hating them? He wanted a son, not a wife. And he didn't have to worry over Galapagos respectability. Between him and Penny Gemeinhardt, they fed the whole town. And stop throwing off rumors about Poppa and Mrs. Sophie *Bandlwurm*. Man visits his half sister-in-law, does her a favor, too, because she was cracked, and people start sniffing sex into it.

INTERVIEWER

Stefan, are you going to deny that Ulrich didn't keep Benno a carpenter?

STEFAN WAX

Nina, I'd waltz myself into a sightseeing bus before denying anything to you. I would. I would.

INTERVIEWER

Shut your mouth, Stefan Wax.

STEFAN WAX

Suppose Benno liked being a carpenter. I can't remember. He was an amateur philosopher and a dictionary man. Think Poppa was going to trust him with his books? And could be Mrs. Sophie encouraged him to work with his hands.

INTERVIEWER

It killed him. The dust from the Mill.

STEFAN WAX

Shove it, Nina. There's an awful lot of peculiar deaths running in that family. If Benno wasn't satisfied, he could have janitored in Penny's bank.

I'd rather get off this, Stefan. What about you and Anatole? Was there any carry-over from the Ulrich-Benno feud?

STEFAN WAX

None. I disliked the brat on his own merits. Following me everywhere, calling me "Uncle Steffie." Kids at school twitting me, saying I had a shadow tacked on. And I caught it from Poppa at the other end. "He's your little cousin. Your only family in America. Don't let the older boys take advantage of him." I had to teach the brat how to scrape the dried snot off his handkerchief. I told him when to change his shirt. I took the knots out of his shoelaces. Nobody bothered about him at home. Mr. and Mrs. *Bandlwurm* drifted through Galapagos with their eyes pushed in. I'd say, "Anatole, it must be bath day. You stink awful. Poppa gave me soap and a dish rag. I'll wash ya in the Spring." And he'd blabber, "Uncle Steffie, Uncle Steffie. Target practice." Nina, what the fuck do you know about Anatole's writing style? I'm the one who taught him his English. Say what you want, and say it fast. That's my doctrine. I'd scrub the dirt off him—you couldn't imagine the crap that accumulated on Anatole's wrists, knees, and eyebrows, inside his belly button, and between his fingers and toes. I'll bet you never smelled belly button dirt. Then I'd go out with him and we'd smack at bottles and cans with my Daisy pump.

INTERVIEWER

Didn't Margaret Chace provide for him, buy him

lunches and pencils, years before she became his mother-in-law?

STEFAN WAX

I wouldn't be surprised of anything that whore does. Mother-in-law? That's the limit. She's been sucking after him since he was five. Perverted old bitch. Got her own daughter to run off with a pimping plumber, so she could have Anatole to herself.

INTERVIEWER

Would you be willing to say that Drexel Fingers, the dead Sheriff, also "sucked after" Anatole?

STEFAN WAX

The only sucking Drexel ever did was at Mrs. Chace's motel. You can't compare the Sheriff with any dilapidated bag of pus. The sweetest man in Galapagos, even if he cracked skulls for a living. Penny gave Poppa his own whiskey cabinet at the Merchants Bank, jabbered with him every single day, but it was Drexel who figured Poppa's needs. Made him an honorary Native Son. Forced his membership right through the buzzards on the screening board. First time in its history that organization cozened up to a foreigner.

INTERVIEWER

But didn't your old man move the Native Sons from a shack off T Street to a renovated mansion near the College?

STEFAN WAX

So what? Penny financed the operation. Poppa only paid for half.

INTERVIEWER

Stefan, would you care to spell out the circumstances surrounding Drexel Finger's death?

STEFAN WAX

Nina, why do you have to take something simple, twist it inside out, and stretch it into a complicated story? The man went into the woods behind town and got himself killed, that's all.

INTERVIEWER

What about Turkey Semple? Weren't the bruises on Drexel's neck a Semple hallmark?

STEFAN WAX

I thought Turkey only bothered to strangle women. Hated them, the old wives used to say, those who weren't getting any. They'd masturbate with Turkey in their minds. Tell me, Nina, you ever see Turkey Semple?

INTERVIEWER

No.

STEFAN WAX

Did anybody in Galapagos talk to him, feel him out?

Suppose I walked over to him and said: "Turkey, can't you claim any snatch without messing it up?" And he answered: "You get a better orgasm from a woman if you close the windpipe. I like to look at them when they're gagging. That's what turns me on. I can't abide raw pussy."

INTERVIEWER

You're disgusting, Stefan Wax.

STEFAN WAX

Hell, Nina, this town needed a bogeyman, so it invented Turkey Semple. Makes it easy. Kid decides to dig the mud for bullfrogs, his Poppa or Momma can shout, "Come on home before Turkey Semple gets ya and eats ya alive." Some society whore up in Oregon lets a bum into her, then hollers rape, and there's a ten-state alarm: Turkey's on the loose. Who knows what Drexel met in the woods? A bobcat? A stray rodeo cow? A deadbeat living in a tree? A junkie from Oakland? His own look-alike? A brother nobody knew he had? One thing, though. It wasn't Turkey Semple.

INTERVIEWER

Stefan, earlier you called Sophie Waxman-Weissman "cracked." Can you clarify that statement?

STEFAN WAX

Cracked is cracked. The town fool. Mumble to herself in the streets. She'd shit in garbage pails. Show her ragged underpants to the old men outside the cigar store. Sunbathe on the old Indian Mound with her brassiere over her crotch. I think she was a bit of a whore too. It wouldn't surprise me any. She'd pull her disappearing act. And Anatole would have to track her down with his nose. He'd poke into every door, alley, and bin sniffing for a vomity glove or a pissed-on hat. You could bet ten to one he wouldn't find her.

INTERVIEWER

What can you tell us about Anatole's later life, when he began to suffer through the horrific, alternating rhythms of cyclothymia?

STEFAN WAX

You mean his highs and lows?

INTERVIEWER

Yes. The manic-depressive episodes that hospitalized him in his twenties and thirties.

STEFAN WAX

You and your technical crap. He was squirrely before he was ten. And lucky to have had a fortieth birthday if you consider the histories of his Momma and Poppa. In addition to which, I'll bet he caught clap of the brain running through Mrs. Chace's whorehouse somewhere between the ages of eight and nine.

INTERVIEWER

His later life, Stefan. That's our concern at the moment.

STEFAN WAX

Nothing special there. You could sum it all up by discussing his stopovers at two institutions: Galapagos Junior College and Minerva State. And if you gave me the pick, I'd rather sit in the hydrotherapy tub at Minerva and pull on myself than listen to the prattle bouncing off the walls of that other place. The baddest thing Drexel did in his life was to pressure the College trustees into making Anatole a campus dick. Those trustees weren't stupid. They wouldn't have been intimidated by Drexel's badge, but they couldn't afford to tangle with a Sheriff who was also grand deacon of the Native Sons.

INTERVIEWER

But putting Anatole in uniform paid off. Wasn't he the hero of the Charter Day riots? Yes or no? Whatever opinions you have about Anatole's head, he was shrewd enough to hold the Native Sons' arsenal in check.

STEFAN WAX

Nina, I swear, I swear, I swear, I'll split open and die if I get one more story on how my little cousin licked Penny Gemeinhardt's ass and shamed the Sons away from slaughtering the College population. Lord, it was the students who trashed the buildings and threw the rocks, not the Native Sons. And just because Penny blubbered a few words about putting flags inside the dorms and cafeterias. He couldn't have enforced his silly flag rule. You humor him, that's how you shake off Penny, but not with hisses and rocks. The Sons couldn't have fired anything except sand farts out of those miserable cannons. I'm telling you. I loaded their shotguns myself. No, Drexel's the dirty one. He shouldn't have steered Anatole toward the College in the first place. If Anatole hadn't become a campus dick, maybe he wouldn't have broken out with lectures and scribblings, and his stopovers at Minerva could have petered off.

INTERVIEWER

Stefan Wax, either you're an ignoramus or a very jealous man. That was an absurd, prejudiced view of Anatole's life you gave us. You're not qualified in the least to comment on his writings. Paralinguistics supports Anatole's belief that personae are interchangeable, thus all narrators are the same; that language is viscous and malleable; that words can gouge, burn, and betray; that the world consists of one interminable sentence we pick up before we are born and utter after we die; that there is no such—

STEFAN WAX

You keep flinging that theoretical puke at me, Nina, and I'll bite your nipples off. Paralinguistics can kiss my ass. I say Anatole's stuff is drivel. Anybody who works on a single story ten years has got to have constipation problems. I suppose I'm not qualified to comment on Anatole's hemorrhoids. You think his Momma and Poppa troubled themselves to toilet-train him? He learned how to wipe himself from watching me. I don't dream on the pot, and I wouldn't devote more than an hour to my cartoons. How much of my life do you want me to invest in one filthy thing?

INTERVIEWER

Now that we've shifted around to you, Stefan, why don't you tell us about your life?

STEFAN WAX

You coy little bitch, you'd love to know why I dumped Wax's Mill and settled in Laguna. Anatole had the right idea when he ran away from Galapagos without graduating from high school. If he'd kept his smarts, he wouldn't have come back. He was a free man, his Momma and Poppa being dead. I didn't have Anatole's options. I had to burrow into the town's gut, do my father's bidding, manage his Mill, become a Native Son, suffer Penny's jokes, sit on my accounts at the Merchants Bank, and wait, wait. Sure, I could have run, years ago, but Poppa staked his whole existence in Galapy, and he would have spooked me. There's no rest for a creature who damages his Poppa's idols while his Poppa is alive. Galapagos was inviolable to him. For me it was a frizzled-out swamp. Poppa tried to glue me, him, and Galapy together. His papers said I could own the Mill but couldn't sell it. I shut the fucker down soon as he died and gave the property away.

INTERVIEWER

Couldn't you have left without bleeding our industry?

STEFAN WAX

Go play with yourself, Nina. I gave the property to that fool College of yours. Ask the trustees why the College doesn't revive Wax's Mill? They're going to level it and build an institute for geriatrics, so they can get retired people to study here. The College farts on industry. They want everybody in Galapy to work for them.

INTERVIEWER

I've never met a more disagreeable man, Stefan Wax. We only occupy a small portion of Galapagos, and you want to make us out to be some crazy empire. You wallow on a beach, draw animated genitals for a porno syndicate, you don't even bother sketching faces, and you call that a life.

STEFAN WAX

I do. Mornings I piss in the sand, bathe, and earn a hundred bills for every cock I draw. I fuck whenever I can, I shit in peace, and I go to sleep with the indescribable comfort of knowing my system has rid itself of Galapagos.

INTERVIEWER

Stefan, have you really given up Galapagos? Isn't it true that you're hooked in with a group of Sonoma provocateurs, who call themselves the Stepchilds or whatever, and operate out of our Flea Market? I've seen "Cocks by S. Wax" at several of the Market stalls.

STEFAN WAX

Never heard of any Stepchilds. You can't keep artwork from circulating in this County. Maybe the grubbers up here are hungry for my cocks?

INTERVIEWER

Vile, Stefan, vile.

STEFAN WAX

Twiddle yourself, Nina, and let's eat.

SHERIFFS OF GALAPAGOS

Galapagos has had more than passable luck with its Sheriffs. Our earliest Sheriffs were mercenaries hired by rich merchants and farmers to look after their personal treasure; they took no interest in the general welfare of the town. Galen Harpending, who served from 1853 to 1861, was the poorest of the lot. He managed to hoodwink his masters, cheat the citizens of Galapagos, and align himself with Joaquín Tiburcio, a Mexican miner-turned-bandit who roosted in Galapagos after 1854. The relationship between Harpending and Tiburcio has become ripe material for Western balladeers; evidently, they shared the same *querida*, a Galapagos brothelkeeper with the name of Charlotta, who succored both of them and once waylaid a band of U.S. marshals in pursuit of Tiburcio by sleeping with every marshal in the band; in 1858 Charlotta took a bullet meant for Harpending and died. In the popular eye, the two men were gruff saviors who longed for an independent California, free of the United States. Unfortunately, historians dispute the balladeers; it seems Harpending and Tiburcio murdered and plundered without giving mind to California or the United States. The Native Sons, organized in 1861, rid Galapagos of these two and their various gangs. With the stink of Harpending still in its streets, Galapagos remained sheriffless for several years. Finally, the Native Sons risked bringing Ezekiel Bagby, an Oakland detective, into town. Our first public-spirited Sheriff, "Big Zeke" proved to be the greatest peace officer of nineteenth-century Galapagos. His tenure coincided with our emergence as the premier hot spring in northern California; from 1871 to 1889 only one homocide was recorded in all of Galapagos. Zeke reformed the local penal system; finding jailhouses abhorrent, he billeted prisoners in his own home; the prisoners worked with Zeke in his pear orchard, and were paid a living wage. Reportedly, no man or woman who "picked Zeke's pears" was ever jailed again. Having kept the peace in Galapagos, Zeke died of natural causes on May 8, 1891, in the security of his H Street house. His stay in Galapagos has been commemorated by a bronze tablet set in an orchard boulder (Galapagos Registered Landmark #7), which now sits in N Street Park. Bagby's successors being competent and unremarkable, Galapagos had to wait over forty years for its second great Sheriff—to wit, Drexel Fingers. Elected in a period of economic decline, Drexel slashed his own salary and saved money for the County by having his deputies collect trash, paint fences, and plant trees on their own time. He repeatedly raided Galapagos' skid row (formerly near Chinatown), apprehending all undesirables and escorting them across the County line. Mindful of our children, Drexel bought kites for orphans, and constructed playgrounds, swimming holes, and a shelter with the help of his deputies. In 1959, after twenty-three years of uninterrupted service, he was murdered while defending Galapagos from a depraved outlaw.

W[OODROW] W[ILSON] KORN

The Other Anatole

My father was a turpentine still operator, a pecan farmer, a trader in bauxite and feldspar, a part owner of two Macon funeral establishments, an off-and-on member of the Georgia Legislature, and a trustee of a barbers' college and a manual training school for black boys and retarded whites. I saw him approximately twice a month. He called me "Little Dubs" when he was sober, "Skinhead" when he was drunk, and after he became an overseer at the barbers' college he wouldn't allow anyone except himself to cut my hair. My mother was a mousy woman who seemed to have had a difficult time being delivered of me, though I believe I was only six pounds at birth. She shuffled through the house clutching her belly, a cigarillo in her mouth, and wouldn't eat unless one or the other of my father's sisters, who lived with us, fed her. She would tuck her napkin in, polish her spoon, and scream, "Helen, Zell, mushy, mush." I was raised essentially by my two maiden aunts, who bathed me and my mother in the same tub, and swore that she had been "witty, honest, and upright" before she carried me.

Having been given authority over the fates of student barbers, my father convinced himself of his own educational acumen, and he wasn't going to let me languish in any commonplace Georgia school. At the age of

eleven I was handed up to one of my father's Macon
cronies, bundled off to Chicago, and registered for the
new Giovanni plan at Giovanni Teachers College:
Twenty of us, out-of-staters, under twelve, would either
be transformed into baccalaureates before our eighteenth
birthday or dropped from the plan with ignominy. I
lived in a boarding house near Hyde Park, under the
supervision of a Mr. Pflaum, cranky tutor-janitor with
swollen hands and a hearing device which he clipped to
his neck. Pflaum wore my father's discards, and favored
me over all his boarders. I was the enviable Mr. Woodrow who had unchallenged rights to the hall privy. The
other Giovanni boys despised me, and I had little use for
them.

A middling Giovannian, more of a Chicago street
urchin than a "baby baccalaureate," I was still cautious
to see that there were at least five boys in the plan with
grades as poor as mine. Overplaying a bronchial cough,
conjuring up rashes and hives, or winning Pflaum with
an open bribe, I managed to stay in Chicago during
vacation periods. I smoked on Washington Boulevard,
rode the Jackson Avenue El to both ends of the line,
lost a sock, a handkerchief, and my school cap to the
petty thieves of Maxwell Street, walked out of Carson
Pirie's with odd-shaped bottles of eau de cologne,
watched near-copulations in Lincoln Park, followed
whores to the edge of the Black Belt, encouraged a
stinking grayhaired lady on the Milwaukee Avenue
trolley to keep her hand in my pocket, and sidled up to
my baccalaureate in five and two-thirds years.

A teacher-in-training, approaching his sixth Chicago
year, I lived on at Pflaum's and groomed myself to be a
master of science as I quacked to the most recent crop

of Giovanni babies, avoiding father, mother, pecans,
and maiden aunts once again. Eight Giovanni semesters
later, after Zell, my more adventurous aunt, threatened
me with a visit, and tiring of Pflaum and Hyde Park
anyway, I contacted the Giovanni placement bureau.
Upon the recommendation of Assistant Provost Seth
Birdwistell, who hoped to apply the Giovanni plan to
young adults at Galapagos Junior College and revamp
the entire curriculum, I moved to Galapagos Springs.

My first interview with Seth Birdwistell wasn't in his
office, or any place near the Junior College. I bumbled
across the Galapagos foothills, in my teacher's suit and
city shoes, and we met in a funicular at the bottom of a
cliff. He wore brakeman's gloves, old boots, and a
patched shirt. He shook my hand, sat me down, tugged
at the cables with a glove, and we screaked up the cliff
at a risky angle, the downward car swerving extrava-
gantly above us, and I was about to wave to the man in
the other car when Seth glowered at me between cable
pulls: conventional funicularism, it was a stuffed sack
wearing a pilgrim's hat, put there to counterbalance our
weight. On later rides I would suck in the Galapagonian
landscape and get to sit with the pilgrim, but now, in the
upward car, catching strips and chops of Galapagos, the
hat unsettled me.

We drank hard cider in Seth Birdwistell's cabin. He
worried over the color in my face. He showed me diagrams and sketches of a college building. "I didn't bring
you two thousand miles to educate farmer boys, Mr.
Korn." I wasn't to be his amanuensis, but a full ally;
together we would push for a new division at the Junior
College, a school that could mingle arts and sciences
with practical life. He needed a precursor, a magazine
to commemorate local talent and convince trustees that

the Pragmatic Letters and Philosophies division was justified. "We'll call it *The Tar Baby Review*." He made me editor-in-chief. He couldn't have missed my groans. "More cider, Mr. Korn?"

"Provost Birdwistell, if you selected that title in deference to me, please scratch it. This is my eleventh year out of Georgia and I'd rather stay away from tar babies."

"Mr. Korn, my *Tar Baby* has nothing to do with Georgia. I was thinking of the Hindu tar critter, who sized up your nature without sticking to you. His handlers carried him from town to town. You paid the handlers their price to look under his cloak, and having no Daddy and no soul, the critter could reflect the honey or the turpitude in each beholder's face."

My mother died of a cerebral hemorrhage three years after my arrival in Galapagos (she may or may not have bumped into a wall on one of her rambles through the house). My father died next, suffering a massive coronary outside his barbers' college. Aunt Helen, who loved to bathe me and my mother, fell asleep in her tub and drowned there. I learned the facts of these deaths from Aunt Zell, who is still alive and sends me a family newsletter most Christmases. I have no idea how she uncovered my Galapagos address. If Zell is correct, my father's properties are being held in escrow for me. Should I tire of *The Tar Baby,* I have the option of returning to Georgia and becoming a pecan farmer or a dealer in bauxite.

The first generation of *Tar Baby*s (the word *Review* was dropped in 1946 at my insistence) were markedly uneventful. We discovered a country poetess, Melvinia Bogardus, who wrote sestinas on the wildlife of Napa, Yolo, Plumas, and Butte counties. Miss Bogardus didn't come across. She married a broom salesman, moved to New Jersey, had four children in a row, changed her style, and sent us a batch of confessional poems (oozing with extramarital glop) which I had to reject. We also published spin-offs from Birdwistell's new Pragmatics division, cheery, mindless articles about the contribution of the sewing machine to modern life, the antinomy of Northern California and Karl Marx, immigrant writers and their exflagellation of America, the pros and cons of making Alaska a vast prison farm, Oakland's slow defedation by its shifty populace, and other matters.

In 1951 I hired a Business Manager, Nina Spear, a fugitive from Georgia like myself, and *The Tar Baby* had an immediate turnabout. We sneaked away from Pragmatics; I sold *Tar Baby*s on the road in order to maintain our independence, and Nina commissioned the Galapagos millman-cartoonist Stefan Wax to design a logo for our masthead and frontispiece. The logo enraged Birdwistell as it failed to resemble his Hindu tar creature. He called it "Korn's nigger baby," but couldn't bitch out loud: he was in the midst of prying money from Ulrich Wax for a Life Sciences Building.

Passing through the college library somewhere in '55 I noticed Anatole, badged, in blue, taking notes inside a shaky carrel. My students must have told me about Sheriff Finger's latest prodigy, a miseducated security guard who was boning up on Wittgenstein and had been given his own carrel because he was an obscure relative of the Wax family. Busy with *Tar Baby* matters, I would have gone by him, but his concentration, notching the details on his chubby face, held me, made me aware that he was more than a Galapagos bumpkin under the Sheriff's thumb. I stopped, introduced myself, glanced at his notes, invited him up to my office. I admit there

was an element of personal gain in my overtures to him.
If I found some clever passages, Nina and I could prune
his notes (on the average we rewrote half *The Tar
Baby*), though I wasn't quite sure that reading him
would be worth the effort of emptying the muck from
my teapot.

My arrogance redounded on me, and deservedly so.
Anatole wasn't making any move to stencil in the rude
facts of Wittgenstein's life; ignoring the conventions
of time, space, and local color, scornful of all facts, he
attempted to reconstruct a weightless Wittgenstein, a
Wittgenstein who might function three centuries from
now, in Rabat, Hong Kong, or Macon, Georgia. He
chose to put Wittgenstein in Galapagos because it was
convenient for him and he didn't want to choke his researches with a more specialized setting. We tore chunks
from the notes, published them without connectives, ex-
planations, or biographical tripe, and kept our hands off
Anatole's prose.

The response to "Galapaga—A Philosophical Nativity" (my title) was thick and noisy: twenty-four letters
of repudiation, including cancelled subscriptions, smug
remarks for Anatole, and obscenities for the Provost
(who was still on our editorial board), Nina, and myself; to balance this we had congratulatory notes from
retired businessmen, a Central American linguist, a convict from Idaho, and two schoolteachers living in a
trailer, five anonymous contributions to *The Tar Baby*,
totaling six dollars and forty cents, and a net gain of one
subscription. Withal, we expected flak from the College;
while Nina made preparations to kill our Winter–Spring
number, Birdwistell came over to our side. "Woodrow,"
he wrote on a sheet of scratch paper, "I don't understand a line by this Waxman-Weissman fellow, but we

must do everything in our power to encourage native talent." Thereupon Nina gathered the "Galapaga" letters for our Winter–Spring "Cries to the Tar Baby" column, I lashed back at Anatole's attackers, and we announced that the youthful Galapagos logomachist A. Waxman-Weissman would pull his Philosophical Nativity together for our readers in a future number.

Did we exploit Anatole, as Birdwistell would later suggest both in and out of our pages? Perhaps. I have no intention of recapping our affairs vis-à-vis Anatole (see "A Waxman-Weissman Chronology," pp. 6 & 7). We published him, shared lunch bags, became his friend, visited him at Minerva State, mulched over his difficulties with the College bookstore, and later we would babysit for him, lend money to his wife, support his lectureship at the College, and become his coffin bearers.

My fallout with Anatole wasn't over *The Tar Baby* (we remained his publisher even after his death). He accused me of joining the plumber Stokie's campaign to steal his wife. I wouldn't have minded confronting him in private. I'd dealt with his rages before. But he broke into my classroom, threw his handcuffs at me, called me a "shit-eating pimp," and ran away. Students attended to the welts on my forehead, and I continued with the lecture. What was my topic? It may have been the tautology of everyday grammar, some territoriality question, or Anatole's prose. Whatever, my face and arms swelled with ugly blueish-red hives, and I was forced to dismiss the class (hives, I hadn't been plagued by hives in forty years). Concerned for me, my students leaked the news that Anatole had been "violence-tripping" in Life Sciences 205. One of Birdwistell's obnoxious underdeans favored depriving Anatole of his badge and teach-

ing post, and removing him entirely from the campus. I
checked the underdean with a handwritten note to Birdwistell (knowing he'd be touchy, I avoided *The Tar
Baby* letterhead), indicating that Anatole merely exer-
cised the prerogative I had given him to demonstrate
radical teaching techniques before my class. The underdean ate crow, but my relations with Anatole didn't
improve. On my part, I wasn't about to forgive him for
abusing me in public *or* for infecting me with hives. I
had a rather good reason to be chummy with his wife.
Someone other than Margaret, who was caught between
her pampered daughter and moody son-in-law, had to
gain Cindy Waxman-Weissman's trust, in order to come
to grips with that chaotic marriage. Granted, I failed,
but does this make me a pimp? Whenever Anatole and I
met on the quad, we'd look down and pass each other
without a word. This went on for two years. Mother
Margaret brought his manuscripts up to *The Tar Baby,*
and I'd send the copyedited pages, with Nina's queries
on them, back to Mother at the Redwood Motel. I
swear, more than once I set out to visit Anatole, to chide
him, woo him, patch things over, with bonbons for
Mother, doodads for baby Bruno; I'd feel the hives
erupting on my arms, turn around, and go home. And
then, before I could shake up the courage to walk the
full route, Anatole was killed.

I'm quite ashamed of the morbid chatter around
Galapagos that has raked over the dead Anatole. Ignorant critics (include Joachim Fiske) and hostile ones
(Seth Birdwistell) scream suicide. As evidence they cite
the muddled snatches, theories, and remarks of nameless
passengers aboard the bus that ran Anatole down. Several claim he was carrying a satchel. Others say both
hands were free. One woman who refuses to identify

herself swears that Anatole waved to her before jumping in front of the bus. Her friends contradict her. They
say Anatole was looking at the ground. Half the bus
would have us believe he was coming from the spring:
his knees were wet; he had moss on his ankles; he was
petting a frog. The other half doesn't remember the
frog; they think his knees were dry. A majority of both
halves favor the idea that Anatole was aware of the bus,
and that his death had to be deliberate. The driver, Mr.
Anthony Bliss, a veteran of over twenty years with
Elbow Hill Transit Co., disagrees with his passengers.
Mr. Bliss is less inclined toward the invention and ro-
mance of tourists and sightseers. "Thought he heard me
coming, but I can't tell. He must have been concentrating
hard on something. He stepped into the road without
looking up. I swung as wide I could. Clipped him with
a bumper guard." The driver's account meshes with my
own impression of Anatole, a man who took delight in
abstractions and could easily void his immediate surroundings. I've seen him peer into himself, dead to
sights, smells, and sounds. He might have been particularly troubled. Perhaps he was running away from
Galapagos in a mad push for reconciliation with his
wife. If so, what happened to the satchel passengers supposedly saw? Did it disintegrate with the smack of the
bumper guard? In any event, I do not think Anatole
walked into Mr. Bliss's touring bus on purpose.

We're all would-be saviors, aren't we? I thicken myself with schemes. I'll marry Margaret, be a grandfather to Bruno. I'll strangle Millard Stokie. I'll violate
Cindy, give her a child she won't be so ready to forget.
I'll close *The Tar Baby*, send Nina down to Laguna
where she belongs. I'll have it out with Birdwistell, tell
him what I think of Life Sciences and Pragmatic Letters

after thirty years. See, not even Anatole's death can stop my indulgences. As Anatole's publisher, what can I say to explain his writings? I'll tell you what I liked best. The number of characters. I've added them up. Give one, take one, Anatole created eight characters per page (nine if you include animals and other dumb beings). Nina is commissioning an article for us on Anatole's exploitation of "the amalgamated noun," the noun that can soak in other parts of speech and will one day make adjectives, verbs, and adverbs obsolete, but has anybody bothered with the commonplace? A simple character-quotient? L/CP. Your loneliness goes down in proportion to the number of characters on a page. Mostly though, Anatole's death has shrunk out Galapagos and Chicago, and left me with Georgia. I drift into Life Sciences 205, nod to students, a finger in my scrotum (Helen's? Zell's? Is that where the hives came from?), a thigh against my chest (crazy mother with glabrous skin, her bush under soapy water), Zell scrubbing my back, Helen singing to us, two in a tub, two in a tub (Why should I have been so afraid my father would catch us? (a) He was never home at four in the afternoon, the hour Helen chose. (b) He wouldn't have cared. He was probably tarring the scarecrows in his pecan orchards, or shandying between his Macon business establishments and one of his philanthropies), are Bailey, Josh, Hank, Potato Stan, Dana, and Bob the Mustache my students or the names of Daddy's scarecrows? A snigger from the upper benches, where the C and D people sit: the option of weaker students to laugh at a professor who dribbles over his lectures notes. The C people sneak out. I excused myself and left via a door near the blackboard.

SLS

The Society of Literature Scientists
Inaugural Convention
Sunday Morning   4 May 1972
The Redwood Motel
Galapagos, California

•

The first annual meeting of the Society will be devoted
to the work of Anatole Waxman-Weissman

•

OFFICERS

PRESIDENT:	*(vacant)*
VICE-PRESIDENT:	*Joachim Fiske*
SECRETARY:	*(Miss) Nina Spear*
TREASURER:	*Dalton Chess*
CONVENTION CHAIRMAN:	*(to be decided)*

•

MEMBERSHIP INFORMATION
   —Please enroll me as a member of SLS for the rest
   of 1972 and all of 1973: $13.50. (Privileges include a
   free subscription to SLS's official publication, *The
   Tar Baby*, for the life of your membership.)

•

CONVENTION ROUNDUP
   —Registration Fee and Breakfast
   SLS Members: $7.00; Non-Members: $8.50
   —Breakfast for spouse
   SLS Members: $2.00; Non-Members: $2.75
   —Room rates for the Convention
   SLS Members: $9 for singles, $13.50 for doubles
   Non-Members: $11 for singles, $14.75 for doubles

•

ARRIVING SATURDAY NIGHT?
   Meet your host, Mrs. Margaret Chace, owner of the
   Redwood Motel, in the Hospitality Room, Bungalow 11

•

SLS
Box 99
Galapagos

abcdefghijklmnopqrstuvwxyzabcdefghijklmnopqrstuvwx

COMPUTER CRAFTSMEN
A DIVISION OF BONNEFROY INDUSTRIES
GALAPAGOS, CALIFORNIA

yzabcdefghijklmnopqrstuvwxyzabcdefghijklmnopqrstuv

FEATURING THE BONNEFROY-PRODUCED
KIT CARSON 99

wxyzabcdefghijklmnopqrstuvwxyzabcdefghijklmnopqrst

COMPUTER CRAFTSMEN HAVE THE IN-HOUSE CAPACITY TO WRITE, DESIGN, AND/OR PRODUCE INDEXES, DIRECTO-RIES, CATALOGS, POPULAR MAGAZINES, AND SELECTED FICTION AND NON-FICTION ON WESTERN LORE

uvwxyzabcdefghijklmnopqrstuvwxyzabcdefghijklmnopq

WE ARE THE DESIGNERS AND PRINTERS OF THE GALAPAGOS TELEPHONE DIREC-TORY, THE GALAPAGOS JUNIOR COL-LEGE CATALOG, PATCHQUILT BOOKS, AND *THE TAR BABY*

rstuvwxyzabcdefghijklmnopqrstuvwxyzabcdefghijklmno

SEE OUR DISPLAY AT THE SLS CONVENTION

pqrstuvwxyzabcdefghijklmnopqrstuvwxyzabcdefghijklm

THIS ADVERTISEMENT AND THE ONE ON THE PRECEDING PAGE WERE WRIT-TEN AND PRODUCED BY KIT CARSON 99, FOR COMPUTER CRAFTSMEN, AT OUR GALAPAGOS PLANT

nopqrstuvwxyzabcdefghijklmnopqrstuvwxyzabcdefghijk

ADDENDA

This, all we have presented to you thus far (plus a few marginal items to follow), was to have been our complete Anatole Memorial Issue. Whatever the limitations of the Issue, the contributors, who stated their point of view in single file, are not be blamed. Blame the editors instead, W.W. Korn and Nina Spear (and particularly Korn), who assembled the special number, revised several of the contributions (though not without notice to our readers), and whose own chagrins and adorations could hardly have been piled into a random corner of our office. Needless to say, we expect you to react to the special number, and we are allotting a decent amount of space in future "Cries to The Tar Baby" for such purposes. (*The Tar Baby* will respond in print to as many of its readers' comments as is humanly possible.) Seth Birdwistell, having had a perfect opportunity to comment on Anatole and *The Tar Baby,* along with its editors (he is one of the contributors to the special number), now chooses to malign us. The Provost, who has not asked for an advance copy of *The Tar Baby* in almost fifteen years, claims that the two of us (Spear and Korn), willfully sneaked out the special number behind his back. "Had I known the company I might be in," he retroactively swears, "I would not have contributed to the Memorial Issue." Splendid. But why the sudden interest in our table of contents, Provost Birdwistell? Owing to the severity of the charges against us, we suspend *The Tar Baby*'s usual policies, and are allowing the Provost to critique our special number within the Memorial Issue itself. And because we want to avoid a footnote war, the shrill clutter of charge and countercharge, which can only serve to embarrass the three parties involved, we offer the Provost's rebuttal cleanly, without snaps, asides, or testy remarks. We make no judgments; for the moment we will keep a private score of our grievances.

In order to accommodate the Provost, we had to delay publication; this delay provided us with an unexpected dividend. We had intended to save Mother Margaret's article, "With Me," which arrived long after we originally went to press, for Summer–Fall. We can now include it in our special number.

—The Editor (with Nina Spear)

SETH BIRDWISTELL

The Tar Baby *Reappraised*

*   *   *

If the Korn-Spear axis expects to lure me into a game of
vituperation, it is sadly mistaken. An utter fool could
see through Korn's miserable bait: goad the old man
into stuttering on paper, have him boil over with rash,
unsupportable claims, which Nina, the businessminded
shegoat, can later sweep aside. I will not dignify *The
Tar Baby* by exploring the reasons for its consistently
shabby treatment of one Seth Birdwistell: drop the old
man from the masthead, beg him for articles and then
butcher them out of recognition, misspell his name in
the yearly index, stir up controversies about him in the
margins, and so forth. Had it not been for the proximity
of my office to *The Tar Baby*'s rooms, and my own good
fortune in spotting galley proofs of the Memorial Number on Nina Spear's desk, Korn might have gotten away
with his hoax. The "Anatole" Issue, as it stands, is
nothing more than an oversong to W.W. Korn. Anatole
is barely discernible in its pages; he pops up in one article, disappears in the next; his presence is that of a
hobgoblin or naughty stepchild—but I'm afraid I may
be running ahead of myself; let me proceed to the body
of my argument.

*   *   *

That spindly, neutered thing on *The Tar Baby*'s front, with breasts and swollen belly, tells more about the "Anatole" Issue than all the hodgepodge between its covers could ever do. Inked by the disgusting Stefan Wax, an ex-Galapagonian who gave up his birthright in order to defecate on a beach, Korn's "tar baby" is mushy, effeminate, and washed over with a pathetic gray. Examine it. Its nostrils and ears are missing. Its toes are illogically splayed. It has runty shoulders and knees without caps. Its eyes, far apart and on a crooked line, have the vacant glare of an idiot. And its genitals, which might be hanging pudenda or penis tip, are so obscured, each possibility seems to cancel the other out and leave the tar baby sexless.

What better signature for Korn, Nina, Stefan, the dead Anatole, and their magazine, than the imago of a wishy-washy golem, without father, mother, or individual character, soft enough to push around and reshape, and who may even have the capacity to hatch itself? —at least that is how I interpret the tar baby's vague, outsized middle. My last chat with Stefan Wax, just before he left Galapagos, might be revealing here. Stefan said the following about W.W. Korn: "That man's been so fucked-over by his past, he's on a lifelong fantasy trip." In my estimation, filial confusions, the fear of being abused and betrayed by grownups, the child's niggling sense of its own illegitimacy, qualities which have racked Korn himself, link him to Nina, Nina to Stefan, Stefan to Anatole, and all of them to the tar baby.

The "Anatole" Issue is shot through with tar baby imagery, from the sawdust covering Benno Waxman-Weissman's body (pages 16 & 17), to Korn's fixation on tarred scarecrows during his rather stagey crack-up (pp. 164–165). To those readers who are suspicious of me and think I have loaded down the Memorial Number with two isolated "tar-babyisms," I offer a more inclusive sampling, viz.

—Sophie Waxman-Weissman's decomposition at the Northern Lights Motel into a tar baby of sorts: "Her eyes were shot with purple, her lips were turning black . . ." (21)

—The thirty-year-old snicker of some of our citizens over Anatole's rummagings on Sonora Indian Mound: "Black as a nigger with that mud and sand on him." (29)

—Millard Stokie on Sheriff Fingers: "Drexel's dust and clay and melted bones." (42)

—Cindy, under the covers, waiting for Anatole, "stiff as a mummy . . ." (44)

—From Anatole's juvenile report on the Pitfaces: "No baby could tell his own father." (54)

"Ugly now and itchy, with scabs on their noses, their testicles, their thighs, the Pitfaces kept to themselves." (54)

"Alive, a Pitface meant nothing to himself or his Pitface brothers. But once he was a rotting corpse, his value went up considerable." (55)

—From Lucian Bonnefroy's critique of Anatole's report: "If a Pitface baby wasn't weaned, who taught it to pee?" (57)

—Anatole's classmate Alana "drawing grime to herself." (58)

—Nicholas St. Justin, believed to be the last Pitface alive, who visits Anatole's class with "tar on his shirt" and "ordure in his underpants." (59)

—The false transvestite Morris Plotch, unable to locate his birthday: ". . . my parents used up so much of their energy in feeding me, they lost track of my chronological age." (96)

—Stefan Wax scrubbing the young Anatole: "You couldn't imagine the crap that accumulated on Anatole's wrists, knees, and eyebrows, inside his belly button, and between his fingers and toes." (144)

—And a batch of wholesale tar-babyisms: "brainchild" (15); "Austrian isolate" (19); "half-man husband" (41); "Cindy No-name" (43); "nigger babies" (70); "maimed doll" (79); "penispoppuh" (89); "talking fetus" (91); "water-bag baby" (93); "rodeo nigger" (109); "baby baccalaureate" (157); "weightless Wittgenstein" (161); etc., etc., etc.

Along with the tar baby mold Korn imposes on us, are the Memorial Number's blotches, distortions, and lies, which I will uncover *ad seriatum*, moving at my own pace from article to article.

W.W. Korn: Speculations on Benno, Anatole, Sophie, and Drexel Fingers

Readers would be wrong to presuppose an overeagerness on my part to attack W.W. Korn. I have little argument with Korn's dour speculations, at least in regard to the Waxman-Weissmans. I can hardly deny that Benno was damaged before he arrived in Galapagos, that his mute style of life contributed to Anatole's slothfulness as a boy and to Sophie's psychic deterioration.

But I take issue with the author's characterization of Drexel Fingers as a "racist, redneck Sheriff" who lusted after Sophie and had cockeyed dreams of restoring Galapagos "to its pioneer grandeur."

I am not volunteering myself as Drexel's apologist or hagiographer. His faults shouldn't have to be candied by Seth Birdwistell or anyone else. Drexel was a frequent whorer at Mother Margaret's (he may even have kept a cabin reserved for him under another name, and he certainly picked up the crabs); he wasn't particularly kind to visiting derelicts; his rule over the Native Sons was often peremptory, though few of us considered him a rigid grand deacon; his various obligations probably forced him into neglecting his family: Mrs. Fingers moved to the State of Washington with her three children almost immediately after her husband's death. In spite of it all Drexel was the complete *homo galapaga;* no one could expect to match his devotion to our citizens, our landmarks, our streets. He enshrined the Sonora Mound, instituted Kite Day for our children, brought the rodeo to us (he dogged the Merchants Bank into scraping its O Street properties for an arena), and administered a welfare fund at the Sons' headquarters for "Galapagonians in trouble." Why so much energy thrown in our direction? readers might legitimately ask.

At the risk of tar-babying Drexel, I present a scatter of facts I happen to know about his boyhood. Drexel's father worked for the Galapagos lettuce growers. He was a sneaky, violent sort of a man who neglected his sick wife (she died of emphysema, I believe), kept his son out of school, and nearly starved him: our oldest citizens remember "that wild boy in rags" found sleeping in a garbage bin off M Street. Questioned by our magistrate, the boy squinted, spoke in monosyllables, and proved to be utterly and profoundly illiterate; unable to read or write, he could only scratch the outline of his thumb on a piece of slate. The town council fed him, housed him, schooled him, made him its ward, and sent old Mr. Fingers away. The rest is quite obvious. Drexel reformed himself, graduated from our high school, stuck with us, and was named our Sheriff and grand deacon of the Sons; Galapagos, in turn, became Drexel's "ward." It should no longer surprise readers that Drexel befriended stray Galapagos boys. And had W.W. Korn bothered to examine the Sheriff's past, he would not have made stupid, damning remarks about Drexel's "overtures" to Anatole.

Dalton Chess: Galapagos

In his cartographic study of Galapagos Dalton Chess commits a major sin: a demographer who turns impressionistic invites turds to fall on his head. So long as Dalton touches ground, he stays out of trouble. His thumbnail history of Galapagos Springs has the charm and resonance of a clean, accurate, and well-defined map. But when Dalton provides us with chats and checker games between Anatole and Mother Margaret, his writing deteriorates and he suffers a total loss of credibility.

Who were Dalton's informants? How does he know that Mother's pet name for Anatole was "runt," that she ventured into the Merchants Bank without a brassiere on a particular day, that she attempted to fleece two hundred dollars out of Penn Gemeinhardt (two hundred? why not five?), that she had a premonition about Anatole being unable to walk up the steps of his school? Instead of cardboarding a day in Mother Margaret's life, he should have mapped more of Galapagos.

I am disturbed by the "new" Dalton Chess. Odd, in going through back numbers of Korn's magazine, I cannot find one other instance where Dalton erupts into a fictive dance: his writing is neat, sober, and impersonal. Though Anatole's death may indeed have moved him, I doubt whether it would have prostituted his style. Nina's scissors, paste, and ball-point, I'm afraid, are responsible for the shifts in Dalton's prose. I can grant that presumptuous bitch her editorial rights to *The Tar Baby*'s style sheet—she has, in all fairness, pried loose clumsy constructions from my own work—but to rewrite an entire article, to construct false dialogues and false scenes, to slander Mother, Penn, Anatole, Freddy Duckert (the present owner of Duckert's Butter Farm), and Dalton with her silly inventions, seems unbearably gross. Why didn't she put her own name over Dalton's contribution? Or say, "touched up by Nina Spear"? Can we spy out Korn in this mess? The man who has control over a magazine's contents page can't be altogether innocent. Aren't his fingers slushing around somewhere in the pork pie that Nina has made for Dalton in the Memorial Number?

Cynthia Waxman-Weissman: Remembrance of a Dead Husband

At least here we come upon Korn in the flesh as he conjures recollections from Anatole's semiliterate wife. The hero of the piece isn't Cindy, or Stokie, her new "common-law husband," or the recollected Anatole, or

Korn, or anyone vaguely human: it's Korn's miracle
tape recorder, his "talk machine," which manages to
tar-baby Cindy and still not "tinker" with her voice.
Korn doesn't need to splice or edit Cindy's "unabridged
monologue." Conveniently, the talk machine is insens-
itive to anything it doesn't want to hear ("I supply a
long dash whenever . . . Cindy's words become indecipherable"). And Korn can leave his own droppings
between brackets; tell us about the wallpaper in his motel
room and other tripe, and have Stokie make the vicious,
ugly, mocking claim that Anatole is Cindy's husband-
father ("Ought to be arrested, putting out for her
natural father and having a child with him"). Instead
of correcting Stokie, the ol' talk machine, who's scientific
and doesn't take sides, plays up Cindy's confusions.
Anatole, the subject and object of the tape, drops off,
and "Cindy No-name" becomes a walking, talking tar
baby spreading bitchy tales about her illegitimacy (". . .
Gemeinhardt . . . hustled the State into believing Galapagos is my father").

Readers, I've been a lay anthropologist over forty
years: I've interviewed backwoodsmen who preferred
the company of wild turkeys, dirt farmers who lived on
hog manure, cowboys, rodeo tramps, eskimos, paupered
Indian chiefs whose worthless bales of shell money once
bought them staggering quantities of fish oil, women,
blankets, and slaves, and I've never had a tape recorder
with me in the field. What you can't take down on pad,
ruled or unruled, deserves to stay lost, in my estimation.
The tape recorder demoralizes an interview, driving a
wedge between the investigator and his informant, and
glorifying speech patterns and tonal values at the expense of camaraderie and quick rapport. Who knows

what Cindy might have been willing to divulge about her life with Anatole, had she not been subjected to Korn's machine? Perhaps it is selfish of me, in light of my negative stance towards the Memorial Number, to insist that Anatole detested talk machines, that he considered it a profanation to put the human voice on tape—but I do so, anyway.

Joachim Fiske: Anatole's Juvenilia

During the Charter Day riots an aroused, ambitious coed mascaraed the entrance to Life Sciences with a note for me: "Mr. Seth, there's only one thing worse than a honky administrator, and that's a mean and smelly grandfather pig." Her grammar was impeccable, and the message has stuck. Seth Birdwistell, you are a mean old man, constipated, sentimental, and squeamish, rotten with prejudices, hatreds, and crablike loyalties; I admit, Joachim Fiske, who shinnied up the ranks of the Galapagos public school system to become my subdirector at Pragmatic Letters, is a favorite of mine. Moreover, I imposed upon Korn, bullied him, in fact, to get Joachim into print: I may have threatened to choke off *The Tar Baby*'s funds in one of my rages. Korn must have known this was a bluff; any financial haggling would have been an embarrassment for me, since I had persuaded the trustees to create *The Tar Baby* and secure its copyright in their name. No, Korn accommodated Joachim, published his articles, reviews, and poems—Joachim *is* an ungainly poet—for different reasons. He gambled that he could trade my "Joachimisms" for his own Anatole mania, that one or two Fiskes could buy space for a fourth, fifth, or sixth version of Anatole's "Wittgenstein." A wiser, less self-centered Birdwistell would have kept both Joachim and Anatole quiet.

Because of my predispositions, I'm reluctant to venture an opinion on "Anatole's Juvenilia." The style of writing is definitely Joachim's, and if I let out that Anatole's junior high school class seems chockful of tar babies (viz., grimy-necked girls, a boy picking "dead skin off his lip," visitors with snot on their hats and crap in their pants, Joachim's pietism about "clumsy language and body dirt"), Nina and Korn might think I intend to accuse them of perverting Joachim. Surprisingly, I am much more charmed by Anatole's report than Joachim is. I admire the death-prone Pitfaces, in spite of their tar baby complexion and Anatole's "shameless coupling of fact and fiction." (Indeed, I wish Anatole had stuck close to his juvenilia. Unlike "Wittgenstein Among the Redwoods," the Pitface report is various, funny, pathetic, and not without its own peculiar logic. Joachim awards Anatole a miserly B for the report; I would have upped it to an A.

Note: In discussing the later careers of Anatole's schoolchums, Joachim is obliged to mention Kit Carson, Lucian Bonnefroy's proofreading, typesetting computer novelist. Out of kindness to me, I feel, Joachim suppresses the fact that I lost my three year war to keep the Bonnefroy machine off campus. Bonnefroy has won the trustees over to his side, softening their heads with input-output figures, quilted economic charts, schemes of a College-wide data bank (likely stories, all), and Kit Carson was installed in a shed behind Life Sciences five semesters ago, with Lucian unveiling his six-fingered threat: Kit Carson means to invent, distribute, proctor, read, grade, and destroy student examination booklets. (I plan to retire before this happens). *Tar Baby* buffs, I ask you not to dismiss me as a cranky mechanophobe with a grudge against all machines. Remember, I built a complete funicular railway on my own—but I despise a machine that usurps human functions and human needs. It is not hard to imagine my pique when you consider that Kit Carson has scanned, designed, and typeset this very page, that Bonnefroy's machine has a sinister hold on *The Tar Baby;* I'd prefer to expose myself to Nina's whims.

Seth Birdwistell: Auguries of Futility

I have nothing to add.

Whatever my assessment of Anatole's work, I'm sure notes will arrive in the "Cries to The Tar Baby" box censuring me. I expect to have a busy year sorting out and responding to attacks from metalinguists, parapsychologists, militant students, and convicts (yes, one of Anatole's greatest admirers is an embezzler at an Idaho prison farm) in this country and abroad.

I could claim that I was duped into contributing to the Memorial Number, that Korn wanted me to tar-baby Anatole's characters in the "Wittgenstein," to reveal their sluggish, puttylike natures—but I prefer not to make such a claim. I would rather Korn tell me, instead, why my article is bloated with eleven footnotes by *Tar Baby* staffers (none of the other articles has more than two or three), and why my biographical sketch, which he and Nina prepared, is riddled with errors. I wasn't born in "Blue Niles, Texas, on January 11, 1907." I'm from Blue Needles, a less exotic town; my birth year is 1905 (did Korn think he'd get more sympathy bamboozling a "younger" man?); and I was never a "Friend of Northern California Drum Majorettes" or a member of "the Rubber Horn." (Perhaps Korn will beg out of the matter, swear he's at the mercy of Kit Carson's magnetized tapes.)

Morris S. Plotch: Some Preliminary Notes Towards a Morphological Survey of "Wittgenstein Among the Redwoods"

I refuse to dignify this honeypot of lukewarm, bastardized mush. The stu-fac directory at E. Arizona State Teachers College shows no Morris Semple Plotch. Morris, I suspect, was conceived inside the console tummy of the Bonnefroy monster, Nina standing by, punching keys with her sticky index fingers. *The Tar Baby* gang needed a mod scholar-schlemiel with a mum tar baby daughter to ballast the "Wittgenstein," and got it all with the help of Kit Carson, who invented noun charts, punctuation profiles, voyeuristic touches, boring erotica, metalingual manure, pinheads, a talking fetus, a humdrum doll who drinks pee, and other tidbits.

Monte Falkes: At the J.C.

I must share some responsibility for Mr. Falkes' contribution. After all, I did encourage him to attend Galapagos JC. He was a confused and bitter boy, as I remember, attached to a deathtrap rodeo, earning his livelihood in a barrel. I chose to ignore his minimal qualifications, allowed him to move in and out of any class, hoping that the College would shag off his rough, splintery exterior, and draw him away from cowboying. Obviously, Mr. Falkes abused my confidence in him. Long gone from the College, he's still "barreling" for the Cummerbund Stampede, and has taken up with the "Royal Sponge," an interchangeable quartet of guitar-playing hustlers who operate out of a hearse, cribbing groceries from farmers, shucking credit cards off near-sighted old ladies, and turning teen-aged girls into prostitutes, in order to support their own filthy life-style. This quartet has grown stealthily, and is now affiliated with the Stepchilds, a tribe of smut-men who have com-mandeered N Street Park and control most of the por-nography traffic in Sonoma County. The Stepchilds do not seem to have an identifiable leader. I wonder about their relationship with the Galapagos police. Why hasn't the Sheriff's Office made more arrests?

That's all I care to say about the Stepchilds or Mr. Falkes (though certain alert readers might note a vague similarity between the mawkish, closed-in despair exhib-ited by Plotch and Falkes at the very end of their respective articles).

Anatole Waxman-Weissman (?): Scrapings

What have we here? Anatole's intimate gambols and quips, or the waxen protuberances of Claude Chardin? This whole fishy enterprise—the French text of Ana-tole's partial autobiography restored to English by our loving Nina Spear—stinks of Galapagos. Chardin, who has crapped up Anatole's image in *Magie,* a nasty little magazine devoted to the geometrics of language, is capable of anything. In *Les Fantômes de Galápagos* he sets out to prove that Anatole was a free-wheeling mystic nurtured and destroyed by a backward, spook-ridden town. For *Souvenirs de l'Année 1971,* he invents a preposterous dialogue between Anatole and himself, with both of them spouting the most current garbage of metalinguistics and referring to obscure Paris bistros (Anatole never stepped outside California). But the Anatole of "Scrapings" had to be blessed by Korn-Spear. Chardin, on his own, would not have had the sense to mask Anatole's voice in the third person (Anatole despised the confessional pap of first-person narratives). And this piece is so tainted with the specific feel of Galapagos, I cannot bring myself to believe that it is the singlehanded product of a French quack who knows nothing about us. I, for one, was charmed by Anatole's map-going and his ritual for peeling eggs, and horrified by his bout with the jays in Margaret's yard. I suspect that "Scrapings" grew out of Nina's own observations of Anatole (was Margaret looking over Nina's shoulder?) sent to Chardin, who embellished them with a structure and story line for *Magie,* and put them into workable French; and Nina, our Nina, able to profit from Chardin's gift for building competent stories, wiped off his errors, his excesses, his anti-Galapagonian views, and presented her "clean" pages to *The Tar Baby.* If I have misconstrued the authorship of "Scrapings," if through some serpentine stroke these pages do belong to Anatole, I ask Mother Margaret, as Anatole's closest adult survivor, to forgive me. The others—Korn, Spear, Chardin—need no mercy from me.

Nina Spear: Conversations with Stefan Wax

Nina's "conversations" irk me more than any other

contribution to the Memorial Number, and not because of Stefan's pokes at Anatole, the Native Sons, Sophie and Benno Waxman-Weissman, our College, and everything to do with Galapagos—frankly, I prefer his brutalism to Nina's utter insincerity. Nowhere are we told that these "conversations" are a lovers' quarrel, that Nina and Stefan had conducted an off-again, on-again affair in Galapagos for over eighteen years (note: "conversation" is a covert term for sexual intercourse), that Ulrich Wax disapproved of Nina and knew of her promiscuity [at one time or another Nina slept with Anatole, Joachim, Dalton Chess, a backlog of Galapagos merchants, postmen, sawyers from Wax's Mill, students, cowboys, and most sadly, myself—I'm ashamed to mention our fumblings in my funicular car one winter night (cramped, with frost on my eyebrows, the cables knocking, I had a premature ejaculation, which Nina has never quite forgiven; ergo, her malicious digs at my sex)], that Nina expected Stefan to marry her after Ulrich's death, and that Stefan didn't come through; he dropped her along with Galapagos, hence the raspy overtones to their "conversations," which took place at Laguna Beach. I invite readers who think I am slandering Nina to examine the sexual motifs, whether veiled, visceral, or exposed, that literally "glut" the text. Or should I give you a page-by-page account?

Page 139: "copulating under a piano"; "socio-sexual underground"; "Fuck America Club"; "areolas of prepubescent girls and boys"

Page 140: None

Page 141: "suckers and hooks and sexual organs"

Page 142: "prickly Austrian skin"

Page 143: "shove it"

Page 144: "I'll bet you never smelled belly button dirt"

Page 145: "perverted old bitch"; "The only sucking Drexel ever did was at Mrs. Chace's motel"

Page 146: "masturbate with Turkey in their minds"

Page 147: "Turkey, can't you claim any snatch without messing it up"; "raw pussy"

Page 148: "brassiere over her crotch"; "bit of a whore too"; "clap of the brain"

Page 149: "pull on myself"; "campus dick"; "how my little cousin licked Penny Gemeinhardt's ass"

Page 150: "sand farts"; "Drexel's the dirty one"; "petered off"; "bite your nipples off"; "kiss my ass"; "one filthy thing"

Page 151: "coy little bitch"; "burrow into the town's gut"; "shut the fucker down"; "Go play with yourself, Nina"

Page 152: "The College farts on industry"; "animated genitals"; "earn a hundred bills for every cock I draw"; "Cocks by S. Wax"

The piece ends with a direct sexual overture: "Twiddle yourself, Nina, and let's eat."

Two of Stefan's remarks also irritate me. He intimates that I was involved in the plan to "build an institute for geriatrics" on the old Wax millsite. Nothing could be further from the truth. It is Bonnefroy and his new regime who are pushing for their "Gerontia House," who want to restructure the College into an intellectual circus-supermarket that will service Californians from birth to death, and entice retired folk to Galapagos. Bonnefroy is itching to study the "biochemical clocks" of eighty-year-olds, so that Kit Carson can prepare a master chart on longevity that will make the College famous and fatten our lives.

Earlier in the "conversations," Stefan comments on Turkey Semple's "bogeyman" status. He claims Turkey doesn't exist. I should like to direct Stefan and other hardcore skeptics to a wanted bulletin inside our Post Office, the contents and format of which I now summarize for *Tar Baby* buffs:

WANTED FOR INTERSTATE FLIGHT IN CONNECTION WITH MURDER, ARSON, RAPE, KIDNAPPING, POST OFFICE BUR-GLARY, EXTORTION, PETTY THEFT, AND MAILING OBSCENE POSTCARDS TO LAW ENFORCEMENT AGENCIES

MELVIN ORMONDE SEMPLE

ALIASES
 H. O. Peck
 Melvin Peck
 Leroy Earle Semple
 Odell Norman Semple
 Cyril Glover Semple
 Raymond Guthrie Melvin
 Gayle Daniel Ormonde-Peck
 Howard Whitelaw Ormonde
 Hugh Everett Ormonde
 Hallie Oscar Semple
 H. O. Ormonde

NICKNAME
 Turkey

DESCRIPTION

DOB November 11, 1910 (not supported by birth records), Male Caucasian, 5'8" to 5'9", 145 to 155 lbs, Steel blue eyes, brown hair, dowdy complexion, medium build

NATIONALITY

American

SCARS AND MARKS

Pigment deficiency on face, chest, thighs, and back of both hands; scar left shoulder, right shoulder; round scar right palm; scar leg below knee; knobby wart above left nipple; tattoo of spur rowel upper right buttock; believed to have humped knuckles and thumbs

OCCUPATION

Former professional rodeo clown and bull rider; has been known to enter amateur competitions under the alias of H. O. Ormonde; often poses as an itinerant cosmetics salesman before strangling victims

REMARKS

May wear powder on face to hide pigment deficiency; uses contact lenses; a strict vegetarian; last seen in a Plymouth Roadrunner with Oregon plates; believed accompanied by a mongrel Pomeranian bitch who answers to the name "Sharon"

CAUTION

Consider armed, dangerous, and psychotic; has been quoted as saying he will not be captured alive; continues to mail obscene postcards from various points; may dress as a woman to avoid arrest

PHOTOGRAPH, FINGERPRINTS, AND SIG-NATURE OF THIS PERSON ARE NOT CUR-RENTLY AVAILABLE

W.W. Korn: The Other Anatole

O, the vagaries of a title. Who can this "other Ana-tole" be?—except Korn himself, the penultimate tar baby, who couldn't be suckled because he crazied his Georgian mother coming into this world, who was called "Skinhead" by his cold, arrogant father, who had fan-tasies of being molested in a bathtub by his maiden aunts, when actually, he must have enjoyed seeing his naked mother scoured and having his little bags rubbed, who rose over his aunties' heads and out of the south-land, who scraggled in Chicago as a baby baccalaureate for ten years, who dispatched himself to Galapagos, climbed the old man's shoulders (I was near forty the day Korn showed), thrived there, developed claws, and has been scratching at my eyes ever since.

Conveniently, Korn recollects word-for-word a con-versation we had on his first visit to my cabin. He tells readers about "the Hindu tar critter" I tried to plant on him, my visionary tar baby "who sized up your nature without sticking to you." It would be presumptuous of me to say that I, too, recollect the particulars of this conversation—my memory is poorer than Korn's—but I am aware of my researches into the "tar baby" phe-nomenon, which have little to do with Korn's stunted, pot-bellied logo.

The tar baby of Old India was seldom a baby at all; it might be a grown man, an old woman, or a monkey, depending on the text, and was often made of wax (or wood chips, blood, feathers, and soft coal). The tar baby performed a thousand functions: votive, seer, voluptuary, scarecrow, caretaker, shaman, murderer, savior, stud, moralist, viper, broom. Hence in one version, from Hemachandra's *Paricistaparvan,* a band of rowdy monkeys fighting over a lone female wastes itself and the she-monkey in its blind attacks; the oldest monkey, wilier than the rest, manages to survive; it ruts the dead female, then sits exhausted on a rock. The rock happens to ooze with bitumen, and the thirsty monkey, dumbed by its fighting and rutting, licks the bitumen, imagining it to be rusty water. A farmer passing the rock sees the bituminous monkey, swears it's a devil, and clubs it to death. The moral, I suppose, is that lust "niggers" the soul. In another version, villagers taking advantage of a blind, lonely jackal, put together a wax woman and place it in front of the jackal's path. The jackal bangs into it, curses the wax woman, breaks off its nose, and the villagers laugh. But instead of melting and sticking to the jackal, the woman begins to speak. She berates the villagers and becomes the jackal's wife. One could easily tease a moral out of all this, but unfortunately, the woman grows into a shrew, and the jackal, blind as it is, would have been better off without her.

The Cherokee, the Zulu, and the Mpongwe of Nassau, among others, also adopted the tar baby; again, these tar babies were complicated, multi-layered beings (dead warriors encased in the hardened blood of their enemies, adulterous wives who were feathered and left in caves, false prophets who lived among cattle and caked themselves with dung to emphasize their disgrace) ; and in suggesting *The Tar Baby Review* to Korn, I was hoping for a subtle, varied magazine that would further the tar baby legend, reflect the voices and faces of Galapagos, and encourage indigenous art; instead, Korn imported Nina Spear, permitted Stefan Wax to befoul our frontispiece, and turned *The Tar Baby* into a flabby, corrupted image of himself.

INDEX VOLUME XXVIII 1971

ESSAYS

AUTHOR	TITLE	ISSUE
R. Berry	A Galapagos deputy interviews himself with last year's Charter Day Riots in mind	Winter–Spring
S. Birdywiste	Moocow down the road: the maltreatment of California livestock by maverick rodeos	Winter–Spring
L. Bonnefroy	Hard times and bad nights for a computer programmer-teacher	Winter–Spring
	The new hominidae: or can machines subsume the human voice?	Summer–Fall
C. Chardin	The phantoms of Galapagos (reprinted from *Magie,* Paris, 1971; translated by Nina Spear)	Summer–Fall
D. Chess	Why Galapagos has resisted the Republican bite	Summer–Fall
J. Fiske	I am the walrus	Winter–Spring
	Where I stand: a word on Provost Birdwistell's impending retirement	Summer–Fall
N. Spear	A layman's exploration of circadian time	Winter–Spring
	Solid-state bliss: flirting with Kit Carson 99	Summer–Fall
	Provost or penny whistle?	Summer–Fall
A. Waxman-Weissman	Wittgenstein among the redwoods (sixth edition, with author's corrections)	Winter–Spring

AUTOBIOGRAPHY

AUTHOR	TITLE	ISSUE
M. Skedgell	Woman-child in Barbaryland (parts three and four)	Winter–Spring

VERSE

AUTHOR	TITLE	ISSUE
J. Fiske	Ode to Sonora Mound	Winter–Spring
	Tea	Winter–Spring
	Below the porcupine's quill	Summer–Fall
	Alphabet streets	Summer–Fall
	A ceasing of the commonplace	Summer–Fall

BOOKS REVIEWED

TITLE AND AUTHOR	REVIEWER	ISSUE
Language Knots, C. Chardin	N. Spear	Summer–Fall
Rodeo Primer, S. Markitivitch	S. Birdwistell	Winter–Spring
The Bifocaled Computer, T. Ritchie	L. Bonnefroy	Winter–Spring
Woman-child in Barbaryland, M. Skedgell	J. Fiske	Summer–Fall

FILMS REVIEWED

TITLE	REVIEWER	ISSUE
"Mickey Lost His Scattergun"	J. Fiske	Winter–Spring
"Cowgirls in Bull Country"	J. Fiske	Summer–Fall

CORRESPONDENCE

LETTERS RECEIVED	ISSUE
S. Belfrom; J. Flaccus; McNabb (2); M. Northcut; G. P. Ormonde-Peck; A. Wenzell Law; L. Zacharias	Winter–Spring
T. Abbick; S. Birdwistell; R. Burt; J. Hawes; S. Markitivitch; O. Medlicott; N. Perrin; T. Ritchie; N. Seinfelt; N. Spear; B. W. Stackpoole	Summer–Fall

DISTRESS SIGNALS

(a poem)

Potted

With namby
grease

I burn
in the run
neled twilight
of Oxnard
street

Catty
corned
and
quartered

Joachim on a
trickle bed

Ass d
  o
   w
    n

—J. Fiske

CRIES TO THE TAR BABY

(continued from page 12)

grammar." Nonsense! Nina herself is the guilty party. She has pissed on all of us. Were it not for Provost Birdwistell's charity and sense of fair play, I would demand that Miss Spear either apologize at her earliest convenience or be goosed, feathered, and fucked by the entire College, and be rode out of Galapagos on a broom.

Disgustedly yours,
Mead Sholes
Piano Tuner
Blue Needles, Texas

THE TAR BABY ANSWERS:

Dear Mr. Sholes,

Grateful acknowledge for your letter of July 7. We would prefer not to enter this controversy at the present moment. Please note that Provost Birdwistell helped conceive *The Tar Baby*, and we have never denied him access to our pages. He has rubbed against Miss Spear in the past, without damaging himself, and we expect his scuffles with her to continue into the future. (Miss Spear informs us that she is allergic to feathers, and has no intention of leaving Galapagos on a broom or otherwise.)

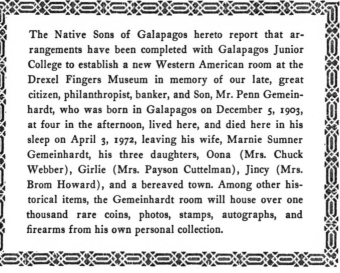

The Native Sons of Galapagos hereto report that arrangements have been completed with Galapagos Junior College to establish a new Western American room at the Drexel Fingers Museum in memory of our late, great citizen, philanthropist, banker, and Son, Mr. Penn Gemeinhardt, who was born in Galapagos on December 5, 1903, at four in the afternoon, lived here, and died here in his sleep on April 3, 1972, leaving his wife, Marnie Sumner Gemeinhardt, his three daughters, Oona (Mrs. Chuck Webber), Girlie (Mrs. Payson Cuttelman), Jincy (Mrs. Brom Howard), and a bereaved town. Among other historical items, the Gemeinhardt room will house over one thousand rare coins, photos, stamps, autographs, and firearms from his own personal collection.

CRIES TO THE TAR BABY

Dearest Tar Baby,

You disgraced yourself by printing Mimi Skedgell. *Woman-Child in Barbaryland* is vile, vile, vile. A burning is what it deserves. I can't match Mimi's age of ninety. I'm a touch under eighty-three. Seven years doesn't prove her an expert on Sonoma. I recollect the trapper Monks. I know what the mountains can do to a man. In Mimi's despicable chapter, "The Self-Anthropophagite of Sonoma Mountain," she reckons just anybody would believe her story how a delirious, starving trapper set on by timber wolves ate his clothes, his hair, his stools, and finally his limbs, for nourishment, and survives because it was easier to roll down the mountain being a stump. Monks traveled with a road show after his ordeal. It was the wolves who ate off his hands and feet. Mimi wrote about him, but I saw him inside his gunny sack. I sat with him, I touched his face. "Missy," he said, "can't trap much with your teeth. Excepting flies. Thisser show's making a freak out of me. I aim to fool them blind. My left hand is growing back. Feel." Lord, a thumb joint started wiggling through the burlap. That's Monks. But you wouldn't guess such from Mimi Skedgell's book. Lies, and I dare her say no.

Elvina Cassidy
Geyserville Rest Home
Sonoma

GALAPAGA:
the official handbook
to Galapagos

Published without interruption
since 1873

Still only 35¢

Incorporating the Galapagos Chapbook, Smuckler's Home Remedy Kit, & Sonoma Earth Manual

Sponsored by the Native Sons of Galapagos, the Galapagos Merchants Association, the Galapagos Businesswomen's Bureau, Galapagos Junior College, & Sonoma Lettuce Growers Association, for the betterment of tourism & trade in our township

Listing pertinent Galapagos names, facts, recipes, dates, & telephone numbers

GALAPAGA will guide you to Sonora Indian Mound, Sheriff's Bridge (formerly tollgate iron bridge), Finnegan's Winery (no longer in use), Bear Flag Plaza, Bitter Water Creek, the old halfway house of Rancho San Geronimo, & other choice historic spots

Under the general editorship of Seth Birdwistell, Provost, Galapagos Junior College

Write:
GALAPAGA
Box 4
Galapagos

RETIRING GALAPAGONIANS

Galapagos Junior College proudly lists the members of its faculty and staff who are retiring this year. Combined, their stay at the College equals over three centuries of service. An asterisk preceding the name indicates that the person hopes to continue living in the Galapagos area, and to take advantage of College facilities.

*Jerome Angelou, College Physician, 13 years

*Arona F. Bagtree, Secretary, Dept. of Health Education, 17 years

*Gunther Bazelon, Assistant Custodian, 21 years

*Seth Birdwistell, Provost, Professor of English, and Director of the School of Pragmatic Letters and Philosophies, 41 years

Jonathan Flaccus, Associate in Anatomy, 18 years

*Anne Sykes Gilder, Assistant, Faculty Typing Pool, 22 years

Katherine Hulbeck, Chief Registrar, 37 years

A. Wenzell Law, College Printer, 31 years

*Isaac Meskill, Director, College Bookstore, 28 years

*Nellis Mosley, Director, College Security, 14 years

*A.R. Bogie Piel, Professor of Nursing, 11 years

Luther Strode, Purchaser, College Business Office, 16 years

*Sanford Varner, Jr., Lecturer in Economics and Practical Arts, 23 years

*Gerald K. Whimzer, Coin Operator, College Cafeteria, 29 years

---

CRIES TO THE TAR BABY

*

THE TAR BABY ANSWERS.

Dear Elvina,

Grateful acknowledgement for your undated letter, which we have forwarded to Mrs. Skedgell. With the help of her grandnephew, Dalton Chess, she writes: "Tar Baby, you tell Elvina to lump it. Denton Monks was a cousin of mine. He never traveled with a freak show. Touched his face, she says. Denton wouldn't permit a boardinghouse whore liberties like that. Why doesn't Elvina admit I mention her in *Woman-Child* as 'the oldest active prostitute in the County'? She's been 'house scrub' at the Geyserville Home for fifty years. What about the meal in Sonoma Mountain? No wolf gnawed on Denton. Monks did all the chewing. Tar Baby, I ask you: If he got his thumb back on, wouldn't he tell his cousin?"

CRIES TO THE TAR BABY

Dear Tar Baby,

Undersheriff Roland Berry's account of the Charter Day Riots (*The Tar Baby,* Winter–Spring '71) is amateurish hokum. Who on your staff is responsible for encouraging such a churlish idiot to interview himself? I consider this the worst editorial lapse in your thirty years of publication. In Berry's words, "a band of politically motivated students attempted to seize the College's new data storage system and pervert it into a propaganda machine. These same students were seen punching out a manifesto attacking the College, its trustees, the Native Sons, and the Sheriff's Office, at the time we recaptured the computer." Could a normal, sentient human being have written the above two muggy, toneless sentences? It's offal language, the cry of a deputized pig who eats and sleeps in Galapagos. All Berry had to do was remove his sunglasses, put down his shotgun, close his mouth, and he would have discovered on his own steam that we were only emptying the card hopper and dismounting a few of Kit Carson's tapes. Where in his jerk-off interview does he suggest that the Sheriff's Office, Galapagos store owners, and the landlords were buying slices of Kit's memory bank? They'd programmed the bastard to keep tabs on us. K.C. was sending us chatty notices about being behind in the rent, about hiding our traffic tickets, about writing neater checks, and pretty soon he'd be clueing us in on who to fuck and what kind of shit to smoke. We had to get in there and rip him off. What does Berry know? If you think I'm lying about Kit's nosiness, ask Professor Birdwistell.

Stevie Bucher
President
The Galapagos Senate
Galapagaos JC

THE TAR BABY ANSWERS:

Dear President Bucher,

Provost Birdwistell has his opinions, we have ours.

Our regard for Undersheriff Berry is higher than yours is. Indubitably. We weren't looking for a sticky, liberal, anthropomorphic interpretation of the Riots. We wanted an authentic voice from the interior. And we found it. (We disagree with you about the merits of Mr. Berry's prose.)

Thank you for writing to us.

The Tar Baby

With Me

Margaret Hatchpaw Chace was born in Galapagos
on February 11, 1913. Her father, a failed tanner,
took her out of school before she was twelve and
put her to work as a scullion at the Half Buck, a
rotting cowboy hangout that had once been a resort
hotel. In 1927, when she was going on fifteen, she
married Arnie Chace, a handsome rodeo bum who
paid Hatchpaw seven dollars for his daughter, and
would have "kicked him shitless," Margaret remembers, if he—Hatchpaw—hadn't signed the
marriage certificate. After abandoning Margaret
one or two years later, Arnie himself was kicked
to death outside an Oakland hooch cellar in a
brawl involving sailors, rum runners, and male
prostitutes. Margaret returned to the Half Buck
as a respectable widow and became its night clerk
and assistant manager. Borrowing money from
Galapagos Merchants, she opened the Redwood
Motel in 1937 at the age of twenty-three. Mrs.
Chace was president of the Galapagos Businesswomen's Bureau for many years; she is now in
semi-retirement, living with her grandchild Bruno
in her private cabin; though most of the other
cabins have been shut down, Mrs. Chace still hosts

conventions and wedding parties at the Redwood
when the feeling strikes her. She will be sixty next
year.

[Note: we would have been glad to have Provost
Birdwistell "appraise" Mrs. Chace's contribution,
but its late arrival at the printers made this impossible; the Provost can get his licks in during
Winter–Spring.—*The Tar Baby*]

Long-distance operator pestering me with her mousy
voice. "Yes," I said, "I'll accept charges for the call. You
can tell Mrs. Stokie, or whatever name she's using, to
stop blabbering and talk into the phone."

"Son of a bitch," she says, "you fart-heavy son of a
bitch." I'd explain her she's getting my sex mixed up,
but she'd only get madder at me. "Piss-poor mother,
what the hell you mean humiliating me, shouting my
business to operators, saying I aint Mrs. Stokie."

"Honey, where you calling from? The wires must be
crossed. I'm getting three conversations at once."

"Mundelain. I'm not sure what State it's in. We've
been traveling in a circle, kind of, day and night."

"That trick husband of yours, he been robbing a
bank?"

"Who gives you these scratchy ideas, Margaret?"

"Why you going in circles then?"

"Millard likes it this way. Only reason I can call is
he's sleeping now. He doesn't want me talking to you."
I'll bet. He's standing behind you with a finger in your
ass and a handkerchief over his mouth, telling you to
put the tap on me.

"How much you asking for?" I said.

"Kiss off, mother. I didn't call about no money. Bring Bruno to the telephone. I want to hear him go googoo."

You little shit, I felt to say, if you kept your nose in your son's accounts, you'd find he's got a vocabulary could bend Stokie's head and yours. Learned himself ten to twenty words. I held low, calculated, and brayed to her, "Mrs. Stokie, you got your nerve. Asking me to wake a two-year-old at four in the morning. Call a decenter hour and that boy will teach you how to roll spit balls over the telephone." I could hear her chewing her sleeve, habit she picked up from me before she was six, and it made me miserable. "Hold on to your pants," I said. "I'm bringing him." I picked Bruno off his crib, him rubbing his eyes and looking mean at his grandma, because he got hustled out of some sleep, but grabbing me anyhow with the legs of his blanket suit. Cindy started on her googooing. "Talk natural," I said. "He understands." Only he mummied up to her. And I couldn't get him to piss a word. "Stubborn, tell Cindy 'bout your fire jinjin and your 'lectric blanket."

"Bruno," she crackled at him, "want to come and live with your mama?" His chin got all creased, and he pinched me so hard, I had to take him to his crib.

"Son of a bitch," she said when I got back. "You been learning him to hate me." He don't need much help from me, honey. He can't tolerate hearing your voice. "I'd take him from you, only Millard won't let me have him. Says a baby'd slow him down."

"Where's he going to, honey, he's got to run so fast?"

There was a bit of quiet, then she said, "Millard's going to strangle you, mother."

"I thought he's asleep."

"He was, but his bladder woke him up."

Heard scuffling, and Millard grabbed the telephone.

"Mother, listen to me. Fat ass. Whole world knows you stuff hundred dollar bills in your twat since the banker man died. Next time I'm in your territory, I'm going to strip you out. I'd have done it last year, but I aint sure what crotch money is worth. Most people couldn't abide the stink."

"Be a pleasure to see you again, Millard. But don't trip over my scattergun on your way in."

He got off, and Cindy came on bawling.

"How much?" I said.

"Fifty, mother. We need it bad. Millard owes this police feller twenty-five, and—"

"You can always come home, honey. Cabin'll hold you."

"*Home,*" she says. "Yeah. So Galapy can dump in my face. Tell stories how Cindy Boom-Boom gave her child away for a street-ass plumber. People be trafficking outside your cabin all day. Bruno and me'd pose for any motherfucker with a camera in his hand. Charge him a dollar. Get me to Galapy? I'd rather be dead."

Girl inherited my loquacious mouth. Could have told her everybody's too busy wondering about the new buildings the College is putting up. We'd have to undress on O Street just before noon hour to scare up enough customers who'd be interested in Bruno, her, and me. But what's the point to arguing?

"Should I send the fifty to the Mundelain jailhouse?"

"Ha, ha, mother." She screamed at Millard. "What state we in?" Then she said, "Send it to the GPO at Mundelain, Mundelain, Illinois, care of Mrs. Cynthia Waxman-Weissman," and she hung up.

Couldn't sleep a bugger's worth. 'Bout eight o'clock Garth Lewis, the credit agent, raps on my screen. Spindly prick is a backdoor man for the Merchants Bank. Used to climb on my girls and vomit in the sink twenty years ago when he was over at the high school, and here he is grabbing at my property.

"Garth Lewis, get your dirty knuckles off my screen. I got a baby sleeping inside."

The prick took off his hat. "I would have come later, Mother, but my schedule's tight. Aint you going to invite me in?"

"State your business where you are."

He put on his finger-licking act, and strummed the pages of his credit book. "According to my records, Mother, the town, the county, and the bank has got liens over you. There's water tax, land tax, rubbish tax, firemen's tax ..."

"Sure you aint composing a few them taxes on your own, Brother Garth?"

"Shame, Mother. After I been picking up your debts. Garth Lewis is one the only friends you have. Old man Gemeinhardt aint alive to protect you now." That's a fact. Left the wife near a quarter million in securities, and not a pip for me in his strongbox. Guess Bruno didn't penetrate his mind. The coffee his widow is sucking up this minute was bought with thirty years of whore sweat, including mine. Garth reads down the page.

". . . charities tax, pavement tax, coroner's tax, tree surgeon's tax, and other taxes owing. Plus butcher bills, and complaints from the bed and crib store."

"You know it takes me three months to pay a bill."

"Mother, some these claims been out over a year. I'm appreciative of your troubles. Anatole dying on you, rotten girl throwing a baby in your lap."

"I'd be obliged, Garth Lewis, if you'd keep your mouth off my family."

"Only looking to help, Mother. Found a buyer for the Redwood. There's a biscuit company in Alameda wants to relocate."

"Funny," I said. "A biscuit company suspicioning a future in a college town. And when did I tell you I was getting rid of the Redwood?"

"No other choice, Mother. Way it is, bank's gonna take it from you."

"And deliver it to the College, I expect."

"Lewis Agency can't afford to put doubts on a buyer. It says 'biscuit company' in my book."

"Well, maybe you're reading the book with crooked eyes, brother Garth, because I believe the Agency's in trouble."

He crunched the hat back on his head.

"Peculiar trouble, Mother? Or ordinary trouble?"

I loved squashing the little prick, flecking off his expectations. "Would I waste my days at the Business-women's Bureau without a purpose?"

"What purpose is that?"

"Securing my property."

"How?" he said with his hands under the credit book.

I stalled him there, watched the book; he couldn't control the shaking.

"Oh, I messed around, Brother Garth, and got the town council to guarantee my property *in perpetuity*. Means I own the Redwood and the land it's sitting on outright and forever, long as I'm still alive." It was mostly cowshit, but it would take Garth a month to get over his fright. The book kept shaking away. If you've started on a bluff, Mother, might as well go at it with every tooth in your mouth. "Brother Garth, want to accompany me to the Merchants' vault? That perpetuity clause is settin' right inside my safety tin."

The prick recovered pretty damn fast; didn't even let the book fall. "No perpetuity clause is gonna pay for Bruno's upkeep or provide for him after you're gone. This buyer of mine, the biscuit company, is willing to lay out sixty thousand—sixty, Mother—over the next twenty years for you and your survivors, and let you keep your mean ol' cabin. Think on it." He rolled his credit man's eyes at my truckle bed, and I had a feeling what was in his mind. *That where Waxy and the old whore used to sleep?* He saw me watching his eyeballs, so he switched to Bruno and peeped into the crib, his nose leanings laying bulges in my screen. He scratched at his jaw and put on that fake look of surprise. "Mother, where's the ol' barber chair?"

"Garth Lewis, had that chair yanked out fifteen years ago."

"Peculiar," he says. "Never missed it before. Morning, Mother."

Shit's on my face now. Prick blabbers 'bout sixty thousand dollar biscuits, and me with a rip in my wallet and two mouths to feed. How much boodle you expect a woman with a long distance telephoning daughter to have? Him gloating over the decline of my property, and the rot in my cabin. Barber chair. Brother Garth, 'member the sign I had,

HANDS OFF

MOTHER ISN'T OPEN TO STRANGERS

Well, I'm going to locate that sign, nail it over my door
for show. Discourage bankers and biscuit company men.
Mother's closed. I bent to collect the trash off the floor,
bottles, filthy spoons, paper bags, and there I was, bawling on my knees, the dust so thick and heavy you could
make patty cakes with it. Shh, Mother, you'll wake the
boy. Only the crib was moving. Bruno sat in a bundle,
entertaining himself, holding a leg on his blanket suit
and biting it with a gurgle, repeating, "Bruno dada,
gran'ma." And I couldn't stop bawling. He had his
father's cheeks, his mother's pug nose, and the independence of a lady deacon. Can't put the scare into
Bruno. Earned his pluck from me. Oh, you got your
Daddy's stubborn in you, but I wish he'd had a bit more
your gall. First time I met Anatole he was maybe six,
and he already had the saddest eyes to him, like a boy
with perpetual diarrhea. He was standing outside this
cabin, his face against the screen. I had half the rodeo
in with me. Blackie Mayhew, Tubs Shorter, Darl Simister, Tadpoles, Turkey Semple, Jim Mullaney, and a few
other slugs from Buzzer Carmody's lot.

"Sonny, hey, where's the beer pail?" Darl said, pump-
ing himself up and down in the barber chair.

"I don't hire runts to carry beer for me, Darl Simister. What's your name, boy?"

He stared at Darl's boots clumping on the footrest;
Darl was naked 'cept for them; man wouldn't consider
whoring without his boots; none my girls minded Darl's
peeling leather 'gainst their ankles and thighs; he rode
bronc or whorewoman with the same devotion. Irma,
LaVerne, and Dorit were crouching behind the runt.
Their scratchings sickened me. But they were my girls,
and I had to comfort them. "Buzzer's party," I said.

"He's paying for it."

"Damn right," Buzzer growled. "Get on back to your cabins."

Darl's the only one who had politeness to him. "Try us next time around, LaVerne. Buzzer's bought up the Sauerkraut Lady."

"And we're willing to wait," Tadpoles said, heckling them. Then he screamed into the back room. "Tubby Shorter, I'm losing patience. Tie on your gut."

"German bitch," Irma said, and the girls marched away. They left the runt, eyes and ears, taking it in. Darl pointed a boot at him. "If he aint carrying beer, Mother, he must want something else. Sonny, come inside and get your lick."

"Surely," I said. "Drexel finds him, he'll think I'm extending invitations to the Galapagos kindergarten. He won't close *you* down, Darl Simister."

"Hell on Drexel," Tadpole said, out the corner his mouth. "Turkey'll shit in his eye."

Turkey was snoring on a stool, far as I could tell, his hair tied in an Apache knot, hat on a peg, whittling knife next his crotch, fingers clutching a shot glass, his long johns soused in rum.

"Runt," I said, "shovel home."

Tubs drifted out the bedroom, mooneyed, hugging his belly.

"My turn," Tadpoles said.

"Ignorant, give her a chance to clean herself."

Darl jacked down the hydraulic pull, stepped off the barber chair, grabbed Tad by the britches, and sat him in Turkey's lap. "I believe I'm next," he smiled. "Anyways, Sauerkraut's been asking for me."

"He always gets second lickings before anybody else,"

Tadpoles said, and he forgot where he was, hunkering on Turkey's thighs. He felt the knife 'gainst his tail next and jumped into the barber chair. "Mother, sheet me up. I'll take shave, mustard bath, finger massage, and whisker trim."

"Asshole," Darl said, strutting into the bedroom, "you know Mother don't operate the chair on Saturdays."

I was still after the runt to scatter salt. "Aint you got no mother to twist your ear and run you home? You deaf? Dumb? Don't they learn you at school to answer your elders?"

I remember correct, Drexel walked in. Wasn't any sporting call either, because he didn't hang up his cartridge belt. He blasted me first. "This a peep show, Mother? What's the little boy doing on your premises?"

"Damn if anybody can tell," Tad said. "He been bugging us all morning. Maybe he's one them traveling deaf boys what beggers from town to town." Drexel threw him out the chair, and settled in. "Didn't ask you. Go and wake Turkey."

"What for?"

"Wake him, I says."

He cakewalked up to Turkey's stool, touched him with three fingers.

"If I wanted his neck tickled, Mr. Tadpoles, I'd do it myself. *Wake him*."

He stood a foot to the side, reached out, and slapped Turkey's face. "He made me, Turkey. He made me."

The shot glass dropped out Turkey's hand. He yawned and spoke with his eyes closed. "My piles is so bad, they dragging under my knees. Sauerkraut roll me over, she'd have a number of jabbers to choose from, all them raw."

Tadpoles yelped at him. "Sheriff's asking for you, Turkey."

"That a fact?" He opened his eyes, sniffed the rum on him, but he didn't make a grab at his knife. "Appreciate it, Sheriff, if you could recommend me a laxative. I figured you might have a little country medicine, seeing how sheriffing must keep you on the road most the day. Something triple-distilled, to grease my turds with."

"Try licorice with onions," Drexel said. "How you otherwise?"

"Nothing to worry you, Sheriff. There's advantages to being a contract clown. I'm paid for every spill I take."

"Buzzer pay you to grow your hair down to your tail? Story is your hair got tangled up in Marysville."

"Can't stock yourself with paper on the circuit, Sheriff. Hair's the best ass-wiper in the world."

"Turkey Semple, your name's scribbled in my public nuisance pad. Man with long hair, it says, rodeo scum, cut up a barkeep outside Petaluma. Thought it was an Indian til they saw the blotches on his face. Another longhaired chump, with skin problems, set fire to a Marysville whorehouse. Got perturbed, they say, when a girl wouldn't rub up against his woolly union suit. Either you're downright crazy, Mr. Melvin Ormonde Semple, or you got some rough bark on you thinking you could stop over in my town for a blow job and a quick shit."

"Talk to a man about your bowels," Turkey muttered to himself, "and he accuses me of taking quick shits."

Boy's pudgy face in the door and Drexel tapping his revolver butt put the spook in me; and Turkey rocking his knees. He'd crushed a mirror, sailed over the barber chair season ago with one of his leaps, and bashed in the teeth of a cattle buyer who was poking fun at his Apache knot. "Turkey's polite to my girls, Drexel. His long johns never got him in trouble 'round here."

"Stay out, Mother. Turkey can answer for the Marysville fire. He aint no mute."

Buzzer got to perspiring watching Turkey's rock. "Sheriff Fingers, aint no complaints out on Turkey. He's under contract to me."

"Mercy," Drexel said, leaning in the chair. "You honor his contract in the next town. Besides, you aint paid the full rodeo policing fee."

"Mailed fifteen dollars to your office, Drexel, day before yesterday."

"Well, there's a subcharge for bringing skunks with you into Galapagos."

Stool toppled and Turkey's feet kicked air, but the rum must have upset his timing, because Drexel smacked him in the head with his revolver butt. Then he hollered into the bedroom. "You aiming to throw a whiskey bottle at me, Darl Sim'ster, think it twice. I'm going to squeeze one into your belly. Hard to pick a bullet out a man's intestines, Darl. Put the bottle down and come out that room."

He made Darl lean over Turkey.

"Spit in your hand and hold it over the crack in his head. We don't want no brain putty on Mother's floor."

He had us all following his stage directions.

"Mother, give the boy your thinning shears. Don't you drop it, Darl. Now loosen the Indian knot and snip off his pigtails." Darl's elbow kept wavering and he couldn't manipulate the shears. "Just as soon put a bullet in your spine, Darl Sim'ster, for obstructing County business."

"Aw," Turkey said, blood on his teeth, "snip it, Darl.

Pay that Sheriff no mind. Damn, have to find another ass-wiper. Drexel, be grateful you'd lend me your star. They say tin is soothing to piles."

"Bend lower, Darl. Kiss him on the mouth. I want to see how an ex-longhair man responds to a little rodeo loving. Kiss him, Darl."

"Drexel," I said, "you stop that meanness. I'll shoo you out with the flies, gun and all."

"Quiet, Mother. Pucker up, Darl. I'm going to count to three."

"Manhandling my men," Buzzer said. "You suppose the Merchants Association is like to enjoy hearing about their elected peace officer humiliating cowboys and dragging away trade?"

"*One.*"

"That Association's got a complaint board, Mr. Drexel Fingers."

"*Two.*"

Darl bent halfways. Never saw a naked man so red. Only part of him without any blush was his boots. Turkey smiled. "I know a bit about kissing, Sheriff." He reached up, put his tongue in Darl's mouth.

Drexel clapped his hands, and he started tossing hats, shirts, belts, and britches off the pegs on my clothing tree. "Everybody, get. There's women in them other cabins. Take your whiskey and your party up the hill." Tubs, Tadpoles, and Darl lifted Turkey out the door, but his long johns caught in the screen, and that mum, goggly boy had to pry them loose; couldn't believe any stiff-legged runt could be capable that much charity; maybe watching us he fell in love with Turkey's hair and Turkey's flying kick. When the cabin was cleared, I shot one off to Drexel. "Miserable son of a bitch, you couldn't tolerate the idea them buying Sauerkraut for the morning. You had to go chicken Buzzer's crew so you could have her to yourself. I don't care how big a piece the Redwood you own. Dipping into the till don't give you exclusive rights to any my girls. Turkey ever bother you? Plenty bulldogging clowns braid out their hair."

"I'm partial to long hair, Mother," the son of a bitch said. "Turkey's a favorite of mine. Go bother Penn. His notion to ditch him. Seems merchants were getting twitchy worrying over Semple's behavior in Galapagos. They'd prefer to live without broken windows, fires, and cut faces. They like the extra trade, Mother, but nobody's crazy about rodeo bums. Have to lock your daughters in the cellar with Buzzer's crows around. Turkey's the one they hit on. Every Sheriff's Office from Ventura to Siskiyou's got his name and 'scription on a card. It's them albino spots on him makes him a giveaway. Suspect his clowning time's been snuffed out."

He dropped his belt and went in to Sauerkraut. Damn if I'd put up with them eyes in my screen another minute. I grabbed a broom and chased the runt down to the edge of Oxnard Street. "You appear again, runt, and you'll be hanging from this stick." He ran backwards, his fingers piggying out his torn pockets, staring at me from behind his fat cheeks. All I could do was wag the broom at him and scowl hard. Only it was the German bitch I was sore at, not him. I expect my girls to be obliging to a customer, but a part-timer, a Monday-Wednesday-Saturday whore who gets wetter with each new man, who can howl for ten cowboys in a row, that's something else. Couldn't fire her, she was in such demand, and she was driving my girls shaky. Caught LaVerne writhing in bed alone, practicing orgasms in front of a mirror, Sauerkraut bothered her so. Pretty soon it'd be me in the parlor, Sauerkraut in back, and Drexel patrolling thirty empty, scrubby cabins.

Broom and evil looks meant nothing to the boy. He scrounged on my doorstep next day. "Mr. Bubble-eyes, want a banana? If you won't talk, might as well fill yourself up." The runt surprised me. Took the banana, peeled it, ate with crackles in his forehead. Near cleaned me out of fruit. Peaches, apricots, and a fig. But his chomping didn't loosen his tongue. When I got tired chattering to him and handing him fruit, I chased him off the premises. Went on for months. "Where you live, runt? Your Daddy one them migrant farmers? Don't somebody worry 'bout your nutrition? Fat cheeks is a bad sign." And I stuffed an apricot into him. My fruit bills came to a considerable amount. I had more troubles too. Doris, LaVerne, Irma, Madge, Bella, and Dorit stopped talking to me. LaVerne, who owed me the most, because I'd rescued her from a rotten, ungrateful husband and taught her not to be ashamed of thigh blubber and kinky hair, left me in February, towards the busy season, with her key wrapped in toilet paper and no note. Dorit's cabin was closest, so I picked on her.

"Where'd fatty go?" I shouted, and Dorit could tell I meant business. Her mouth dribbles wasn't any play. "Jumping off like that. I'll see she's locked out every decent establishment in this County, and the bunch surrounding it. Think I won't stick Drexel on her? He'll leave his mark. She'll have to shove her burnt hide into Colorady to get work."

Dorit was always dependable after a cry. So I sat on the couch and waited her out. "She suffered, Mother. LaVerne wouldn't disappoint you, if she could help herself. You hurt her pride, Mother, favoring Sauerkraut. Why didn't you station any of us in your cabin? Keep Sauerkraut, you'll send this place to rot."

"Wash up," I said. I couldn't allow no street whore like LaVerne to dictate terms to me. Stewed in my cabin for two days. Forgot to order fruit for the runt. I sat in the barber chair sniffing shaving lotions. Drexel visited me. "You must have skipped a page in your calendar book. Sauerkraut's in tomorrow." He spun the chair around, squashed my face into the head rest. "Drexel," I slobbered out, my mouth sucking metal. "You don't stand to gain disfiguring me. How you going to afford imported cologne without Mother?"

"Dumb bitch," he said. "Where'd you find her?"

"Who? Sauerkraut? She wandered in one day. Crazy look to her. But a real handsome woman. And her accent aint going to cost her any in bed. Let my face up, Drexel. I've been meaning to chat with you 'bout her. Maybe you two can work out a private arrangement, using my cabin during off hours, but I've got to let her go. My girls are deserting me. They can't compete with no sex-hungry woman."

"Whoreshit, you shouldn't have hired her in the first place. Know who she is? She's Ulrich's sister-in-law."

"Glory," I said. "How come you couldn't tease that out of her? You're with her three mornings a week." I sucked metal again. "Drexel Fingers, you want me to ask my girls to fill out questionnaire in the future?"

He was so preoccupied with other matters, he forgot to leave me space for breathing. "Ulrich traces her here, I'll have to throw my badge in the sewer. Get rid that woman."

"I'll do it, Drexel, soon as you let me swallow some

air." He took his hand off me. "If she didn't volunteer nothing, where'd you get her biography?"

"From that fat little bugger you're always feeding. Caught him snooping in Chineetown. Told me he was looking for his ma. Said she takes five hour walks."

"The runt belongs to Sauerkraut? Imagine, whoring with her own boy on my porch. Drexel, I swear, that's the last time I hire any refugee. Worse than a nigger when it comes to morals."

Well, I fixed her on Saturday. Oh, I let her perform. I wasn't going to lose a day's wages. She came out the bedroom with that tired, unnatural look of hers. And I figured, no wonder poor LaVerne couldn't keep pace with her. Professional girl don't go unconscious for cowboys and Galapagos strays. I'd listened hard, concentrating on Sauerkraut from the barber chair. That woman was crawling, scratching, and moaning herself to death on my truckle bed. Wasn't fair to the customers, way she was using them. "What the hell you mean coming here under false pretenses? You looking for slaughterhouse work, take your carcass somewheres else." Would have punched her silly she'd been LaVerne, dragged her to the other side of town, but I got to pitying her on account the boy and the miserableness of her swollen, run-down body. "You can whore in Guerneville or Freestone if you want. But let me catch you operating out any motel near my district, I'll lay you out." And I helped her on with her coat.

Didn't see the runt almost a year. Then he poked his nose in my door. "Scram," I said. "Nobody you know lives here. I can't afford your stares. It's a poor time for motels." He was talkative these days. "Auntie," he said, "give me a banana." That's how we got to be friends.

Asked Drexel 'bout Sauerkraut.

"She's in Yolo most Saturday mornings."

"How'd you track her to Yolo?"

"Track her? Mother, you are the stupidest. I arranged for it. My deputy drives her there."

"Drexel Fingers," I said, "you'd make money off a dead log."

He would too. And pimping Sauerkraut off to another County didn't hurt him any. Ulrich supported his re'lection campaign, and with the Native Sons, the Merchants Association, the Wayneflete Electrical Parts Company, the Mill, the College, and the Bank squatting behind him, town near but handed Drexel his Sheriff's stool. Only Strotter Martin, eighty-year-old Mormon lettuce farmer who troubled himself 'bout the slot machines nesting in the drugstores, run against him. I guess he suspicioned Wayneflete Electricals distributed them machines and Drexel got some kickback money. Well, Strotter was a baby when it come to Galapagos politics and Galapagos chicanery. Bank owned Wayneflete Electricals, College was its landlord, Ulrich was its contractor, Merchants Association was its steadiest customer, and Drexel was its advertiser, footman, and collection agent. Now I aint indicting anybody. Maybe the College is a bigger baby than Strotter. Expect any poketown trustee to tell the difference between electrical parts and slot machines? But how come four those trustees sat on the Merchants Association, and one of them, Penn, was a Wayneflete director? Drexel's kickback from the Electricals was nothing but slop. Strotter ought to have looked into his other activities. Drexel collected pieces from every hotel, motel, restaurant, bar, package store, and filling station in Galapagos township. Levied a

Sheriff's tariff on whores, whiskey, gasoline, and side-walks without the County's permission. Made you pay according to the heads, bottles, or turnips he counted. Cost me a fortune on account my choice location. Strotter Mormonized against the slot machines, and he ran a dreary campaign. Nobody except his family and a dozen lettuce growers voted for him. I surely didn't. Better Drexel. Knew where you stood with that son of a bitch. Some County investigating team might fall on you un-awares, Strotter ever got in.

Drexel had a house and twenty acres in the foothills, wife and three childs, whores, tariffs, and a Sheriff's car with revolving lights and siren to play with, but two things upset him. Turkey was one. Drexel shouldn't have pushed him out of rodeo, buzzed other Sheriffs on him, so Turkey couldn't show his albino face in a decent town. Turkey had to embarrass Drexel to keep his self-respect. Can't run from the man who outlaws you. He made forages into the County, stole a school bus in Freestone, sent notes to neighboring Sheriffs about Drexel, accusing him of being a scumsucker and a whore boss, robbed filling stations near the township, broke into a widow's boardinghouse, gagged her, put on her jewelry, and touched her tit, according to the widow's report, but he had enough smarts in his head to stay clear of Galapagos. Drexel showed me a picture postcard Turkey mailed him. Dropped it in a rural delivery chute without a stamp. Had a rodeo scene on the picture side, with a brahma bull, and Turkey scratched out the bull's horns and drew a cross and an arrow around its balls. "Sheriff, I am going to chicken you just like that some day soon. Truly yours, Melvin Ormonde Semple."

"Drexel, you shouldn't have pulled on his *chongo*."

"It was Darl who did the pulling."

"You made him, Drexel. And you had no business hurting his career. Good bullhazers come scarce."

"Shut up," he said, and he tore the card, stuck the scraps in my hand.

Other thing was Sauerkraut. Being pimp, jobber, and gigolo didn't satisfy him, it seems. Idiot had to go scratchy over her. He'd moon in the parlor, swiggling gin and Coke on my barber chair, ignoring LaVerne who'd come back to me a couple seasons after Sauerkraut left. "Drexel, you can't expect proper love from a woman who's interested only in depreciating herself."

LaVerne wanted to take him into the bedroom. She touched him in the wrong place and he spit gin at her. "Leave my prick where it is." She rushed out, slobbering and screeching, stood around the cabins and let the gin soak into her blubber, so she could prove how Drexel wounded her.

I grabbed my plunger from the toilet and held the rubber end over his head. "Don't you mess up any my girls again, Mr. Drexel Sheriff."

He closed his eyes, drooped in the chair. "Mother, put your club down. Condition I'm in, you could take me with your hands."

True. Saturated with Sauerkraut, he forgot to count heads and collect his whore tariff. Oh, she'd put out for him all right, but you weren't going to pull much affection off that woman. He decided to court her, and he dragged me and the runt along for cover, to give himself a show of respectability. We sat in the gadget-crowded Packard the township lent him, four in the front, Sauerkraut on the far side, him at the wheel, runt and me in the middle, food hamper on my knee, Drexel's scatter-

gun cradled against the back window, in case we met
Turkey on the road. Runt fondled the knobs on Drexel's
shortwave radio, I warmed the chicken legs in the
hamper, Sauerkraut didn't say a word.

"Where we going, Drexel?"

"Any place, long as I can get Ulrich's buzz saws out
of my ear."

We stopped and had a picnic in the Sonoma woods. I
was only a woman of thirty, thirty-one. Don't you suppose I was jealous watching Drexel up close? Desire
twitching him, putting bumps along his arms, none of it
aimed at me. He took Sauerkraut on a nature hike, and
I got mustard, napkins, chicken bones, and the runt.

"Where's your pa?" I asked him.

"Milling," he said.

"Can't you speak without confusing a person?"

"Milling is what he is, and what he does."

"My, aint you nasty for a ten-year-old."

"Won't be ten until November."

That's how the picnic went.

Anatole's pa died the next year, but it didn't seem to
give Drexel any more leverage with Sauerkraut.

"Easier to marry a widow, Drexel. Of course, you'd
have to dispose of your wife, put your daughter and your
sons in boarding school, adopt the runt, and move to
Solano County. Citizens here won't tolerate a woman-
swapping Sheriff. And Ulrich might take it harsh having
a new brother on his hands."

"Do it anyhow," he said, "if it pleases me."

But I didn't see him give away the Packard, his wife,
or his badge. He sat still, and Sauerkraut deteriorated
meantime. She got to be a boozer, she'd spread her legs
and piss in front of children in the street, and no respect-

able whorehouse would take her in. Drexel dropped her in the middle of '43. LaVerne swears he latched onto a barmaid from Petaluma. I aint so sure. His attitude 'bout the runt kept shifting. "An'tole? Saw the prick on J Street, carrying diggings from the Indian Mound. Wasn't even worth my hello." Day or two later he'd leave County assessors, assorted bagmen, petitioners, deputies, and clerks waiting in his office and drive the runt to Mount Helena on an expedition for volcanic ash. Sauerkraut got worse and worse. Station agent catch her at the depot, Old Crow poking through her overcoat, punched tickets in her hand, he'd call the Sheriff's Office, and a deputy'd bring her home. Other times she'd sneak by the agent, climb a bus to Vacaville, scurry roads for a week. Couldn't fool a donkey with them sightseeing trips of hers. She was working the flophouses, going down for stragglers to keep herself in booze. Disappeared altogether one day. I guess she forgot to come back. Ulrich wasn't too happy having relatives on the Galapagos missing persons' list, so Drexel sounded the County alarm. Found her dead in Yuba City. Papers said something about mysterious circumstances. Nothing mysterious to me. Sauerkraut went to Yuba to piss, drink, and die. LaVerne got Drexel wrong. That whore-taxer was still in love with his German bitch. "Might have saved her, Mother. Had suspicions she was grubbing it at the Northern Lights."

"Close your mind to the subject, Drexel. Sauerkraut knew what she was doing. Can't repair a body that's inert."

He was so damn low he wouldn't even accept a rubdown on my barber chair. "Thanks, Mother. My skin's so dry. Might crack if you touched it."

Town gave the runt to his uncle, but they couldn't get along. Drexel blabbed Ulrich's side of it. "Ought to be grateful, unorphaning him, buying him shoes, giving him a room, cooking, and laundry privileges, and the boy looks at him mean, with his cockeyed scowl. Ulrich don't need it. Up to me, I'd shove him into a County Home, where he'd have to show respect, put on gray trousers and do gardening."

"No you wouldn't. You'd deputize him and let him chauffeur your whores to work."

"Aint in that line of business any more, Mother," and he rapped my teeth. I got a sore mouth, and the runt couldn't stay put. He ran from Galapagos. Didn't even leave a dent in the population. Barely a soul missed his fat cheeks. Council might have scrubbed his name off the town roll, if Ulrich had given them permission, but the runt was too persistent. He was only gone eight-nine months. Drexel spotted him bumming near the County line, and drove him back. Never met a Sheriff who had such a knack for locating people at the proper time. Town couldn't badger the runt, because he reached lawful age before he came in off the road. He roomed with Mrs. Kwat on F Street for a while. Hired himself out as an attic cleaner, a junk collector, and a window wipe. Never stopped by to ask me for work. I would have paid him good wages to be my cabin master. I guess Mrs. Kwat didn't want the town drudge living with her. The dirt on his hands and face made her crotchety. She accused him of pilfering from her attic, and the runt had to sleep in jail overnight. Drexel shoveled him over to me. "Give him a cabin on the fringe, Mother. But you allow him to mix with your girls, I'll break your cheek."

"What happens when Ulrich memorizes his new address?"

"Can't be helped, Mother. Nobody wants him. Goodbye."

Runt kept staring at me. Same cords in his neck, same fatness, same expression on him when I chased him from my screen twelve years before. Only his hairline was new. Whoever heard of a boy balding at eighteen? He had no belongings except the clothes he was wearing and his attic sweeping tools. We'd grown estranged, I guess, and I couldn't buy a word from him or get rid of his mope.

"Place is yours, runt. Just put in a claim for a bungalow. Glad you got Drexel for a reference. Don't hurt to have Sheriffs on your side. Hope you won't kick LaVerne out of Number 8. She's partial to that bungalow."

"Name's Anatole," he said. "Don't call me runt." And he wasn't through with his squinching. "I'll take the southernmost cabin, if you don't mind."

Take my ass, I felt to say, with your hotshit words and chubby fists. But he didn't stick around long enough to let me put a sentence out. Runt went his way, and I went mine. He got so dirty squatting in attics and drudging there, my girls could sniff him a hundred yards off. LaVerne bitched about it. "Mother, I'm going to strangle on that stink." But she was polite to him. "Anatole, why won't you work for Ulrich?" He hissed at her, and she learned to hold her nose when he was in the area. "Can you imagine sleeping with him? Bet he'd leave grist on your belly. Makes me shudder."

Anatole took to visiting the College library, but the librarians complained about the thumbprints on books he handled and the bad air around his seat. The stink

must have got to the Sheriff's office after a couple of
years. Drexel finagled with Penn and the College,
cleaned Anatole up, and installed him as campus security
guard. The students didn't mind looking at a fat cop,
and Anatole liked his special library privileges. Wish
Drexel could have done half as much for himself. Sauerkraut splotched his ambitions. "Wasn't Drexel supposed
to be elected County Prosecutor?" people asked. "I
hear the Governor's been paging him on the telephone."
But Drexel set his limits in Galapagos. He'd stand for
Sheriff every four years, that's all. He was satisfied being head deacon of the Native Sons. He tooled in his
office, let his tariffs run dry. His deputies did his policing.
Most of them weren't so roundabout. They just grabbed
inside your pocket. You'd ask them, "Where's the Sheriff
today?" They'd wink at you. "He's painting trash cans."
And it wasn't a lie. Drexel aimed to slap a clean face on
us. He added ten more feet to the grubby little park on
N Street. He arrived one day with ladder and spray gun
when caterpillars attacked the pepper trees in my yard.
He stood thigh-deep in garbage potting rats off Sonora
Mound, and turned the place into a shrine. Not even
Turkey's threats and Turkey's postcards could get his
ass away from Galapagos. Only pleasure trip he'd make
was to my barber chair. He wanted a hair trim and company. "Turkey must be sending an awful number of postcards to your deputies, Drexel. Every widow in town
knows about them. Say they're going to sit tight until
you punish him."

"How's the boy?"

"Anatole? Never see him. He takes the southern
route to school. But he's pretty regular. Find his rent
money wadded under my screen last day of the month."

Drexel left me a dollar tip. Run him down to the street, I was boiling so. "Drexel Fingers," I shouted, "you ought to look to your manners. You growing formal on me? Take your dollar back."

He shrugged, but he wouldn't take the dollar.

Jarold, his chief deputy, cuckooed him.

"Any albino threaten me on a picture card, Mother, I'd be after him in a streak."

"Well, Jarold, why don't you pretend a little?"

He looked at me suspicious. I don't think Jarold owned a brain could accommodate too much pretending.

"Surely," I said. "Pretend you're the Sheriff, and let's see what happens."

"Don't you involve me in it, Mother. Personally speaking, I got nothing against Turkey. All I care he can squat in Sonoma woods till the century runs out. Aint no slur on me." And he wasn't too shy to strip down my pocketbook before he put on his hat.

You'd hear the buzzings in town. "Drexel sleeps and Turkey mows. What you expect from a five-term Sheriff?" Turkey had his off years too. He'd sneak around in Oregon. Barely mailed out a card. Then they'd come in batches, and there'd be reports how Turkey was wintering in Sonoma again, crawling into boarding-houses, spooking the woods. Merchants Association cried to the Sons. They swore the Turkey Scares drove their trade away. Maybe business was bad, and they needed an excuse. Maybe it wasn't the Sons who got Drexel to act. I saw him from my porch, carrying a back scratcher and his scattergun, mothers parading behind, hugging their brats and following him to the edge of town. An older boy stopped on my porch and jeered at Drexel. "Sheriff, you going to walk Turkey out of the woods?" I chased him off. "Scratch yourself." Only got a sideways view of Drexel, and I can't tell you much. The ear I saw was twitching. The eye looked straight out, over hecklers, gawkers, and buildings. The mouth, nose, and chin were unnatural white. Blame it on Turkey, if you want. I don't. Drexel wasn't reckless. If he'd really been afraid, he would have brought a deputy along. I'd say that pasty color came from fifty years of Galapagos goosing his skin. I could be wrong. The paraders deserted him near O Street, behind the rodeo grounds. Every child in Galapagos knows the rest. Drexel reached the woods, all right, but the trouble is he stayed there too long. His deputies carried him out with a broken neck. Drove him through town in a hand-cart. Jarold gave the order. He seemed fairly pleased with himself. Somebody'd taken off Drexel's boots. Pricks had to show a dead man in his dirty socks. Drexel got his dignity back, I suppose. Governor almost came to his funeral. The Sons wore their mourning shrouds, and they dedicated the College museum to him. The Merchants grew religious on us. Claimed they didn't want to defile Drexel by scattering his personal name. So we got Sheriff Park, Sheriff Street, Sheriff Bridge, and Sheriff Road.

A scroungy witch visited me a few months after the naming ceremonies. She had peculiar hair, crooked tits, bandaids on her fingers, and a net over both eyes. "I'm not hiring this year. Go away." Damn persistent witch. She scratched on the door, so I had to look up. My double inspection paid off. "You scrump. Got your nerve. I aint no boardinghouse widow to play with. Lunatic. Go roost in your woods."

"Mother Chace, I'll thrash you, you don't quiet down."

"If you're that desperate, Turkey, come on in."

He stepped out of his shoes and gingham dress. Two
rotten grapefruits plopped on the floor. He ripped off
the net and the shag of horsehair on his head. Son of a
bitch stood with a year's dirt behind his ears and a stiff
prick peeking through his long johns. "Who's that?"

"My daughter."

"Adopted or natural?"

"Natural," I said, and it hurt my pride to answer.

"How old?"

"Nine in September."

"What's her name?"

"My, you got an awful lot of questions for an outlaw.
Cynthia's her name." She was sitting under the window,
chewing the wax off her shoe strings.

"Don't she ever smile?"

"She's in mourning for Drexel," I said. And I swear
Turkey moaned.

"Mother, I been gone too long. Who's her father?"

"How the hell should I know. I wanted a child, so I
had it."

"You used to be more careful than that, Mother."

"Maybe Penn Gemeinhardt's her dad. I don't keep
tabs. Could be Buzzer or Drexel or anybody. Give or
take a few, I'd say there's three dozen candidates just
about. I was more active in them days. You hadn't been
off outlawing, I'd put you on the list too."

Must have pleased him, because his prick got stiffer.

"Anyhow, Drexel was nice to her. Bought her dresses.
Took her places."

He slapped his face, on the side where the blotches
were. "Shit. Wish somebody had told me. I wouldn't
have kicked him so hard. But he didn't leave me too
much selection, Mother. He sat under my tree four days
straight. Cracking hard-boiled eggs and scratching his

Sophie Waxman-Weissman (?)

Anatole despised photographs; he seldom allowed any to be taken of himself; none were found among his papers, except the one above, which seems to be of Sophie Waxman-Weissman long before her marriage to Benno. Joachim Fiske believes there is "little discernable resemblance" between this photograph and the Sophie he remembers. I disagree; the look about the woman's eyes does remind me of Sophie. Is it Sophie in her Lithuanian schoolgirl's uniform at the age of twelve? Thirteen? Fourteen? None of us can be sure.—The Editor

PHILOSOPHY 001.   **Introduction to pragmatics**   **3 credits**

Mr. Waxman-Weissman.   TuTh 2:10 — 3:26   Auxiliary Shed

Caution: Students interested in esoteric subjects should not register for this course.

An examination of phenomena out of our everyday lives: eating habits, speech, evacuation, modes of dress, body carriage, care of teeth, nervous tics, mating habits, and sports preoccupations will be touched upon and considered for discussion. Frankness on the part of all concerned is definitely a prerequisite. Field trips will be taken in and about Galapagos, so that the student may reacquaint himself with his surroundings. How much of what we allow ourselves to see is motivated by improper breathing and cramped bowels? Part of each class hour will be devoted to physical exercise. Students should bring their own towels, sneakers, and sweatshirts. Lemonade will be supplied by the instructor free of charge.

      The listing for Anatole's course in the Galapagos Junior College Catalog of 1963 (the first year Anatole taught). The Catalog material was written by Anatole, under the supervision of Seth Birdwistell and W.W. Korn.—The Editor

. . . .

SUBSCRIPTION BLANK

Business Manager   CHECK ONE
THE TAR BABY
Life Sciences Building   ONE ISSUE: $1.75 ☐
Galapagos Junior College
Galapagos 1   TWO ISSUES: $3.00 ☐
California
                                  SIX ISSUES: $6.00 ☐

          LIFETIME SUBSCRIPTION: $12.00 ☐

Published at frequent intervals

    Please enter my subscription to *The Tar Baby* for_____
issue(s), or Lifetime ☐, beginning with the current number.

                              NAME _____

                              SEX _____

                              STREET _____

                              CITY _____

                              STATE _____

                              AGE _____

                              OCCUPATION _____

                              INTERESTS _____

    Sorry, we do not have the facilities to bill subscribers; please
enclose check, money order, or postage stamps for the proper
amount and list any additional information or gripes at the bottom of this form.

. . . .

back. Singing to himself. Can't tell me it was any accident he picked the right tree. He knew I was up there.
He expect me to say, 'Drexel, lend me an egg?' Didn't
jump on him, I would have starved to death. Taught me
a lesson, Mother. You can rob the fuckers blind, jiggle
every Post Office in the State, steal the underpants off
their wives, but you touch one of their heroes, and they'll
never let you alone. Must be a thousand Sheriffs hunger-
ing for me. Have to shit on my feet. Can't afford the
sitting time. Drag my piles wherever I go. Mother, any
baby cream in the house? Baby cream's the one thing
what soothes them."

"Sorry to interrupt you, Turkey, but you don't strip
down this minute and bathe, I'm like to die. Only so much
body rot a woman can take. And I wouldn't want my
daughter puking. You don't have to be embarrassed in
front of me. I've seen the spots on your chest."

Took us a quarter hour to peel off his long johns. And
he left pieces of skin in them too. He wasn't so fidgety
after his bath. "Mother, first long sit I've had in months.
Where's LaVerne? Aint heard a door slam since I got
here."

"Had to let LaVerne go. Bank's in cahoots with the
College. Trustees angling to shut me out. Don't want no
whores' colony putting scum on their precious campus.
Figure they'll throw up a dormitory over my bungalows."

"What about that rodeo lover Gemeinhardt?"

"He aint much interested in my welfare any more.
But you won't catch me worrying. Never met a trustee I
couldn't beat when it comes to stripping bark. One thing
they can't tolerate is bad publicity. Hurt their image
jabbing me with a stick. Redwood's been around too
long. They'll starve me slow."

"I'll scoop out their gizzards, one by one, you permission me, Mother. Hate the word trustee."

"Turkey, it aint worth your time."

We crouched over the tub, steel wool in our knuckles. He scrubbed dirt rings away and let me stare at the birth marks on his prick. "Turkey," I said, "I'll just close the door." Cindy'd sucked her shoe laces dry. She had fly paper wrapped around her chin. "Can't you recognize what's candy and what aint? Go on. Play with the ham in the ice box." I climbed into the tub to satisfy Turkey. Can't recall another man who had such a hate for beds. When I reached for a pillow, he growled.

"Turkey, faucet's going to gnaw your back."

"Let it gnaw."

He stuffed my pillow in with the rags and dirty clothes under the sink. But he was gentle otherwise. Rather have Turkey with me in a tub, porcelain ripping my bottom, than be stuck with a Galapagos merchant, his drool on your belly and his cuff links on a chair. Wish somebody would outlaw me. Maybe I'll move to the woods. Or burn down a couple of Post Offices. I admired his straddling. Because with Turkey on top, it wasn't one poke and a kiss goodbye. And he didn't smuggle his way out with any shitsticking five dollar bill. He left his long johns in the parlor, so I wouldn't forget his strange coloring, and he proposed to me, I swear. "Mother, ought to leave this rathole. No future in Sonoma County for you and your daughter. Attach yourselves to Mr. Odell Norman Semple. That's my rodeo name. We'll jump on the circuit near Marysville, and I'll earn enough for the three of us clowning and biting steers. If I run shy, Mother, I can always bag the day's receipts."

"Appreciate the offer, Turkey, but I just couldn't get that close to rodeo again and keep alive. My late husband was a bulldogger. Seeing the crippled horse sleds, brahmas bleeding from their asses and mouths, it'd only sicken me. And I wouldn't be much of a woman to you."

He hugged himself, crawled out of the tub, his skin crackling and shivering. "Woe to me, Mother. They're comin'." He was in his long johns before I could sound him out.

"Sorry I upset you, Turkey. Didn't mean to downgrade your rodeoing."

"Woe to me." Bumps came up in the splotchety part of his face. "I can smell it, Mother. They're comin'."

I sucked wind, but I couldn't smell a thing except his scrubby long johns. "What's that you're sniffing, Turkey?"

"Sheriff sweat." He bobbled the grapefruits, and I had to fix his bosom for him, button on his gingham dress, manage his horsehair wig.

"Nothing to worry, Turkey. Nobody'd ever recognize you. Not Jarold Hawes. Must be the laziest and stupidest Acting Sheriff in the country."

"Mother, they got bloodhounds, magnets, 'lectric eye, and all the latest crime detecting junk. Told you they never let a bugger rest."

I walked him to the ice box, stuffed him with goods. Cindy laughed at the banana wiggling through his sleeve. "Your girl's livening up, Mother." Short of presents, he pulled a bandaid off his fingers and gave it to her. She was pleased with it, and he started to cry. "Shouldn't have killed him, Mother."

"Aint worth dribbling over, Turkey. Wasn't all that much love between Drexel and me." And I shouted at him. "Turkey, you forgot your face net." But he was five bungalows away, horsehair scattering on his shoulders, his gingham dress attracting burrs. Sure enough, a Sheriff's fleet cruised by, Jarold sitting in the lead car, jawing with County officers and looking pious. Son of a bitch had a tracking hound inside the car, its droopy forehead pushed against the window, its muzzle wetting glass, only it must have been trained to sniff out a man in between snores. Otherwise what was it doing asleep? Jarold kept his eye off my porch. He didn't want them County officers thinking he'd associate with any old motel owner. An Acting Sheriff with more sense would have stopped the fleet, pinched the hound, and come inside. Cindy wasn't much better than a tattletale. She'd have told him about the banana in Turkey's sleeve, and our sit in the tub, and that hound could have run Turkey into the dirt. Jarold waved the fleet up Oxnard, hound slobber from the window on his glove.

Having my thoughts. Maybe I was foolish turning Turkey down. Aint been many suitors since. Unless you want to count Chesbro, that shoe salesman from Laguna Beach with a sideline in pornography. Had a thriving business packing his shoe boxes. He'd smuggle skin flicks, slides, and picture books into the northlands, and catch me on the way up. He was scrumpy, with hair in his nose, fat lips, and tiny feet, but he knew how to stroke a woman while she was watching his slides on her parlor wall. Almost got used to the corns on his fingers. And you can't condemn a man for having piggly toes. "Margaret," he'd say, "rather screen for you than anybody. My wife isn't so appreciative. Sophistication is what I value. You screen for a lumberyard slut, she giggles where she shouldn't, and I can't stay hard." Chesbro's a millionaire today, but I had to give him up several years back. On account of an accident. Near spooked me with one of his movies. There he was, humped over his projector, looping film, anxious, his thumbnails plinking the lamp, so our shadows rolled and tweaked in my parlor. "Brought you a pisser, Margaret. Part of a cameraman's estate. I purchased it off his widow. She lacked your eye. Satisfied her with a year's supply of shoes. It's a smudgy old print, so be careful you don't miss any details." Gloating over his swindles, he caressed the projector, and didn't have a hand left for me. Got my own ten fingers to choose from, I need a crotch rub. I concentrated on the wall. That widow deserves more credit, is my opinion. She wasn't so dumb to trade for shoes. Skin flick ought to have some punch to it, not just nibbling, dribbling, and a swad of cocks. Wasn't one costume in Chesbro's movie. Plenty of scratches, hairlines, and bubbly dots, so you had to push on your eyeballs to match a body with a face. Trouble is, the actors bothered me. I'd seen them before. In my own parlor, I suspicioned. Embarrassing to say, but I recognized Darl Simister by the tilt of his prick. Got easier after that. Couldn't mistake Blackie Mayhew's tucked-in balls. Rump scars belonged to Tadpoles. Buzzer Carmody must have signed a contract with the film-maker. Had his stock and crew working for him. First off, Darl comes in riding a bull calf, Blackie and Tadpoles massaging its thighs. Darl slides back, sits on the calf's hipbone, and with Blackie twisting its ears and Tadpoles cracking its tail, they knock the calf off its feet while Darl pretends to bugger it. Scene changes, and now they're spraddling a baby heifer, and this time it's Blackie who does the buggering, Darl snapping the heifer's teats. Film goes cloudy, projector rattling, and they come out again in a spraddle, but the heifer's gone, and Chesbro's got a finger in my ass. That man's always entering me backwise. The three cowboys are sucking and poking the woman under them, Chesbro on me, copying Darl, sputtering out my name. I'm following the woman's body through the hairlines and the bubbles, liking Chesbro a little more, and her face jerks up between Darl's ankles. No hairline's going to hide them soggy bones and that tired sneer. "Chesbro," I screamed, "get Sauerkraut off my wall." I roughed his projector, ripping film with my teeth. He crept into his pants.

"What the hell you mean bringing a dead woman into my house?"

"Crazy bitch," he said, "I'll sue," and he locked the projector in with his shoehorns. Last I heard from Chesbro.

Cindy beat my luck in suitors. At least for a while. She switched the pompoms on her tail at the junior and senior high, and half the population in the township got stuck with blue balls. Only she lost the pompom somewhere, and parts of her skull. "Found me a marrying man."

"Haw," I said. "One of those snively boys from the College I bet."

"Bullshit. He's middle-aged."

"You been letting bankers guzzle you?"

"Don't scatter your filth on me, Margaret."

"If it aint a banker, who then?"

"Anatole."

Couldn't help myself. Dropped a turd in my drawers.

"That damn twitch? Aint said a word to him in five years, and he lives twenty yards away. You'll be honeymooning in the fun house and putting slick on his badge."

"Mind your business. I'm marrying him."

"Need my permission to marry."

"You don't sign the certificate, Mother, I'll run off with him and leave you dry."

That marriage of theirs rubbed out my revenue. Anatole was my only lodger. Had to give them a bungalow rent free. Rather croak in an unmade bed than listen to people twitter, 'Poor Mother, she's running with the dogs. Being supported by a girl.' Tried to make peace on Cindy's account. Thirty-six, the certificate said, and he was still a runt. His bald spot couldn't touch my eyebrows, and Cindy's only a quarter inch shorter than me.

"Won't do ignoring each other, Anatole. One day we're going to have to say hello."

"Hello, Mother." And he quit for the rest of the month.

Marriage couldn't have agreed with him all that much. His head got skunked after six weeks of bride-grooming. Tore through J Street, winking at merchants, tickling his badge, bought a trunkful of creams and face soaps for Cindy, ordered a gross of mousetraps for me, and I had to drive him to Minerva State. He crunched himself up in my automobile, sniffed a doorknob, nudged the steering column. "Mother, I've been here before."

"Surely," I said. "It's an old Sheriff's van. Got it at the County auction last year. After Drexel died, they stripped down the gadgetry and used it to truck garbage and manure. County begged me to take it. Nobody wanted a stinky Packard. It shits gas. Drexel took you on rides. You rode in it once with me and your mother."

"With your mother," he said, wiping his fingers on his chest.

Anatole got into this habit of being a parrot. It annoyed most people. I didn't mind. His ward doctor

said it comes with his disease. Had an urge to echo
everything he'd hear. I aint convinced of that. Seems to
me he was pretty damn particular about what he echoed
and what he didn't.

In and out, out and in, wearing labeled pajamas under
his coat, sucking berries from a stand in the foothills,
that's Anatole's roadbook. And I stank up his home.
Should have been more suspicious of a plumber who
wouldn't advertise his rates. Hired Stokie to fix a
clogged pipe, and he stayed on. "Mother," he said, "you
need a handyman," and he poked around in my drawers
before we could settle on a wage.

"It's poor business, Millard, taking liberties with
your boss. I might sack you any minute. What would a
woman my age want with a squirt like you?"

"Give some, take some, Mother, I'm going to fuck
you tonight."

"Millard, I didn't ask you for a song. Just clear my
drain."

Pitied him, he could scarcely keep a wrench in his
fingers, and I let him park in my bungalow. Might have
figured he'd sniggle up to Cindy while he went snaking
through my pipes, but I had Anatole on my mind.

"Ought to visit him, honey. Bring him custard, sham-
poo his chest. He gets tired soaking in a tub without his
dictionary."

She wouldn't go. "You're the one he misses. He
scratches his groin whenever I'm there."

In the hydrotherapy room at Minerva I got to like
Anatole all over again. Twenty tubs in a row, without
screens, the attendant didn't care if you peeked at a par-
boiled cock, long as you deposited your visitor's chit in
his lap and gave him a dime. Patients wore ice collars

around their necks, so they wouldn't catnap in the tubs and drown themselves. One of them leaned too far or closed an eye, the attendant batted him with an iron ruler. "Mr. Fourteen, you know you're not supposed to snooze in here. You can pull off, you can sing, you can kiss your big toe, that's about it. Already costing you thirty cents in fines." He made his rounds, ruler on his thigh, and stopped at Anatole's tub. "Mr. Eight, how you going to work up a sweat frowning so hard? Smile, Mr. Eight. I'll pry open your mouth, if you don't behave. Hate to get germs on my ruler."

"Leave him alone," I said, and I stuffed his pocket with dimes. "Just sit in your chair and play with the visitor's chits. You can stack them or trace them on paper. I'll guard the tubs."

Water hissed and bubbled around Anatole's knees. Scratchy hair under his lip was blobbed with snot and eye crust. Paid that prick attendant to wash him and shave him, but I'll bet he spit on him and scraped him with his ruler.

"Anatole, should I drop the heat? Only take me a second to locate the proper knob."

"Heat's fine, Margaret. But you can hold my hand."

Damn peculiar sight, chilled fingers coming out of a boiling tub. Sucked his thumbs to warm them. The attendant bleeped at me through the megaphone by his chair. Embarrassing to have a little shit scold you in front of twenty naked men. "None of that, mam. You advise her, Mr. Eight. This is a public institution. No twiddling allowed." So I held Anatole's hand underwater. Couldn't understand how he got that chill. Bubbles stung my wrist. "Exercise time, exercise time," the attendant croaked. The men jacked themselves up, making their ice collars stiff, and howled in the tubs. Near took my ears off. The attendant wasn't satisfied. He dawdled over his stopwatch, clocking the howls. "Left side of the room is letting up, gentlemen. Screams aint landing right. Mr. Sixteen, Seventeen, and Eighteen, use your thorax. Mr. Three, take the frogs out of your mouth. Breathe, you cocksuckers, breathe. Cost the State a boodle to pay your water bill." A few of them kicked their feet out and rotated their necks. One old man paddled with his elbows. Anatole howled with the rest. A twitch got caught in his throat.

"Anatole," I said, "don't let that little megaphoning shit abuse you. I'll rub his shoulder. Raise my skirt and piss on his watch." But he wouldn't release my hand. So I sat out the exercises, with an earache, a frown, and a finger burn.

"That boy knows what he's doing, Margaret. Can't relax without learning how to scream. It takes the kinks out of your belly."

"May be," I said. "But I'd still enjoy pissing on him."

"Cindy coming to the dance?"

"She don't, I will."

Yapped at her over an hour, but I couldn't even leave a scratch. "You seen him in the therapy room, I say, with his ice harness and his raw complexion, smelly old scrags farting from the other tubs, this little shit of an attendant forcing him to scream, you'd pity your husband more."

"Pity aint much of a cuddler, mother. Too bad. You expect me to dance with boobies? Do the idiot crawl? Without a live band? Bet it takes them a week to scare up a phonograph. They'll put it in a wire cage, so the boobies won't rip off its arm, because you can't tell what moves a nut will take on the dance floor. Thanks for the invitation, mother. You go."

"Margaret be your stand-in, honey," Stokie said. "She's a better mixer." He picked his teeth with a runty knife.

"You 'honey' my daughter again, Millard, I'll bite your ass."

"Suit yourself."

Forget about Millard. Should have listened harder to Cindy's bitchings. She wasn't that far off. Didn't need a wire cage in the recreation hall. Music came through the ventilator. Taught myself to squiggle my hips in rattling air. Wouldn't have minded it at all if the dance master had been tolerable. Sour man in an orange bowknot, he slapped numbers on our chests and ordered us around. Couldn't select your own partner at the Minerva dance. The master flicked his bowknot and coupled you off. I got strapped to a blind duff who knew every foot in the hall. Pingpong tables stacked near the door, and I couldn't figure why we were creeping near them, rubbing wood, until I felt the splinters along my arm. "Mr. Pallister, risky business dancing with you." At the next go-around, the master switched me to a boy with wet pockets who walked me into a corner so he could play with his fly. Warned him gentle to shut his britches or I'd be obliged to tattle on him. "You wouldn't dare," he sniggered, and he waltzed away by himself. Danced with a woman who wore lacquer on her face and stuck an elbow in my crotch, before I caught up with Anatole. "Wish you'd be my partner for the rest of the night," and I tore off our chest numbers and crumpled them in my fist.

Enraged the master seeing us numberless. He poured

green mouthwash into a cup, slurped, tipped his head, gargled, spit it out, and shouted at us, grease on his chin. "Restore your numbers. Or else." No Minerva bowknot man could ever make me give Anatole back once I got him.

"Kiss off," I snarled, and the crackle in my mouth must have told him who I was and where he ought to go, because he didn't waste his time gargling. We just took ourselves out of his dance pool. Other folks switched partners, mooned under the ventilator, scraped against the pingpong tables, dragged their feet to the master's calls, and I stood with my fingers in Anatole's scalp.

"Sorry about disappointing you, Anatole, but Cindy has a runny nose. She'd be here otherwise." Thought a lie might sound more natural. Cindy was always catching colds, and I didn't have the guts to tell him she wouldn't shake her precious can to ventilator music.

"Margaret, I'm happy shuffling with you," and he held my ribs and smiled. Lost him for a second in the switchings. Anatole ducked under the boy with wet pockets and grabbed on. Couldn't stop him from inspecting my face. We were dancing eye to eye. Hugging him, extra thighs clinking me after every go-around, the master grumbling at us, sucking mouthwash, I had to snort it out, thirty years of shit. "Whored your mother, Anatole. I was the one. Snuck her in the back while you clawed on the screen. Encouraged filthy grubbers to climb her. Don't blame you for disliking me. It's your privilege to rip my throat." I slobbered on his hospital shirt. Couldn't have heard me too well, because he tickled me, right under the arm, and it wasn't harsh. We just about cracked the master's hold on the floor. When the dancers saw us huggling, a finger in each other's

armpit, they forgot the go-around and kept their partners. The master smashed his cup and called downstairs
to shut the music off. Nobody cared. Scrubbers came in
and herded patients out of the hall. Would have gone
with Anatole, into the wards, but the tub attendant
spotted me and broke us up.

Couldn't get through the day without another long-
distance hassle. This operator had a froggy voice. "Collect call from Mrs. Dillard Stokes. Will you accept?"

"Put her on," I said. And I could hear her bawling
and sniffling and chewing her sleeve. "Must be having a
piss, honey, disguising your name like that. Bet they put
up Millard's face in the Post Office. Wouldn't want to
buy a stamp with his mug looking down on me. You still
in Mundelain?"

"No," she said. "Can't remember where we are. Some
Niggertown. Don't serve you nothing but chitlings. Aint
proper food for a living person to digest. And the
shower stall's got spiders in it."

"How's Millard's plumbing business since I spoke to
you last?"

"Don't bring me down, mama. Enough people poking
me around here. Millard bought himself a pair of handcuffs. All he does is lock 'em and unlock 'em."

"Peculiar present to buy, you ask me. You sure the
Niggertown Sheriff didn't slap them on?"

"Can't you stop?" Twitched my ear with her sniffles.
"Miss Bruno, mama."

"Should I paste him in an envelope, send him special
delivery, care of Mrs. Stokes, Niggertown, USA? Might
feel cramped traveling that far. Scream his head off."
Couldn't tolerate the slabber she made when she took to
her sleeve. "Don't crap your pants, honey. I'm bringing

him. You can googoo at him, if you want." Only I
couldn't locate that boy. I crawled under the bed, because it was his prime hideout, but all I found was
Anatole's old policeman's shirt, with dust balls in the
pockets and a rip in the chest. Bruno must have been
sampling his teeth on it. Picked it out of the closet, I'd
say. Thought he might be eating rust under the kitchen
sink. But he wasn't anywhere in the bungalow. "Hiding from your grandma, Bruno? Ungrateful little brat."
Usually can sniff him from the dirt in his drawers. But
shit smells don't carry much upwind. Maybe he got
curious about his father and went over to the bus route
for a look. Anatole, did you have to lay down in Coronado Road? Were you worried about completing your
water therapy? Could have bathed you every day in my
tub. Aint such a disgrace to have a runaway wife. Had a
husband once who preferred poking steers and rubbing
boys to sleeping with me. I survived. "Bruno?" Couldn't
leave Cindy stranded in Niggertown. How you going to
tell a mother her child is lost? So I walked to the phone,
dandled my arm, and said, "Hang on, honey. Here he
comes." And I googooed for her. Gnawed my throat but
it made her happy, them goos.

"Honey, like to hear him again?"

Heard a man shout at her end. Must have been
Millard, tired of his handcuffs. She said, "Gracious,
mama, I got to go." And I stood with a dead wire,
dandling my arm, expecting Bruno's head to pop out and
break open my fist.

Dalkey Archive Paperbacks

FICTION: AMERICAN

BARNES, DJUNA. *Ladies Almanack*	9.95
BARNES, DJUNA. *Ryder*	9.95
BARTH, JOHN. *LETTERS*	14.95
CHARYN, JEROME. *The Tar Baby*	10.95
COOVER, ROBERT. *A Night at the Movies*	9.95
CRAWFORD, STANLEY. *Some Instructions to My Wife*	7.95
DOWELL, COLEMAN. *Too Much Flesh and Jabez*	9.95
DUCORNET, RIKKI. *The Fountains of Neptune*	10.95
DUCORNET, RIKKI. *The Jade Cabinet*	9.95
DUCORNET, RIKKI. *The Stain*	11.95
FAIRBANKS, LAUREN. *Sister Carrie*	10.95
GASS, WILLIAM H. *Willie Masters' Lonesome Wife*	9.95
KURYLUK, EWA. *Century 21*	12.95
MARKSON, DAVID. *Springer's Progress*	9.95
MARKSON, DAVID. *Wittgenstein's Mistress*	9.95
MASO, CAROLE. *AVA*	12.95
McELROY, JOSEPH. *Women and Men*	15.95
MERRILL, JAMES. *The (Diblos) Notebook*	9.95
NOLLEDO, WILFRIDO D. *But for the Lovers*	12.95
SEESE, JUNE AKERS. *Is This What Other Women Feel Too?*	9.95
SEESE, JUNE AKERS. *What Waiting Really Means*	7.95
SORRENTINO, GILBERT. *Aberration of Starlight*	9.95
SORRENTINO, GILBERT. *Imaginative Qualities of Actual Things*	11.95
SORRENTINO, GILBERT. *Mulligan Stew*	13.95
SORRENTINO, GILBERT. *Splendide-Hôtel*	5.95
SORRENTINO, GILBERT. *Steelwork*	9.95
SORRENTINO, GILBERT. *Under the Shadow*	9.95
STEIN, GERTRUDE. *The Making of Americans*	16.95
STEIN, GERTRUDE. *A Novel of Thank You*	9.95
STEPHENS, MICHAEL. *Season at Coole*	7.95
WOOLF, DOUGLAS. *Wall to Wall*	7.95
YOUNG, MARGUERITE. *Miss MacIntosh, My Darling*	2-vol. set, 30.00
ZUKOFSKY, LOUIS. *Collected Fiction*	9.95